# A Question of Resistance
# Part I
## Jacques Story

Paul Smith

Published by Wise Grey Owl Limited
www.wisegreyowl.co.uk

Farthings, Main Street, Staveley, Knaresborough,
North Yorkshire HG5 9LD UK
publish@wisegreyowl.co.uk

Dedicated to Nick killed in a motorcycle accident in October 2008.

A great biker, a good friend and a good companion.  We had some good times in France and Spain burning rubber that I'll always remember.

God bless you Nick.

# Tuesday 5<sup>th</sup> May
# Grandfather's Blues

My friend, Georges, and I were travelling to Brittany in northern France today by motorcycle. We were both English but had French roots having started our life in Brittany and moved to England when our fathers, who both worked for the same firm, were relocated when the French subsidiary of their company was closed. Georges and I were bilingual as a result and we spoke French when we were alone.

I always saw my grandfather and grandmother before I left. I was close to both of them but I had a special relationship with my grandfather. We had been close all of my life and I loved listening to the tales of his time during the war in France for both of them were French and now lived in England. My father was English and people told me I had a good English accent with a hint of French, which had always been attractive to the girls, much to my benefit. My French dialect was of northern Brittany without an English accent. That pleased me but it especially pleased my grandfather and he never spoke in English to me, though his English was as good as mine. At that time, I did not understand how he could have been so fluent.

I entered my grandparent's house, knocking gently on the door as I entered and shouting, "It is me, Jacques".

Grandmother was in the kitchen preparing breakfast, for it was early as we were leaving at nine o'clock and had to catch the afternoon ferry. For a woman of eighty years of age she had maintained the elegance of her youth. She was short in stature but held her head high and this gave her an aristocratic look, despite the wear lines that told of her long life. She was, as always, immaculately dressed, even at this hour. She came forward and hugged me and kissed me on both cheeks. Her eyes welled up and she hugged me again. I asked her how she was and she told me of her aches an pains and then smiled. In her eyes was something different, something I had not seen before. I would have found it difficult to describe at the time but now I see it as 'a knowing', almost a foreboding of things to come.

Grandfather, hearing me enter, came through from the garden where he had been tending the vegetables. Grandmother remonstrated and told him to take off his boots. He grumbled, as he always did, but came forward beaming with his hands outstretched and hugged me kissing both cheeks in the Gallic manner and shook my hand firmly.

"Jacques, my boy, oh it is so good to see you. It is today you leave for your jaunt, is it not?."

Grandfather's eyes moistened also and I was surprised at this. He was a strong man and although emotional in a Gallic kind of way, he rarely showed the kind of emotion he was demonstrating today. In his eyes too there was something new.

"A coffee, and have some breakfast," said grandmother.

I nodded and she set another place at the table in the conservatory. It was May, in fact the 5$^{th}$ of May, and the sun was warm, even at this time of the morning. Grandfather came over to talk to me and he beckoned me to sit at the table. He washed his hands at the sink with grandmother shooing him away. They had a very close relationship and I worried what might happen to either of them when one of them died. Grandfather was eighty-three and sprightly but age was slowing him and I had noticed the difference in the last few years since I left the dark tunnel that was adolescence. I was nineteen at the time and considered myself to be an adult, though I was to learn soon how that was to be tested.

My grandfather was a strong man, emotionally and physically. He had towered over me most of my life but now I felt taller, though I was the same height as him. His slight stoop, and it was only slight, and expanded waist line, gave me the edge over him now. I loved him dearly and he was a constant force in my life: my role model, my guide, my mentor and he took the place of my father who had died when I was twelve, in a motorcycle accident. My mother was distraught when I followed in his footsteps and started to ride motorcycles when I was seventeen. I found it strange that neither of my grandparents had admonished me when they discovered that I was riding, even though it was their son that had been killed in the accident. In fact they rarely mentioned it.

Breakfast with my grandparents was a delight and we spoke of small things like grandfather's vegetable garden and the larger things like the politics of the day and the world situation. My discussions with grandfather, particularly, were always a pleasure. He and I thought alike and I valued his greater experience. Time went too quickly and I soon had to leave for I was to meet Georges at his house.

Leaving my grandparents house was very difficult. I look back on it now and recognise what it was that was different. Then, though, it left me feeling empty and uncomfortable. Grandmother hugged me and kissed me to the extent that I felt that she did not want to let me go. She did so finally, after many minutes, relaxing her grip. She was crying with real tears gushing and running down her face. She made no attempt to dry her cheeks and appeared quite distraught and it left me alarmed. Then came the response of my grandfather to my departure and I was completely unprepared for it. I have never seen grandfather sob in the way that he did that morning. Even when his son had died he had been more controlled. He hugged me and, even as I was leaving the house, would not let go of me and dragged me back for one last goodbye. I heard his uncontrolled sobs as I left and I heard grandmother comforting him. She continued to cry, even as I closed the door. I almost turned back as it was so disconcerting to see them like this. I wonder now how different things had been had I followed my instincts and not left that day. As it happened, my commitments to my friend Georges took priority over my feelings to my grandparents. I shook as I left my grandparents but tried to put the feeling of a foreboding from my mind. Having something on one's mind and motorcycling are incompatible.

Georges and I had been friends all of our life mostly because our fathers shared the same occupation. We had lived close to each other in Brittany and now did the same in England. I viewed him like a brother and our birthdays were within days of each other. Georges was very French. He was tall, slim, muscular, had dark eyes and dark swept back hair and was very good looking and he knew it. Myself, I was a pretty ordinary nineteen year old. I was pretty fit, in the athletic sense, dark unruly hair, green-grey eyes and average height and not really exceptional in any way. I seemed to play second fiddle to Georges most of my life but I had grown accustomed to it and Georges and I were inseparable. I had ceased trying to compete with him, for I knew I would lose, and in any case Georges did not compete back, why should he, and a one-way contest is most unsatisfactory. I met with Georges but did not mention to him the strange departure from my grandparents. He sensed something was wrong but did not push me to explain. With, Georges, empathy was not his strongest feature.

Both of us had what is called an 'enduro' motorcycle. One that is designed for off-road use, though rarely used like this in my experience. We were intending to camp and Georges was providing the tent which he had strapped to the pillion seat. He was performing what he called his 'pre-flight checks' as I pulled up and I blipped the throttle to let him know that I was there. I came to a halt close to him. He looked up and beamed. I raised my gloved hand and he tapped it, high-five style. I removed my helmet and sat on the bike, engine still ticking over and emitting the burbling noise that a large single cylinder machine often does. I flicked the keys and the engine died.

We spoke to each other in French.

"You ready?" I said, after the usual pre-amble that is the protocol of the French language.

Georges took the leather jacket that was hanging from the throttle grip and slid into it. He put on his black and white helmet and fastened the chinstrap before adding the leather gloves to his protective clothing. I replaced my helmet and restarted the engine Georges mounted his motorcycle in a single effortless motion. Georges had warmed his engine before I arrived so, as he flicked the starter switch, his engine roared into life. He gave me a nod traditional of bikers and left and I followed a few score yards behind. We both had satellite navigation kits with large displays attached to the handlebars and we had agreed that we would meet at the entry to the ferry port should we lose each other, which we did not. In any case we had mobile phones in our bags so we would always be able to contact each other. The ride was as good as it could be as we were riding on motorways which neither of us enjoyed and we were pleased to see the turn-off to Portsmouth and the ferry to Cherbourg. It did not rain and that was a bonus.

The ferry to Cherbourg we had chosen was a high-speed ferry and its superstructure was made from an aluminium alloy. I always worry about boarding a ferry on a motorcycle even though I am quite experienced. The deck can be like a skid pad and there can be patches of diesel, which is always a challenge for a motorcycle. This boarding went without a hitch and we were soon strapping down our bikes so that they would not move during the short three-hour crossing. In what seems like a blink of an eye now we were sitting on the bikes, engines roaring and ready for Cherbourg, the journey through Normandy and then to Brittany. It was May 5th and still sunny.

# Friday 5th May

## *Dangereux*

We took the coastal route, avoiding the auto routes and the busy *route national* roads with their convoys of lorries. The Normandy coast was pleasant and we travelled through what had once been small fishing ports with their centres unchanged. The outskirts showed signs of urban sprawl but not to the same extent as elsewhere in Europe and especially in the UK.

The ride was pleasant and the weather warm. Normandy has some hills but they are not too demanding. The biggest problem in France is Napoleon's tree lined boulevards, as Georges calls them. He always says that they would stop you in a hurry and best avoided. At the end of long straight roads are sharp bends. I enjoy this kind of riding and today, with its perfect conditions was one of the finest.

We turned the corner into Brittany past the *Mont Saint- Michele* and on towards *Saint Malo*. This large town with its old central quarter is difficult to avoid so, rather than following the bypass with the rest of the traffic, we went right through the centre. *Vive la moto*!

Before too long we were heading towards northern Brittany. The sun was still shining and all was perfect, too perfect. We were heading for the pink granite coast where we were to camp for the night; after we left *Saint Malo* we still had a few hundred kilometres to go.

We turned for the coast again and followed the route as close to the sea as we could.  The road was long and straight and parts of the coastline were rugged and cliff topped.  We stopped for a break along the top of one of these cliffs and looked ahead on the road.  A fret had formed and the temperature was dropping.  We could see the mist ahead and it moved towards us blocking out the sun as its edge hit us.

We could barely see 20 yards and Georges said, "Where the hell did that come from.  I hope it doesn't last.  It'll make riding a pig".

"Come on," I replied, "let's see if we can get through it.  I'm cold".

We re-mounted and rode into the mist.  My visor fogged quickly from the inside so I was continually opening it and wiping the inner surface with my gloved finger.  I was pleased when we left the mist behind.  The road surface had changed as we exited the fret and it was much cooler.  It had rained as the road was wet but it was no longer raining.  The wind blew and this surprised me.  I remember thinking that sea fret normally forms when there is no wind.  It was darker too and the sky was filled with clouds and displayed menace.

Georges was ahead so I flashed my lights for him to stop.  He pulled to a halt.  I rode beside him, stopped and raised my visor.

"What the hell's going on?  Where did this shitty weather come from?" I asked.

"Fuck knows, Jacques," answered Georges and he gave me one of his shrugs.  "Let's ride on and see if it clears."

Georges looked down at his sat-nav screen to see how far we had to go.  He gave me a puzzled look and said, "Looks like I've lost the satellite. This thing's playing up. What does yours say? How long before we get there?"

I remember looking down at my screen and I saw the pop-up window telling me that the sat-nav was out of contact with the satellites. I looked around to see if we were in a gulley that would block the signal but no, we were in the clear. I shrugged also and cancelled the pop-up window on the display. The screen reverted to the image of the map of northern Brittany. I nodded at Georges and he twisted the throttle and his big single cylinder motorcycle roared into life. I followed close behind.

The road surface was very different now. It was still a good road but the surface was a different colour and had a greater aggregate content. We reached a section of what Georges always calls 'twisties' where we can have some fun. I noticed that there was no traffic on the road at all. The traffic had been light since leaving the main roads around *Saint Malo* but now there was none. We were enjoying the bends in the road and I followed Georges maybe ten yards behind him watching his lights and, past him, the road ahead. I think I spotted the road block in front before Georges did as I remember a gap opening between George and myself as I slowed. Georges braked soon after.

I noticed that military personnel manned the roadblock and I wondered what was happening. I slowed and pulled up beside Georges a distance from the soldiers. We looked at each other and it was clear from his expression that he was as perplexed as was I. Georges flipped up his visor and I followed. I looked over to the soldiers and they were showing signs of agitation.

"What's this about?" Georges snapped at me.

"Not sure Georges," I replied, "they look serious. Maybe we should go over and find out?"

"Either that or we turn back?" George said.

"We've done nothing wrong, Georges," I said, rather lamely.

"There's something not quite right about this," said Georges, "I don't like it. My senses are prickling. Look Jacques, just get ready to go when I give the signal. We may have to get out of here quickly."

I looked at Georges thinking that he was joking. I should have known better and Georges was serious, very serious. Georges was driven by his instincts and I knew him well enough to know that they were telling him to flee. We pulled up to the roadblock and noticed that the soldiers were armed and were wearing German army uniforms.

"Papers," exclaimed the soldier at the head of the pack. The remainder of the soldiers were moving forward and seemed to be intrigued by our machines.

I pulled up my visor and shouted at Georges who had also raised his visor, "These are German soldiers, is this some kind of piss-take?"

Georges looked at me and I could see that he was worried. The concern was fleeting and he grinned at me and said, "Gun it Jacques, we're getting the fuck out of here".

With this he snapped shut his visor and I realised what he was going to do so I slammed my visor down too and opened the throttle following Georges as his bike leapt through the small gap at the edge of the roadblock. We opened up and were racing down the road. What happened next surprised us both.

There was a crack and I felt a bullet come close, too close.

"The bastards are firing at us," I remember yelling into my helmet and to nobody in particular. Georges was also aware of what was happening and he opened his throttle another notch. I joined him and time slowed as we raced to be out of range of the guns. Georges kept going. He rode like the wind and I did too. We felt the road and took each bend in our stride and at speeds that we would not have believed were possible. People from the villages watched us and I was vaguely aware of them but I was more aware of the next bend in the road.

Georges indicated right and I followed. We were heading up a track and our speed decreased as the road condition worsened. I could see that Georges was heading for a coppice of trees. He stopped and dismounted and I did too. Georges lifted his visor and motioned to pull the bikes into the woods just off the track. We did this quickly so that the bikes would not be seen. I pulled off my helmet. I was sweating, despite the cool of the day so I opened my jacket.

"What the fuck was that about?" asked Georges, rhetorically.

"They shot at us Georges," I said.

"Did you see them? They were dressed in German uniforms. They shot at us, the bastards, and they nearly killed us."

What happened next gave us little time to worry about our near miss at the roadblock. Out of the woods came a group of scruffily dressed and very rough looking men. Our ears were unaccustomed to dealing with stealth and they had surrounded us easily. In fact, they must have been watching our approach.

"What are you doing here?" said one of the men.

"What are they wearing?" said another, "they look very strange".

As he said this he stepped towards me and opened the front of my jacket to look inside at my fleece. I flinched and stepped backwards and the group tensed because of my action. I noticed at that point that they were armed. One had a bren gun that I recognised as a favourite of my grandfather. Another had a sten, the semi automatic that my grandfather said jammed too often for his liking. At times like this the mind races and I found myself subconsciously counting the number of men surrounding us. There were ten in the group and all looked very fierce and some of them emaciated.

"Just kill them," said a bear of a man and he smiled as he said it, "they look like spies to me."

I tensed and looked around slowly. All eyes were on us. Georges went to open his jacket and I heard a click as the safety catch was disabled from one of the rifles. Georges stopped in his tracks. This looked sticky.

"We mean no harm," I said lamely. I think my *Brettagne* accent may have helped.

The first man who had spoken yelled an order to the group. It was clearly an order and the safety catch was re-engaged. This man was the leader.

"Good day. I am Bernard. You're from Brittany, I see. What is your name and what are you doing here?"

"My name is Jacques," I replied quickly, "and this is my friend Georges."

Bernard nodded towards Georges.

"How do we know they are not *Milicens*?" another of the group snapped.

My senses were alert now. I had heard this word before. My grandfather had used it. The *Milice* were French collaborating agents during the war. French spies for the Germans, my grandfather had said. He had hated them. He told me they were responsible for the death of many a partisan and in the most appalling of circumstances including torture. He had always spared me the detail but had spoken venomously of the *Milice*. It was one of the few times I heard my grandfather use English and had often used the English word 'lice' to describe them which amused me then.

I jumped in quickly and explained what had happened to us. Georges filled in some of the detail too and added viciously, "The fuckers shot at us, they could have killed us. Bastards!"

"What did you expect?" said Bernard, "you ran a road block. You were lucky but you will be marked. Do you have papers?"

I motioned to my pocket. Bernard snapped an order to one of the group who he called Luc. Luc stepped forward and checked me for weapons. He was satisfied that I was not armed and nodded to Bernard. I pulled my passport from my pocket and handed it to Bernard. He looked at the front and opened it, flicking through the pages until he found the page holding my photograph. He fingered the plastic coating and looked puzzled. I had a British passport with me, as I had not renewed my French passport. He passed the passport to Luc and then onto a spectacled and earnest looking young man whom he addressed as Roger.

Roger examined the passport methodically.

"What is this?" he said finally, "I have never seen papers like this before. Why is your picture in colour and how was this done? It does not look painted. And what is this film over the page?"

He continued, "What is this European Union? It says you are British and yet you speak good French with a *Bretagne* accent. Explain."

I could not explain but I was formulating something in my mind. The delay in my answering Roger seemed an eternity to me then as I examined my impossible thoughts. My brain was working quickly and I glanced at Georges as I fumbled with the concepts in my head. He looked back at me but I could read nothing in his face except a kind of resigned bemusement and a little fear. So many strange things had happened in such a short time and adrenalin was still coursing through my veins. It made me sharper and, although what I thought seemed so improbable, I felt that I my analysis was correct. I asked a question.

"Tell me, what is the date?"

"5th May," answered Roger, "why?"

"What is this," said the bear of a man, "we haven't time for this, just kill them."

"We are not the boche, Henri," snapped Bernard, "we do not kill indiscriminately. If they are British then they are our allies."

Henri's interjection had made me more certain so I continued, "And the year?".

"Why, 1944, of course".

"1944!" exclaimed Georges, "is this some kind of piss-take?"

Roger continued, "Why do you ask Jacques?"

"Because this morning, Roger, it was 5ᵗʰ May 2009," I replied, "take a look at the expiry date of the passport."

Roger rifled through the passport again until he found the expiry date and said, "He is right Bernard. The date of expiry is November 2015."

Roger mused, stoked his chin and said, "But that is impossible."

"Impossible it may be," said Georges, regaining his composure, "but that is the truth. How else can you explain how we are dressed."

I thought Georges was very calm and inside me I was screaming that this could not be. I hoped that my voice was not quavering as I said, "Take a look at our bikes. Do they look like they were made in 1944?"

I turned around to find two of the group examining the bikes. Their faces had a look of incredulity. The sat-nav screens were still in their 'on' position and a map of where we had been when we passed through the mist was displayed.

"What is this?"

It was Pierre who had spoken. He was tall and painfully thin with a long face. None of the group was clean-shaven and all looked dishevelled like they had been sleeping rough. Daniel was Pierre's companion. Daniel was good-looking and his good looks shone through the grime.

Bernard retorted, "If what Jacques and Georges say is true we should not be standing around here. The boche will be searching for them. Cover up the bikes Daniel, Pierre. Jacques, Georges, collect what you need from them. You're coming with us."

Georges took his luggage off the bike and I did the same. We removed the sat-nav. Looking back, this was a silly thing to do. They were not going to be useful. The day had been strange though and I was not thinking correctly. I could hardly believe what seemed to be happening and I was experiencing life through a stupor. Georges removed the tent and I was pleased because I had a feeling we would need it.

Bernard ordered Luc to remove the tyre marks made by our bikes as we had travelled up the track. He did this with some branches that he then used to camouflage the bikes, which were pushed deeper into the coppice of trees. As I looked at my trusty steed I wondered if I would ever see her again. I noticed Luc touching the fairing. It looked like he had never seen a substance like it before. He had a mechanical mind and the long upside-down forks of the enduro fascinated him.

We marched up the track through the coppice of trees and then into a forested area into the hills. We marched for two hours at least and this was tough terrain when dressed for motorcycling. The air was cool and damp and I was sweating so I was wet from both sides. Georges had tried to talk to me but Henri had told us to be quiet and had separated us. Bernard was distracted so he was not around to protect us from Henri.

Finally, we reached a stream spanned by a fallen tree. At the far side the forest was thick. Bernard whistled a blackbird sound, which was returned. He whistled again, a bird sound I did not recognise. The return was the blackbird sound again. At the far side of the trunk spanning the river the leaves parted and two men armed with sten guns stepped forward and shouted a greeting to Bernard.

The party leapt over the make shift bridge and along a track which opened into a small clearing. Around the clearing was chaos and it was clear that a group of men were living rough here. There was a cooking area with a camouflaged canopy over it. Bernard told me later that this was to stop the Luftwaffe from seeing the camp from the air. The sleeping quarters were in among the trees and were improvised from tarpaulins and what looked like parachute silk. All of these were hidden using tree branches and leaves. The parachute silk had been darkened with a home-made dye.

The camp was not tidy and had it been discovered accidentally it would have been clear that it was in daily use. The smell of the latrine was overwhelming too and the toilets were far too close to the camp. Had these guys never watched the survival expert, Ray Mears, I pondered. Quickly afterwards, I mused that if this really was 1944 then Ray Mears had not been born. For that matter, nor had I.

Having arrived, Bernard told us to find a place to sleep and sent Roger to accompany us. Georges' tent was green and not the bright orange he had wanted to buy. I had dissuaded him and was now very pleased with that decision. Roger watched us erect the tent. He was an inquisitive and intelligent person. His eyes were an intense blue and he had fair hair swept back in an unruly and dishevelled style. His spectacles sat on the bridge of his nose at a slight angle. This added to his look of distraction; he gave the impression of his mind being somewhere else all of the time.

George's tent was the quick erection type. Georges had commented to me that the last thing any guy wants was a quick erection. I remember that we had laughed like small boys at the stupid schoolboy humour until the shop assistant had arrived.

We laid out the all-in-one tent, put together the bendable fibreglass poles, hooked on the tent using the plastic eyelets, put the flysheet over the top and pegged down the tent. This took only ten minutes. Roger clapped when we finished and Georges, ever flamboyant, bowed.

"That's impressive," Roger said, "what are those poles made from? They look too flimsy to take any strain."

I told Roger that they were very strong and were made from fibred glass. He looked puzzled. He came over, rolled a pole between his fingers and muttered something that we did not catch. We had camped under a tree branch so there was no need for camouflage. I looked at the branch and hoped that it would not fall.

"Come on," Roger said, "Bernard wants to talk."

I had not had time to unpack so I placed the motorcycle luggage inside the tent. Georges did the same. We followed Roger back to the clearing, which was empty. Roger suggested that we sit and I could see that there were logs and tree trunks that had been cut for the purpose. Georges and I sat on a tree trunk. Roger left us to fetch Bernard. George and I were alone.

Georges looked at me and I looked back. There were a myriad of questions welling up inside but neither of us said a word.

# Friday 5th May

## Acceptance

"I am not sure I understand what is happening," Bernard said, "but if you are indeed British, then you're welcome. The British are the allies of the Free French and I am sure we will be liberated, and I hope soon."

Bernard was every part the leader even dressed as a peasant as now. He wore a beret and I guessed he was in his mid to late thirties. Not a handsome man but he had earthy good looks and a strong physique. His hair was dark and greying at the temples and his face showed the signs of a hard life and the responsibility he bore. He sat before us facing Georges and I, leaning forward and his legs splayed.

What he said next surprised me.

"We have another two Englishman here too. They are from special operations and are here to help us with the maquis. Gabriel is a liaison officer and Marcel is the communications officer. You will meet them this evening."

It was the word maquis that caught my ear. My grandfather had been with the resistance during the war and the maquis were fighting groups spread around the country. I remember grandfather saying that the resistance organisation had been 'a shower', as he put it, at the start of the German occupation but that it had sorted itself out later. Grandfather had said that the best fighters were the *Francs-Tireurs et Partisans Français*, that he said were known as the FTP. Grandfather had said that he could never join them because they were communists but he respected them for their clear focus, if not their politics. He had said that they took their orders from the Russians and he could not forgive them for that.

"Is this a maquis?" I asked.

Georges looked at me and it was clear that he had no knowledge of the maquis nor the maquisards, as the members of the maquis were known.

"Yes Jacques," replied Bernard, "you are now members. You must earn your keep."

Bernard continued, "There are some here who think you are *milice* and think you should be killed as spies. To me, you do not fit that mould. You're not *milice* I am sure, or you would have been killed already. You're strange people indeed and if you have travelled from the future then we have much to learn from you."

Bernard's eyes twinkled as he said this and it was clear that he did not believe our story but was puzzled by the nature of our arrival and the things we had brought.

"Tonight we have a drop. The nights are getting shorter so we do not have very much time to do the collection. I want you to prove your worth and help us this evening. Luc will be along shortly to tell you what you need to do."

Bernard stood and left briskly with a slight bow of his head. His final words were, "Until this evening. Don't let me down."

Georges and I were alone again. Georges asked me about the maquis and I told him what I knew from my grandfather. I told Georges that the maquis were part of a complex resistance movement during the German occupation. I told Georges that the word 'maquis' was Corsican and meant inner woods and forests. I also mentioned that the Germans had introduced a slave labour regime called *Service du travail obligatoire* requiring young men to work in Germany; many had refused, of course, and this swelled the ranks of the maquis. Until then resistance was a more clandestine operation performed in the shadows by men and women who returned home to their families each evening.

"Do these men live here all of the time?" Georges had asked.

"Yes," I answered, "though they travel to the villages and farms for tobacco, food and drink. Grandfather often said that the maquisards went to the villages to show off their weapons and to brag of their adventures, mostly to impress. He had said that they were fools and they put others at risk by their folly. Grandfather did not suffer fools."

"Like you Jacques," Georges has added.

Luc arrived before we had completed our conversation. He told us about the 'drop'. British aircraft were due this evening and this had just been confirmed by a transmission broadcast by the BBC.

"They broadcast 'We are playing a song for little Jean who has a broken leg'," Luc had said, "which is the expected coded transmission. So we are on for this evening."

Luc had repeated what Bernard had said; the nights were shorter so we had to act quickly. He told us that sunset was around half past eight this evening and sunrise just before five thirty. I had looked at my watch and it was four thirty already. Luc had brought us some clothes as he had said that we looked strange in what we were wearing. I remember thinking that the clothes he gave us looked stranger. He told us that there were no boots so we would have to manage with the boots we wore. Luc said that boots were scarce and if we killed a boche we should take his boots as we would be able to sell them for a good price.

Luc went on to explain what was expected of us. The planes would arrive a couple of hours after sunset and would drop cylinders from parachutes. In the cylinders were arms, ammunition, tobacco, money and sometimes luxuries like chocolate. He also said that we were expecting some jeeps this evening too and that this was a rare occurrence. We were to join the maquisards and detach the parachutes and collect the cylinders and take them to the ammunition store where another group would unpack them. Luc said that Gabriel, the British liaison officer, told the maquisards to bury the parachutes but nobody did; the parachute silk was precious. He went on to explain that there was a risk in having parachute silk because the Germans associated possession with resistance and resistance was punishable by a bullet in the head.

Luc said that we would join him and Henri to make a team of four. Henri had worried me because I thought it was he who wanted us shot as spies. Henri had not been welcoming. I think my concerns must have shown to Luc because Luc had said that Henri was 'as solid as a man can be' and there was no one better on your side. At that time, I remained to be convinced.

The drop zone was a few kilometres away so we would leave as soon as the sun set. Luc recommended that we slept because we would not be sleeping that night.

When Luc left we decided to put on the clothes he had given us. They fitted us because they were baggy and loose fitting. Georges laughed out loud when he saw me dressed. I told him that he looked worse; Georges has a knack of looking good in anything, and he did even in these clothes. We had berets too. It is one item of French clothing that I had always liked so I was pleased to put it on. Georges pulled the front of my beret down over my face and said that I looked like a prat. I ignored him.

Luc arrived with Henri as dusk was arriving. He was accompanied by Gabriel who spoke to us in English. We took this as a test so we spoke back in English.

"You've caused quite a stir," Gabriel said after the formal introductions had been done.

"I've not time to talk to you now", he continued, "but after the drop, maybe tomorrow, we will have more time. You'll want to sleep though so I wouldn't mind catching up with you at lunch. Luc here will come and fetch you so can you make sure you're ready for twelve."

Although politely delivered, this was an order rather than a question and we both simply nodded. With a swift goodbye and a good luck wish for this evening's drop he left and we saw him catch up with Bernard and they spoke together in unaccented French. Even after this brief meeting I could see that Gabriel was an impressive character who exuded authority. I found myself looking forward to our next encounter and hoped that I could convince Gabriel of the honesty of our story.

We were ready to go and Luc beckoned for us to follow him. Henri said nothing and I could tell that he would prefer if we were not in his team. It was still light as we left so the path was visible through the woods. It soon became darker and I found myself following in Henri's footsteps until even Henri was difficult to see. I pulled an LED torch from my pocket, one that I had recovered from my pack, and clicked to light up a single LED.

Henri turned to look at me and struck me and I fell to the ground. The torch was flicked from my hand and landed next to Luc who was taking up the rear.

"You fucking idiot," Henri said, "you want the boche to see us? Maybe that's what you do want."

Luc picked up the torch and put his hand over the front to stop the light whilst he fiddled with the switch to turn it off. He clicked through turning on the LEDs in turn until the torch went out.

"Interesting lamp," he said as he handed the torch back to me.

"Leave Jacques alone," Georges said and stepped forward. George was always protective of me though I can look after myself.

Luc intervened, "Henri, leave it. Give these guys a chance. Jacques didn't know."

Luc turned to me and said quietly, "Be more careful Jacques. This is a dangerous game we are playing. If the boche catch us we are dead, and so are our families if they find them. This is real."

Henri had lost interest and was walking on. I followed behind him with Georges next and Luc was the back stop.

"We will see better when we are out of the forest," Luc added as we set off again, "the moon is a good one tonight and it has cleared from earlier."

This was just as well because we heard later that drops can only be done when there is a good moon so that the pilots have good visibility. Despite the earlier cloud and rain the evening sky cleared.

We continued and I rubbed the blood from around my mouth where Henri's blow had hit me. I was determined at that moment to even the score.

I was still stunned by what seemed to have happened to us and I could not understand why we were here in strange clothes in a strange time trundling through a damp forest and the chill in the air starting to make me feel cold. It seemed to me that we had joined the French Resistance, or the *Force Françaises de l'Interieur* as Luc insisted on calling it, with all that that entailed and without us being conscious of it. We were becoming more deeply committed though, at that time, I felt little but fog.

We left the forest and stuck to a path along the edge of a hedged field.  Luc had said that we could tuck into the hedge if a boche spotter plane flew overhead.  I could not imagine how the spotter plane would see us in the dark though, even with the brightening moon.  I could hear voices ahead, French voices speaking in a low and hushed tone.  Luc said something that I did not catch and started moving ahead at a quicker pace, taking the lead.  Georges and I kept up easily leaving Henri as the back stop.

We caught up with a group of maquisards who were gathered at the edge of a large field.  This was the drop zone, I was told.  I noticed some carts for the transport of the cylinders to the ammunition store.  The men were smoking and it was possible to see the lit ends of the cigarettes waving around as the men articulated their discussions.  I was surprised at how loudly they spoke.  If Germans were around we would be sitting ducks.

Almost imperceptibly at first we heard the drone of the incoming aircraft.  At that time I did not recognise the sound enough to identify the plane as a Halifax bomber.  As the noise became more distinct several of the maquisards rushed towards the drop zone.  They lit the signal lights which formed a rough cross shape.  The aircraft circled once , flew low over the field and then banked sharply before climbing again and then disappearing over the horizon.  This was repeated four times with different aircraft.  I could hear the roar of the engines as the aircraft left the dropping zone.  I looked up, gestured to Georges, and pointed.  There were large cylinders hanging from parachutes luminescent in the bright moon.

Luc yelled for us to move so Georges and I followed him and Henri to where a container was hitting the ground.  Henri detached the parachute skilfully and then, between us, we manhandled the container to a nearby cart.  The cylinder was taken from us and whisked away to the ammunition dump. The containers were heavy and I learnt later that they were around seventy pound; some were even heavier, though not the ones that we intercepted.

This continued for a part of the night and Georges and I were engrossed in our enforced work and for the first time since we arrived I forgot about our plight; I just focussed on the job in hand. I worked with Henri during the night and, despite being in very close proximity to him, he never lost his coolness towards me. I tried to talk to him and each time he replied in a monotone or not at all.

When all of the cylinders had been retrieved we were sent out to try to disguise the plough marks in the fields where the containers had been dragged along the ground. This was mostly done with branches and leaves to break up the outline so that spotter planes would not be able to see where the cylinders had fallen. This took a little time in the dark though the moonlight was bright enough for our work. I caught sight of the dawn rising as we finished and Luc beckoned for us to join him and the other men so Georges and I ran across the field towards Luc, leaving Henri walking behind us.

He thrust a bren gun in my hands and passed one to Georges. He gave us several rounds of ammunition and told us to look after the guns because they were the only ones that we would be given.

"Welcome to the maquis," he said as he passed them to us.

I had done some hunting in France during my youth so I had used a gun before, as had Georges. In fact, we had been hunting with our fathers when we were younger. Neither of us had ever used a sub machine gun, let alone a bren. I thanked Luc. I was surprised at his gift. It meant that Luc and some of the men had accepted us. I wondered what Henri would think. I did not have to wait long.

Henri noticed the guns as soon as he joined the group. He scowled when he saw them and muttered that he though it premature to arm us. It was Pierre who spoke first. I had not known that Pierre was with us but I recognised him in the moonlight and Daniel was next to him.

"They helped us with the drop," Pierre snapped, "that makes them with us until proven otherwise. In any case, Gabriel said that they are to be trusted. He said that they were British and that is good enough for me."

"You trust too much," barked back Henri, "have you forgotten so soon?"

Pierre stepped forward to close in on Henri and Daniel stopped him.

"You dishonour me Henri," he said and waved his outstretched hand in front of Henri's face.

I could see that Pierre's finger nails were torn and many missing. His hands were badly scarred.

Henri backed down and his voice trembled as he replied, "I am sorry Pierre. I have not forgotten your sacrifice."

"Nor me yours," said Pierre stepping back, "come, let us drink to this success."

"And to the end of the boche."

I heard a cork being removed from a bottle and then another. The bottle was passed around and we all took a swig. I was tired and yet exhilarated. I had never felt this alive in my life. The bottles were emptied and thrown into the bushes and we made our way back to camp. The sun was rising and I followed behind Daniel with my bren gun slung over my shoulder.

Back at camp Georges and I unzipped the tent and I unpacked my sleeping bag. We were in a daze and spoke little to each other. This seems surprising to me now. We had left a normal home only yesterday and today we had taken part in a drop of arms to a clandestine maquis group in Brittany. We had been shot at by

Germans, nearly killed as spies by the French Resistance and now had arms to defend ourselves.  There were many questions but we were just too tired to ask them.

I slipped into the sleeping bag and was asleep immediately.  I did not hear Georges preparing for bed at all.

# Saturday 6th May

## Assimilation

I woke on the 6th May warm and comfortable in my sleeping bag with the sun lambent upon the canvas of the tent. I turned over and the sleeping bag followed me. Georges' head was not visible and he was tucked inside his bag. I pulled my arm out of the sleeping bag and looked at my watch. It was late at eleven thirty. I could hear some movement within the camp but it seemed far away. I was hungry.

I lay back and put my arms behind my head. My mind raced as I remembered what had happened in the previous twenty four hours. I was aware that we had somehow joined a maquis group and that put us at risk if we were caught. Somehow that did not matter. My grandfather had told me of some of the atrocities that the Germans had done and, of course, I had been taught at school of the history of the twentieth century. That had seemed so remote and now it felt very real.

The interchange between Pierre and Henri was on my mind. It was clear that Pierre had been tortured and, from Pierre's remark, Henri had suffered a trauma of some kind. It was difficult for me to empathise with Henri for he had been antagonistic since our arrival. I avowed to find out more, even though conversation with Henri was stilted. I wondered whether Gabriel would be able to tell us more. Then I remembered that we were supposed to be seeing Gabriel today, at lunch, whenever that was to be.

Georges stirred.

"You awake Georges?" I said.

Georges head appeared from the sleeping bag and he replied, "I am now Jacques."

"How you doing?"

"Not sure yet, mate," he replied, "God, I'm hungry. Did we eat at all yesterday?"

"I'm hungry," I replied, "and we are supposed to be seeing Gabriel at lunch."

"What time is it now?"

I told Georges and he uttered an expletive. Georges sat and rubbed his eyes. He was dressed in his underclothes; these were his twenty first century underclothes and he looked like the old Georges again. I could almost imagine that we had had a bad nightmare but Georges broke the spell.

"Wasn't that great last night?" He said.

Georges surprised me as this was not what I was expecting to hear. He was right though. The sense of comradeship and the real feeling of vitality was not a prior experience.

"It was," I replied lamely and I smiled.

He ruffled my hair as he often did and pushed me back on the bed. I sometimes felt like Georges' younger brother though we were the same age. I was accustomed to this though and Georges' beaming smile meant that I could not be cross with him for long.

"Come on then," he said, "let's find some grub."

He slid out of the sleeping bag and picked up his maquis clothes and then unzipped the tent door and was gone. I followed him quickly. We dressed outside the tent. It was a warm day and the dew of the previous evening had evaporated. There was nobody near the tent but we could hear voices towards the centre of the camp so, after a brief stop for ablutions, we headed towards them.

There were just three men sat around the camp on the logs we had seen earlier. They were drinking what looked like coffee and Bernard asked us if we would like one. He shouted an order and I heard a noise from behind us. A fresh faced young man, more a boy really, came through the bushes and was carrying a couple of tin mugs full of a hot liquid.

"We have milk today," said the youth smiling, and he passed me a cup and then handed one to Georges.

"Jacques," said Luc, rising from his log, "this is André."

I shook André's hand and he shook it back warmly. He had a warm and friendly, almost innocent, face and a delightful smile.

"If you need any more, just ask," he said as he left.

"André feeds us," said Bernard, "and he has a knack of getting produce from the farmers in these parts."

"How could anyone resist him," said Gabriel and I noticed a trace of an English accent that I had not noticed at our previous meeting.

He continued with, "He really is very disarming but don't be fooled. He is cunning and wily under that façade of purity."

"Good morning Jacques and, Georges, isn't it? Well it is only just morning but you had a long but successful night I am told. And you handled yourselves with honour."

Gabriel paused and then said, as an afterthought, "Despite the provocations."

"I can't say that I understand why you're here or, if you really did come from our future, how you came to be here. I am going to take your story at face value because I haven't time to do otherwise. What is clear, though, is that you haven't the right papers to be here so I have asked Bernard to organise you some forged papers. You will not get very far here without papers."

He pondered for a moment and then continued, "Since yesterday we have made some enquiries about the nature of your arrival. It appears that the boche was surprised that you ran the road block. I hadn't realised that you had strange motorcycles and strange helmets on at the time and the boche have no idea who you are, nor what you look like. This means that you are not marked so you will not be recognised in any of the villages."

Bernard interjected at this point, "What age are you?"

"We are both nineteen," replied Georges.

"That is against you because you should be doing *Service du travail obligatoire* in Germany."

I had heard of this from my grandfather. This was the German's slave labour regime requiring young Frenchmen to work in German factories feeding the war machine. It also explained why many of the maquis, and in particular André, were so young.

Gabriel took over again, "This means that you must be careful and must not be caught in the open where the boche are."

Bernard interrupted again, "Luc, here, will look after you and teach you the ways of the maquisards. You need to learn quickly. Have you used a gun before? And where are your weapons?"

I realised that we had left our newly acquired guns and ammunition in the tent.

Gabriel realised what had happened and snapped, "This is a lesson you must learn quickly. If you do not you will be dead. If we are discovered here by *Milice* or the boche the only option we have is to fight and we have to be ready at all times. If you're captured you will be tortured and then shot. Better to die quickly as man and take a few boche with you. I will forgive this transgression this time but this is your last warning."

"We are sorry. This is new to us. I am still dazed by what has happened in the last twenty four hours. Our world is a safe world, or at least our part of it. We are not used to this kind of existence at all," I said, stumbling my words.

After I had listened to what seemed like someone else talking, I realised how pathetic was my reply.

Georges was not prepared to take the rebuke and snapped, "Fuck you. We didn't ask to be here."

"You prefer that the boche look after you. It can be arranged."

It was Henri who spoke. He had walked through the clearing and, seeing us there, had stopped to listen.

"Enough," said Gabriel, "I'm sorry but you must learn, and learn quickly."

He turned to Henri and said gruffly, "You have work to do Henri. We will talk later."

Gabriel stood, nodded towards Bernard who also stood, and said to Georges and I, "Come with us. We will go somewhere where we can talk without being overheard. I have much to ask you.

We walked away from the clearing and we took our coffees, well more a coffee substitute really, with us. As we were leaving André appeared with a handful of buttered bread and he passed it to us and disappeared back into the shrubbery. It was very welcome and I was famished after our night of toil.

Gabriel led us to a roughly built shack with a tarpaulin roof covered with a camouflage of branches. The sides were open to the elements and inside was a flat table top and rough cut benches. Otherwise, the shack was empty though it was soon clear that Gabriel had been sleeping here and that this was what he considered to be his quarters.

Gabriel switched to English; Bernard spoke English also though his English was very accented.

"This will make sure we are not overheard," he said.

"I am going to assume you're telling the truth and that you come from our future. I find this improbable but, to be honest, everything that has happened in the last few years I would have thought previously couldn't have happened."

"You have no idea of the atrocities that these animals have committed," he spat out the words with venom.

"Not first hand," I said, "for sure. But I know my history. And you probably know nothing of the things that will be found when this war ends too."

Gabriel look surprised and he replied, "Oh Jacques, just repeat that will you?"

It was a rhetorical question so I stayed silent and Gabriel continued, "So many of us have lived through this and we do not speak of the end and you talk of it nonchalantly as if it is a fact."

"To us it is."

"Before I ask you any questions let me explain Henri to you. He is a good man but he distrusts, for good reason."

Gabriel went on to explain and what he told us was harrowing. He explained that there had been a maquis in this area originally, the *Maquis de Saint-Marcel*. It was disbanded because it had been infiltrated with spies from the *Milice* and German sympathisers from the despised Vichy regime. Gabriel explained that the group that they had joined were not a formal maquis, as such, but continued the work of the abandoned maquis. They were often referred to as maquisards, and they did not object to this, but they saw themselves as simply freedom fighters.

Gabriel went on to explain that the hated spies had arranged a German ambush and the maquis had been caught off guard. He told us that the Germans arrived early in the morning and the most of the maquisards were arriving back after a drop of the previous night. The maquis was poorly defended because most of the men had been occupied with the drop. The guards were overrun quickly and one of them had his throat slit. Gabriel paused at this point and I caught sight of a tear forming in his eye. Gabriel was a consummate professional soldier and he must have seen much in his short life; to see this sign of emotion from a proud man was humbling.

Gabriel recovered quickly. He told us that many of the men were lined up, made to dig their own mass grave, kneel along side it and then shot in the head by German soldiers completely indifferent to their plight.

Bernard entered the conversation at this point telling us that he had to break the news to the families of the dead. Bernard had been away from the maquis when they were ambushed and this had saved his life.

Some of the maquisards were taken by the Gestapo to be interrogated and tortured. Most were killed but the remaining maquisards had managed to rescue Pierre and Henri. Pierre had been brutally tortured; he had had his finger nails torn back one by one. His genitals had been mutilated and it was unlikely that he would ever sire children. Bernard was in the rescue party. It had been a daring attack on an armed Gestapo prison. Bernard's glee was evident when he told how he had strangled the chief of staff of the Gestapo using a garrotte.

"It was for all of my comrades who had died at the hands of those pigs," he explained, "I am not proud to say that I enjoyed his death. I would do it again willingly today. He died like the coward he was, pleading for mercy. I showed him none."

My cheeks chilled when Bernard said this. I was starting to feel some hate now, and that was to grow in me. I was not prepared for what Gabriel told us next and my hate deepened with the telling.

A number of maquisards were killed in the raid on the prison. Gabriel explained that this was the price that had to be paid. Henri was among those that was freed, as was Pierre. Gabriel said that Pierre was in a really bad way and had to be helped back to relative safety. Henri had been tortured also but his interrogation had been at an early stage so it had not reached the worst level of brutality. Henri was known by some of the *Milice* and a party had been sent to his home.

Henri had a five year old child, also called Henri but referred to as little Henri.

Gabriel paused again at this point and I could see that it was difficult for him to continue.

Bernard stepped in, "I will continue."

"No, Bernard, thank you but I will finish. This is difficult for me. Henri and his family hid me from the boche when I arrived and they are good friends of mine."

Gabriel went on to explain that the Gestapo had visited Henri's home soon after Henri had been taken.

"I should have given orders for them to be taken to a safe house," Gabriel said. Bernard patted Gabriel's shoulder.

Henri's wife, Aurora, had been home with little Henri.

"The bastards raped her in front of the little boy and beat her senseless," Gabriel was crying now not even trying to hide his tears.

"But then," and he stopped and swallowed, "they hung little Henri on a hook and slit his stomach open and left him to die, dripping blood down the wall. I can never forgive them. They did this with Aurora watching and screaming for them to stop. The pigs then shot her through the head. And they left, laughing at what they had done."

Gabriel went silent and put his head in his hands. He sobbed quietly. The battle scarred soldier crying is an awe inspiring sight.

I felt hate for the perpetrators of this crime, for that is what it was, like I have never felt it before. The hate was growing.

Bernard continued, "Maybe you can understand Henri now?"

There was a period of reflection and I looked at Georges who was unusually quiet. He looked morose. Georges had a large family and was devoted to them and I could see the trauma in his eyes at the unfolding of the tale.

"Henri distrusts strangers, all strangers," added Bernard, "it is not just you. He is a formidable fighter and he has a score to settle."

I remembered that I had a score to settle with Henri for the blow he had given me. All thoughts of settling this score had now disappeared.

"How could they do this," Georges said quietly, "they are no more than animals. We have heard of the things the Germans have done, of course, but hearing this first hand, so fresh, it is sickening."

"You are here," Gabriel continued, his tears drying now though he did not try to dry his face, "and I don't know why. You need to prepare yourself for being here. You are British and that makes you an enemy of the boche, whether you like it not. To me you seem a strange mixture. There is heath and fitness in both of you and strength. Yet there is also a softness, a weakness of mind. You are not accustomed to hardship. You must learn and you must learn quickly."

"Gabriel," I said.

"Yes," Gabriel replied.

"Today is the 6th of May 1944 is it not?"

"Yes, what of it?"

"Well, one month today is 'D' day. This is the date that the allies will launch their invasion. It will be a while before the war is over, in fact the Germans will not surrender until next year, May the 7th. Paris will be liberated this year, as will Brittany. It will be over soon and you must have faith. The world will be a better place, though not perfect by any means."

Bernard looked shocked as I said this, though it was Gabriel who spoke first.

"I don't know why Jacques, but I believe you and you give me great hope. Do you know what is our role in this?"

"I think you do, Gabriel," I replied, obtusely for I felt I had said too much.

"Yes, you are right, I do. We stop the boche from reinforcing themselves. We smash their supply chain. Sabotage, yes sabotage."

"You would be surprised at the disruption a few people can make to a society," I said, but did not elaborate further. I was thinking about the terrorism I had witnessed through the television screens only a few days earlier. Now I was advocating terrorism. I think it was Menachin Begin, an Israeli leader, who said that one man's terrorist is another man's freedom fighter. If it was him, he was right.

"We join your fight," Georges interrupted for he had been deeply moved by little Henri's story, "we need to learn from you and we have little time."

"You have no knowledge of weapons," Bernard said.

"You have no idea what the boche is capable of," he continued, "if you are caught you will be treated brutally. They regard us as scum; they are the master race we do not matter."

"I will learn," Georges said, "we win, we do. Jacques is right. We will win Bernard and we will win soon."

I was surprised at Georges but there was something different about him. Georges was my best friend and my closest companion for most of my life. I knew him well but I could not say that Georges was a man of commitment. If anything he had always been a hedonist. Altruism was not his style and, since he grew, I had watched at the smooth way he manipulated people, apparently without their knowledge, to his own end. He used this approach as his seduction technique and he had been pretty successful too. This was a more direct Georges and there was a vitality in him. Georges was on a mission and I knew better than to stand in his way.

Bernard looked at Gabriel. Some unconscious communication passed between them and Gabriel nodded. Bernard was the one to speak.

"I will ask Luc to teach you to fight. Luc is good in close combat and you will need that. You must know how to use the bren though. Henri is best here but I think we could not ask Henri to do this. Luc is good enough and he knows how to stop it jamming. That could save your life. You know that we have limited ammunition, I'm sure. You will learn how to use the gun but you will not be firing it, except if we engage the boche."

"Jacques, if you are right about the invasion then your intelligence knowledge could be invaluable to us."

I nodded. I was beginning to wish I had taken more notice of my grandfather and stayed awake more during the history lessons.

Gabriel looked at his watch and told us that he was meeting with what he called an SOE contact and had to go but that he would like to continue the discussion later. I discovered later that the SOE was the 'Special Operations Executive'. This was a part of Britain's war machine and its role was to encourage and facilitate espionage and sabotage behind enemy lines. Gabriel, I was to learn, was a key SOE officer.

Bernard led us out of Gabriel's offices to find Luc. Our training was to start today and there was no time to lose.

Georges and I spent the rest of the day with Luc. The day was becoming warm and Luc had stripped to the waist. He was a short man with bulging muscles created by hard work, not work-outs in the gym. He was blonde with startling blue eyes and a pleasant smile. I guessed his age to be around the same as ours; I was wrong by a couple of years as he was twenty one.

He taught us a lot that day and the following two days. He was very strong and Bernard was right about his close combat skills. He seemed to enjoy teaching us and he admonished us and encouraged us when we needed it. I grew to like Luc, as did Georges. We improved over those two days and I found it remarkable what could be achieved with the right focus. Both Georges and I became totally committed to Luc and his mission in those two days. We created a bond unlike any other that I had ever known in my previous life.

We learned how to look after our bren too; how to clean it and how to stop it jamming. Luc had said that we should treat it like a woman; when you need her she is always there.

As we awoke in our twenty first century tent on the 9th May 1944 I mused at the gulf between what we had been only four days previously and what we were now. I had not had time, yet, to grieve for what I had lost for in my mind I knew I would return. Georges awoke besides me and rolled over in his sleeping bag. He broke my spell quickly.

"I need a shit," he said.

# Tuesday 9<sup>th</sup> May

## Love, perhaps

This was the day that changed my life forever. It started early and, for the first time since we arrived, Georges and I were separated. There were two jobs to do and Luc had said that one was pleasant and the other very unpleasant and he emphasised the 'very'. We drew straws, literally, for the jobs and Luc and I drew the long straws leaving Pierre and Georges with the worst of the tasks. Luc looked at me in a manner that suggested that he had fixed the odds and, if he did, I was grateful.

I learnt later that the unpleasant job was to fill in the current latrine and create a new one further away from the camp. This day brought double good fortune for me, if not for Georges.

The day also brought our papers and we were made 'official' and my date of birth was now 1925. As it happens, this was the same year as my grandfather's birth and I found that amusing.

Luc and I were to visit the farm of Louis Martin for some produce and we were to take a wheeled cart with us. Luc said that there were two daughters at the farm of about our age and he laughed that we needed some more attractive sights than were available at the maquis. It took an hour to drag the cart to the Martin's farm and it rained. I remember from my history that the D-day landings had been delayed because of bad weather and we were now experiencing that weather. I learned on the way that Louis Martin's wife had died at the start of the war from an infection in her chest which became pneumonia. I pondered on how she would probably have been saved had this happened in my own time.

The journey took us through a wooded path over some hills and Luc was at pains to keep us hidden. Always the teacher, he explained the ever present danger of being discovered by the Germans or being spotted from the air. He was at his most nervous when forced out into the open because of the terrain. We made a burst of speed whenever we found ourselves in this predicament. I thought it unlikely that a spotter plane would be flying in this weather but I humoured Luc. He was fun to be with, had a wicked sense of humour and we laughed a lot on the journey made more difficult by the rain.

The farm was quiet when we arrived and Louis Martin was out in the fields. He managed the farm with his two daughters and his son who was eleven years old. Élise and Claire were the two daughters and Alain was the son. We were soaking and cold as we knocked on the Martin's farm door. I looked around as we waited for the door to be opened. I mentioned to Georges afterwards that I saw new-old equipment everywhere. What I meant by that was that the farm implements would have been relics in our age but were new here.

Claire opened the door and said immediately and without the usual 'good day' that is normal when the French meet, "Come in, you must be freezing. Look at you, dripping in the rain."

Claire was seventeen and not the 'about our age' that Luc had said. She was a mature seventeen but had an innocence about her that teenagers in my time lacked. Élise greeted us next and she was stunning. Her dark long hair tied in a pony tail made the most of her symmetrical oval face. Here eyes were dark and her lips moist. She had an elegance about her and a beauty with a defensive personality that said 'keep your distance'. She was definitely 'about our age' and I learned later that she was nineteen.

Élise welcomed us and kissed our cheeks. She greeted Luc like an old friend and Luc introduced Élise to me. Élise smiled as she was introduced and replied with the formal French 'enchanted'. She kept up the formality for the whole of our visit except for one moment when I saw her guard drop.

Claire had brought some of her father's shirts and had told us to change into them so that she could dry our clothes on the range. I pulled off the top and handed it to Claire. I caught Élise looking at my bare chest and I swear I saw a look of approval on her face. Luc said later that I was hallucinating and laughed telling me that Élise would not be interested in me when she could have him any time. I was certainly interested in her. It was not just that she was pretty that attracted me, though she was beautiful to my eyes. It was more that she was interesting and intelligent. I detected this in Élise from the moment I met her and I was to be proven correct in my assessment.

Élise made us some coffee and offered us a calvados, the local brandy distilled from apples, and we both accepted gratefully. The range made the kitchen warm. Claire stoked it with more wood as we sat at the large central table. Élise put cheese and bread on the table and some cured ham. We started eating as she added some apple chutney to the collection. The food was great; simple peasant food that I ate with relish. I was hungry.

We sat in the kitchen, our clothes steaming on the range when Monsieur Martin arrived. I refer to him like this because, in all the time I knew him, and looking back now that was a long time, I never used his first name. Luc referred to him as 'Sir' and I followed his lead. We stood as he arrived and he greeted us warmly shaking our hands and asking questions of our welfare. He mentioned other members of the maquis to us, for that is how he referred to it.

Though our leaders had abandoned the term 'maquis', nobody else had done this.

Finally, he asked questions of me and Luc introduced me to Monsieur Martin. Luc was sparing with information when he described how Georges and I had arrived but did describe us as 'British SOE'. I guessed that is was how he saw us.

"I would not have known," Monsieur Martin had said, "your accent is from Brittany. You speak French well my boy."

My grandfather would have been pleased. He liked my command of French and had communicated with me in French all of my life. I was starting to realise how much I missed him and my memory of our recent parting was disturbing me.

"My grandfather is French," I said, "though he lives in England now."

I was about to start to explain how I had lived in France in my childhood but realised quickly that this would have made no sense now and it would have been difficult to reconcile some of the dates so I left it at that. Monsieur Martin asked no further question of my past, seeming happy with the explanation and moved on to activities at the maquis.

I could see that he was a passive resistance fighter. He had no truck with the Germans and hated them and their occupation. He did what was required to keep them at bay, providing them with produce when required. Mostly he tried to keep out of their way and help the 'real resistance', as he called us, in whatever way he could. Luc had told me that resistance to the Germans came in many forms. He told me that families like the Martins risked all if they were caught and that they were very brave.

Claire fussed around us during our visit and Élise sat at the table with us. She addressed Luc at first but spoke directly to me when I joined the conversation. As we spoke I began to realise that Élise knew more of the work of the resistance than I would have expected. We spoke of the drop and Luc asked Élise for any news she may have heard in the villages or from other maquis. We were told that there was a rumour of German troops being recalled to this area. The Germans were expecting an allied push though they did not know when nor where. I kept the information I knew to myself. Luc said that he would pass the information back to Bernard.

Élise, I was to learn, was an active resistance fighter. This was not in the sense of bearing arms, for she did none of this. Élise was a messenger and I was to learn how important was this job. This was a time of poor communication and a force of occupation that monitored all radio transmissions to discover its source. Élise told us of an SOE communications officer who had been careless and had not moved his transmitter often enough. The village in which he was working had been surrounded and sealed before dawn by the Germans and his house had been raided. He fled, leaving his equipment behind but was shot dead as he left.

"He was better dead," Monsieur Martin had said, "for they would have tortured him, British Officer or not, and goodness knows what he would have told them. Few men are strong enough to resist what these pigs can do to them."

I was to learn that the village was to pay a high price for their collaboration. Nobody would tell the Germans who owned the house that the SOE officer had used so they picked out five men randomly, made them kneel, and shot them in the head in front of their families.

The hate in me was growing stronger.

We went on to discuss lighter things and I watched as Élise spoke. She was clever and articulate and very strong willed. In her mother's absence she was running the home and she did it well. Looking back now, I realise that I was attracted to her from that very first meeting and I was hoping that she was interested in me too. I was so pleased, for once, that Georges was not with me. I always felt second in line when Georges was around. Luc did not seem a threat at all. Élise treated him very much like a good friend and no more. I kept my thoughts to myself and did not share them with Luc. Luc was more perceptive than I expected. He asked me later whether I liked Élise and I did not answer him honestly. He laughed and I could see that he knew better but did he not pursue it.

This was the most pleasant day I had spent since we arrived. I am not sure now whether it was the varied company, the calvados or the scent of romance in the air that made that day special. Special it was though and I still remember it fondly as a turning point in my life.

We filled the cart quickly with produce and Luc handed Monsieur Martin some money. The rain had cleared now though the sky was heavy and grey. The ground was sodden and it made dragging the cart harder. We were both young and strong and we made it back to the camp in just over an hour. I was excited by my day when we arrived and showed it in my demeanour.

Not so Georges and I laughed as he said, "My day's been shit."

He had the smell to match his day. As I was covered in mud from the trip we both bathed in the stream and were joined by Luc and Pierre.

We were starting to settle in and with the events of the next day we ceased to be 'outsiders'.

# Wednesday 10<sup>th</sup> May

## Sabotage

We rose early and it was raining which made the camp unpleasant. André had used a tarpaulin to make a dry area for Georges and I to sit and eat. Bernard was eating when we arrived. André smiled at us and handed a cup of steaming coffee to each of us. Coffee was black today which meant that André had no milk.

Bernard asked us to sit. Luc was there already and it was clear that he had told Bernard about the news from the Martin's farm. We ate some bread, cheese and some fruit provided by the beaming André; André was a delight to see and he seemed always to smile and I cannot recall a time when he was sad nor negative. People like him seem to make a difficult situation, like that morning, much more bearable.

"Georges, Jacques," Bernard said, "I need to discuss this with Gabriel first, of course, but Luc here would like you to accompany him this evening."

I nodded and I noticed that Georges did too but neither of us spoke.

"We are going to hit the fucking boche where it hurts," said Luc, and he grinned.

Bernard looked at Luc and smiled and then added, "The Martins said that there is likely to be troop movements into this area. If what you said is right Jacques, about the allied attack I mean, then we need to stop the boche from getting up here."

"OK," I said lamely.

George added, "What do you want us to do?"

"We are going to close the railway line."

In my time, closing a railway line would have been inconvenient but not terminal. Now, of course, the railway was the most important way of moving men and materials. Moving high volumes of both by road without the benefit of the motorways and reliable trucks would have been very difficult. It seemed that the master race was vulnerable after all. I was pleased.

"And how?" Georges responded.

It was Luc who spoke next, "A team are going on the up line and are to send a locomotive towards us on the wrong track. We'll send a loco in the other direction and, if we get our timing right, they'll meet in the cutting. With luck, they'll block both lines. I'm not going to rely on luck though. We'll send another train a few minutes later, fully loaded with coal. It should hit the wreckage and block the other track too."

"The boche don't have many big cranes so we think they'll not be able to unblock the line before the invasion," added Bernard.

"Where do we fit?" I asked.

"I've a contact at the station," Luc said, "and he's a sympathiser though he isn't active as such. He'll not stand in our way but he will not help directly. I want you to start the other train once we've set the first loco going. You up for it?"

I felt that this was a challenge to us and one that we could not or should not refuse.

"OK," I said again, still sounding lame.

"We haven't driven a train," added Georges, "a steam train presumably?"

"What other kind of train is there?" asked Luc and he then thought better and added, "OK, I guess you have different types but yes, they are steam trains. Just one handle to pull Georges and then you need to jump clear and make sure you do. We'll go through the plan with you today. Are you up for this?"

I was definitely willing and I needed to earn my spurs so that I could impress Élise. George was keen to join the team and he said so to Luc who shook his hand and then mine warmly.

"Who are in the other team?" Georges asked.

"Henri is leading it. The others, you haven't met yet. Pierre cannot make it this evening as he is helping Gabriel otherwise he would have been with Henri," replied Bernard.

"We will meet up with the other team on our way back. We have a rendezvous arranged," said Luc.

That was all it took for us to be involved in our first sabotage mission. I was to become a terrorist, a term I had associated with irrational fundamentalists in my prior life. Now it seemed justified and I wondered whether the mindset of terrorists in my time was like mine now. I rationalised it to myself; I was not intending to hurt anybody.

After breakfast Luc took us to Gabriel's quarters. Gabriel was away and Pierre was with him. Luc had said that this was the driest place in the maquis. We ran through the camp and we were all pretty wet when we arrived at Gabriel's place. Water was dripping from my nose and Georges shook his head as he arrived and water flew in all directions. He reminded me of my dog shaking the water off after a dip in the lake.

We settled in quickly and Luc told us about our mission this evening. There were just the three of us to the west of the cutting and two to the east. Henri was to lead the eastern team and Luc our team. He wanted a small group to avoid detection by the Germans and he needed three people. One was to stand guard, one was to start the locomotive going and the other was to start the coal train a minute later. Henri had only to start the loco from his end. There was not to be a second train from the east.

Luc said that he wanted Georges to stand guard and I was to start the first train. He explained what I was to do and drew out the controls of the steam train. He told me that his contact at the depot, whose name I never knew, would assist me in getting the train going. He also told me that I was to strike the contact and tie him up so that the Germans would not suspect that he was implicated. I was not sure about whether I could do this. I need not have worried.

Georges was unhappy about acting as guard and Luc stoked his ego and told him that it was probably the most important role of the mission. Georges is not stupid and could see that he was being patronised but he let it pass.

We were to leave at 22:30 and the first and second locomotives were to be despatched at 23:30. The coal train was to leave at 23:31. Rendezvous with Henri's team was to be at 00:00 and the meeting point had been pre-arranged; we would stay put at the camp until after dark. If Henri's team did not to arrive within fifteen minutes of the agreed time we were to go into hiding and not return to camp until the following evening. We were not to be allowed to return to camp until we were sure that we had not been spotted by the Germans. We were not to put the maquis in jeopardy nor risk identifying its whereabouts.

We went over the plan several times and Luc asked us to repeat details back to him to make sure we had understood. He checked the times with us and he checked contingencies. Georges called these the 'what-ifs' and the term stuck. We had so many what-ifs that I was beginning to lose sight of the main plan. I focused on the key parts of the mission and decided that I would let the what-ifs, should they arise, take care of themselves.

As the time to leave approached, I checked my kit. I was nervous as I checked over the bren gun, knife, garrotte and grenades. Luc had taught us to use all of these and his close combat training had been good. Good enough I hoped. I was fit and strong and Luc's training had been rough; I had coped well, as had Georges. We both learned quickly and we were about to be put to the test. I had never killed anybody, nor wanted to and I was still not sure whether I could kill. Survival, however, is a very basic instinct.

As we left in the half moonlight I was shaking. Luc had said that it is good to be frightened as it heightens one's senses. He was right. I was aware of every noise and my senses were acute. There is a balance needed: fear can overwhelm if you let it. I controlled my fear instead of letting it control me. I learned this skill quickly and I was pleased that I had.

At the edge of the clearing we paused and lay on the ground, the three of us, side-by-side, in a line. I could see the lights of the small railway depot opposite. A wire fence separated us from the yard. Luc cut the wires to make a small opening. We needed to cross the railway lines to reach the edge of the depot. I could see a lone locomotive and a coal train; these were our targets.

"Remember where you are," Luc whispered, "we need to come back this way. Line yourself up with the lights and the depot building and don't make a mistake."

What he told me next surprised and frightened me, "Jacques and I need to leave the brens here. We can't be seen with them in the depot. Georges, you position yourself behind that building and guard us. Shoot if you need to but try to miss us, will you."

We still had our emergency grenades, knife and garrotte. I did not see how that would help me if the German guards opened fire. I did not see any German guards but that did not mean that there were none around.

Georges left the edge of the wood first and made it quickly to his position. I saw his sign that he was in place and Luc hissed for me to go with him. I remembered the plan now and started to put it into action shedding the what-ifs which were merely clutter.

We crept slowly over to the first locomotive. I felt vulnerable when crossing the line. At the side of the huge engine I felt secure. The beast hissed, almost alive and its metal was warm and inviting. Our contact was there and he showed me the controls. It was not dissimilar to what Luc had drawn. He pointed at the pressure gauge. It had a good head of steam and was ready to roll. The safety valve hissed regularly releasing the pent up energy of this dragon. I now had the unpleasant task to perform. Our contact told me to hit him and make it believable. I surprised myself and hit him hard. I learnt later that I had fractured his jaw and he was in pain for weeks. The blow was hard enough that the Germans never suspected him of being involved in the sabotage. I led him to the engine shed out of the cold and tied him firmly. I could see that his face was swelling and that he would have bruising the next day. I felt remorse for what I had done but it did not last long. I returned to the locomotive and looked at my watch. Three more minutes to go. I looked at the coal train and I could see Luc in the engine cab. Two minutes to go. I looked around from my vantage point in the cab and saw a German guard cross the line heading towards the station. He did not look my way. I looked back to where Georges was hiding and saw him raise the gun in readiness.

I prayed that he would not pre-empt and fire too early. He did not. The guard carried on to the station building and I saw him go inside. One minute to go. A light in the station building came on and I saw the silhouette of the German guard having a leak. Thank God, I thought.

It was time. I pushed forward the valve and I heard the creak as the brute came alive. Take off the brake, do not forget, I had been told. I released the brake and the creature lurched forward. A few miles an hour at first and then it started to accelerate. Time to go, I thought and I leapt across the cab and was out of the other side, rolling on the embankment. I was disorientated for a few seconds and lined myself up with the building. I could see the clearing. The locomotive was accelerating now and I could hear its sound becoming fainter as it headed down the valley. I made my way gently and slowly towards the clearing. I could see Georges at his post as I recovered my bren gun. I wanted to join Georges and cover Luc but this was not in the plan. Luc was to return and Georges was to be the last to leave. That was how it was to be. It was only a minute before Luc started the coal train but it seemed like an eternity. Adrenalin was surging through my veins and my senses were keen. I wondered how Georges was feeling. I had no way of knowing as I lay on my stomach clutching my bren gun and waiting for Luc to return.

I heard the coal train start, slowly at first and then accelerating. I hoped that Luc had jumped clear. The coal train was soon in the distance but there was no sign of Luc. The what-ifs came into my mind. Georges was still in position. I looked over towards the station. I could not see as clearly as I had before but I was sure that there was no further activity from that quarter.

It was a full five minutes until Luc arrived and he gave the agreed call as he approached. He lay besides me and gave the call sign again so that Georges would hear. I saw Georges look around and then he crawled over to our position.

"Is it done?" Georges whispered.

Luc said that it was done and Georges added, "Lets get the Fuck out of here."

We withdrew with great stealth at first and then simply quietly. Luc shook our hands warmly when we had reached a safe distance from the station depot.

"Well done chaps," he said in heavily accented English. Luc knew little English and this was one of his few stock phrases.

We headed towards the rendezvous point and I hoped that Henri's team had done as well as us. The mission required the locomotives to leave both the west and east depots at the same time if they were to meet in the cutting where they would cause maximum damage and be most difficult to retrieve. The coal train was an insurance policy. It would ensure that the Germans were kept busy for weeks.

We heard the crash. I think villages for miles around heard the crash. It was spectacular and lit up the night sky. A couple of minutes later there was another loud explosion as the coal train hit the wreckage of the two locomotives. Mission accomplished I thought. If only I had known.

"Now we are in for it," said Luc, "this place will be crawling with Fritz soon. We need to get a move on now and lie low."

I knew the plan and I knew the reason why we had to hide but I was so exhilarated that I wanted to tell the world how clever we had been. Now was not the time for this. It was still important that we used stealth and we were careful to cover our tracks. We headed for the meeting point and made it five minutes early. The clouds were spreading and the moon peered out behind them, tentatively at first but then in its majestic glory providing a half light that lit our way in shades of grey.

Our rendezvous with Henri's team was to be at a rough track at right angles to the path on which we had been travelling. We were to meet up and then hide in a cave complex at the top of the path, a distance of around eight kilometres. The caves had a hidden entrance and a labyrinth of tunnels leading to several exits, also hidden. These caves were unknown to the Germans so they represented a good place to conceal ourselves. I was not so sure myself, as my instincts were telling me that I would rather be pursued in the open than scuttling down some subterranean warren. I accepted the maquisards' experience though and did not register my concerns.

Our world then turned upside down. We heard the sound of a motor vehicle coming from down the track. Then we saw the dull lights and Luc told us to lay on the floor and close our eyes and keep still. I wondered why we had to close our eyes and Luc told me later about the reflections of our eyeballs in the light. We would have stood out like cats eyes on the road. I lay on the damp grass shivering in the cold with my bren gun to hand and heard the vehicle approach. It was difficult to know what type of vehicle it was but I was hoping that it was one returning to the farm a mile up the track. It did not sound like a tractor and in any case I had seen few tractors since I arrived. The vehicle sounded more like a jeep. Luc said later that Germans did not have jeeps and that the car was a *Kubelwagen* or soft top bucket car though I did not know this at the time.

The car drove past us, its lights visible through my closed eyelids and I heard it labour up the rough path. I opened my eyes as it passed me and I thought the danger was over. I then heard the car manoeuvre a turn up the path and head back down the track so I closed my eyes again. It then came to a halt twenty yards away from where we were laying pointing down the track and adjacent to the opening from which we were expecting Henri to emerge; the engine was stopped and the lights extinguished. Henri was an experienced maquisards and would see the vehicle, we were sure, especially in the half light of the moon.

I wondered what was happening and why this vehicle was here. As my eyes became re-accustomed to the half light I could see that this was a German vehicle with a soft top which had been lowered. I could see two people in the front of the car but not clearly enough to identify any features. I tried to relax my muscles for I was tensing.

I soon found out the purpose of their visit. The German was speaking in broken French with a dreadful accent. The person with him was French and female. We had to endure the sounds of carnal pleasure from our hide-away as I watched the French tart mount the German soldier and them both writhe to climax. I would normally have found this erotic and Georges and I have watched enough pornography to know this but that night I found sickening and I wondered how a French woman could even entertain a German soldier, let alone do what they had done.

When they had finished they sat back into their seats and lit a cigarette and I could see the ends of the cigarette glowing red in the dark. Then I heard a rustle from the far track and I hoped it was not Henri's team. With the soft top of the bucket car down the German heard it too and I saw him pick up his rifle and open the door of the car. He opened the door slowly and the click was barely perceptible. I could see his tall form moving cat-like towards the source of the noise. He stepped back away from the car so that he had a better view and I saw the woman crouch down obviously fearful of what was happening.

He was now just ten yards from where we were laying and I tensed; he was right in front of me. To the side of the clearing I saw someone emerge and recognised Henri immediately from his characteristic gait. It seems in slow motion to me now but I remember the German raising his rifle to shoot. I leapt up and must have startled the German and he lost his concentration for a moment. Just long enough, I remember thinking. I did not have time to aim and fire my gun so I spun it round and hit his head with all of the force I could muster. It left a mess of his face and the blood spurted and he fell immediately. Henri leapt forward and finished the soldier off with his knife.

The woman, seeing what was happening, opened the car door and was trying to escape. Henri was quick to evaluate the situation and he leapt after the woman and dragged her back, brandishing his knife. I knew his knife was razor sharp. Henri thrust his knife towards her and I closed my eyes fearful of what would happen next.

"We are not the boche, Henri," Luc hissed.

I opened my eyes again and saw Henri pulling at the woman's long golden locks and cutting them aggressively.

"You tart," he said venomously, "you disgrace France."

Henri picked up the body of the German soldier and threw it roughly into the car. He followed with the woman who kicked and screamed. She stopped yelling when she saw Henri's face close up and the sharp knife glinting in the moonlight. I heard her whimper like a child and the sound chilled me further. The woman landed in the rear seat. Henri took the car out of gear and deactivated the handbrake and gave the light car a push using his mighty strength. This took such a short time that the car was travelling quite quickly downhill by the time the woman managed to raise herself from the seat. I could see her transfixed as the vehicle hurtled down the hill.

We found out much later that the car exited the path, crossed the road and tumbled down the rocky edge into the forest below. The remains, such as they were, were not found until after the war. We were not to know that now.

"Such a waste of a car," said Henri.

# Thursday 11<sup>th</sup> May

## Hide

It was after midnight by the time we had despatched the German. Georges came over to me and, uncharacteristically, threw his arms around me.

"You were fucking brilliant," he said.

I smiled and the adrenaline was still coursing through my veins so I was on a high.

"The bloody tart. Did you see what she was doing to that Fritz?"

"Leave it," I replied, "it makes me puke."

Henri came over to me and he said, "You talk so strange together."

It was a softer, less aggressive Henri with a hint of sadness.

What happened next took me by surprise. Henri kissed me on the cheeks and shook my hand.

"Thank you," was all he said and that was the last that he ever said to me about the events of this night.

He then kissed Georges on the cheeks and shook his hand saying nothing at all. Henri had accepted us and he was to treat us like one of the maquis from that point onwards. It was not possible to be too close to Henri, he did not allow this, but I learned to respect him and we became lifelong friends.

Luc asked, "where are the others?"

A look of angst came across Henri's face and I could see that the news was bad. He was a man of few words so he expressed what had happened succinctly.

"The job was done but we disturbed a German patrol. I tried to save them Luc but they perished."

"Were they taken?"

"No, we fought like tigers. They were killed."

I could see now what I had not seen before. Henri's left arm was dripping blood. He had been shot.

"I was in the rear and that is what saved me. I escaped into the woods after the shoot-out. The pigs shot me in the arm. It is nothing, just a surface wound. They followed me but I know this area better than them and they lost me. I had to detour which is why I was late. I didn't want those bastards to follow me here."

"Let me see the wound," said Luc, pulling off his backpack.

Henri took off his shirt and I illuminated the wound with my LED torch. Luc looked at me, still impressed by the torch. The wound looked messy to me but it cleaned up well as Luc applied some iodine solution. Henri winced as it was applied.

"Hold the lamp steady will you," Luc barked to me.

It was a surface wound and the bullet had missed the main veins and artery and the bone mostly because Henri was well built with large muscular arms. The bullet had passed clean through and Henri had been very lucky that night. I was worried about infection in this dirty environment so I was pleased when Luc applied the stinging liquid to the wound. I had a first aid kit in my bag with some sterile gauze bandage. I had brought it 'just in case' and was pleased that I had. I moved Luc out of the way and applied 21st century antiseptic and plaster to the wound and bound it reasonably tightly to stop the bleeding. I told Henri to keep it clean but I knew that was difficult. In normal conditions, and these were far from normal, Henri would have required stitches in a wound like that.

Henri barely flinched during all of this time and the wound must have hurt him. He was not one to complain about his own problems.

With Henri patched up, for now, we had to move on as dawn was early and we did not want to be out in the open when the boche arrived to find out what happened to their comrade that we had dismissed down the track. We decided that we would spend one day in the caves and would then make our way over the top of the hill to a thick forest. We would need to do that at night because there was a section that had to be traversed in the open and, with what we had just achieved, that was too dangerous.

It took us an hour to reach the caves. Luc was right that the entrance was concealed. I would not have found it at all without Luc's knowledge. We went inside and Luc was very careful to conceal our tracks. We had enough produce for three days in our packs if we conserved our supplies and we had picked up some water on the way from the stream. We would not live well but we would live.

Inside the caves were damp but not airless. Far above, a tunnel led to the surface like a chimney. It was not unpleasant but it was cold and we would need to venture out during the day to warm and dry ourselves. For now we slept on the damp straw strewn onto the floor. It smelt musty but I did not care; I was exhausted and, despite the insanitary conditions, I slept well and woke to find light pouring down the chimney, giving the cave an altogether different perspective. Judging by the quality of the light it was after 10:00. I looked at my watch and I was right. I was becoming more accustomed to my situation and reading the environment better and was less dependent upon my 21$^{st}$ century toys. I thought about how I had been reliant upon these trinkets, especially my mobile phone, and how quickly I had adapted to being without any of them.

I needed to relieve myself so I made my way towards the entrance to the caves. Georges spotted me and said, "You going for a piss?"

"Yes," I whispered, not wanting to disturb the others.

"I want one too," Georges continued, "I'll come with you."

The morning was bright and warm. There were menacing clouds on the edge of our vision but the sky overhead was a startling blue and the sun shone brightly.

As we stood, peeing into the bank, Georges said, "Henri was lucky yesterday. You did a good job Jacques and you were quick. I barely saw you move. You were like a gazelle. Shit you were fast."

I smiled though I confess I do not remember much of it. Instinct seemed to take over and it appeared to me like somebody else had taken over my body. I heard a noise and looked behind to see Henri heading towards us. He joined us just as our stream was finishing. I did the shaking ritual, buttoned up and wiped my hands on some grass, as did Georges.

I heard Henri finish peeing and he also wiped his hands on the grass following our lead I believe, for I had not seen anyone do that before. He handed me and then George a packet of gauloises cigarettes. I did not smoke but this was the first real time that Henri had acknowledged our presence so it felt churlish to refuse. I took a cigarette from the package and handed it to Georges who shrugged and also took one. Henri passed us a box of matches and I puffed on my first cigarette.

Henri was a taciturn man and we stood, drawing on our cigarettes, mostly in silence. When Henri did speak he gave nothing away of himself but spoke of the climate and our surroundings.

"How is the arm?"

"It is fine. It will heal," was all he replied.

I longed to ask him more about himself but I did not on that occasion. He had let us in and I was grateful for that and I felt that I must let him open up in his own time. Luc joined us and headed for the wooded area. It was evident that he needed more than a pee and he was not about to do that in front of us. Later he joined us in the sunlight at the hidden entrance of the cave. It was a good vantage point as we could see down the track if anyone was coming. There was sufficient shrub and wooded area to hide us if we needed this.

"The boche will be mad this morning," Luc said, "I hope they don't take it out on the villages."

I had read in my history books of men being rounded up and shot in front of their families after an attack like the one we had accomplished. The brutality shown by the Germans to innocents was an attempt to deter future sabotage missions and to alienate local people from the maquis. In other parts of France it did this but, I found out, not here. The *Bretagne* were made of sterner stuff. Luc had told me that there were many ways to resist and that I should not judge people harshly because they chose to stay at home.

We ate from the produce we had brought. We did not light a fire so we used the water for drinking. Luc said that we would be able to replenish our produce once over the hill at a farm he knew. We warmed in the sun for several hours and took in the relative silence of our surroundings. All of the sounds were natural; birds were singing, insects buzzing and leaves rustled gently. For the moment it was idyllic.

Then we heard a less natural sound. It was distant but unmistakable.

"Dogs," barked Luc, "Fuck, we need to go. Get your things together and make it quick."

I did not have many 'things' so I went to fetch by backpack and weapons with Georges and Henri. As we returned I saw Luc take something from his bag and I could see that it was some wire and a grenade. I saw him pee along a line of the track and then into a path through the shrub. I was puzzled. I then saw him set a booby-trap perpendicular to the track of his pee. He did the same at the entrance to the path.

"It gives something for the dogs to follow," he said to me, seeing that I was puzzled, and then added, "damn, two grenades gone."

"I have some," said Henri, "three left still."

The sound of the dogs were still distant though becoming closer. Luc was impatient for us to leave; despite this he made good the cave entrance and hid our tracks. He also brushed around the entrance with the leaves of an aromatic shrub.

"It'll confuse the dogs," he said to me and winked.

"This way."

I followed behind Georges who was following Luc. Henri was at the rear and one would not have known that he had been wounded. Luc led us down towards the river which flowed in a deep gully around the caves. We entered the river and walked upstream. I now understood. Luc was a professional and he impressed me greatly. The water would mask our scent to the dogs. It was hard going though and the water was fast flowing at times. We were walking at barely a quarter of the pace that we would have on dry land. I knew Luc was right though; we would have been tracked easily by the dogs.

We had been trudging through the stream, over boulders and up small waterfalls, for an hour when we heard the first explosion. The grenade trap had worked. Then the second explosion. Miraculously, both booby-traps had been triggered. We stopped to listen after the sound of the explosions had passed but could hear nothing.

"Another half hour," said Luc, "then we can exit the stream. We can then hide out until dark and then head for the forest."

We stopped to listen again as we dragged ourselves upstream. Still nothing heard. Our luck was holding.

Finally, we exited the stream into a densely wooded area. It was damp and small rivulets of water flowed into the main stream.

"This way," said Luc.

We followed him, Georges still in front and Henri at the rear. In the densest part of the wood was a hut. I really would not have seen it had Luc not pointed it out. The camouflage was good and in the darkness of the wood the hut was difficult to spot. We went inside. It had six small bunks arranged two up on three sides of the room. On the other wall was a rough table and a reasonably clean pan and some dirty mugs.

I was exhausted after the trek upstream. I had a spirit stove in my bag; this was another 'just in case' item I had packed as was the small amount of spirits I had with me. Georges was impressed when I heated some water and added some sachets of Nescafe instant coffee that I had stolen from a hotel. To preserve our supplies I added only half the normal quantity of coffee and there was no milk.

"It tastes like piss," said Luc and smiled as he took the first drink, "but I like piss."

"Your piss saved our skin," said Henri.

"Plus a couple of grenades," said Georges and laughed.

Henri smiled and this was the first time I had seen his guard lowered. He drank the coffee without further comment.

"We leave for the upper forest after dark," said Luc, "we should get some sleep. Once over the hill we'll be away from the danger zone I think."

We did sleep and I was surprised to be woken by Georges.

"Come on you dozy bugger," he said into my ear, "we're ready to go."

I was disorientated but alert immediately. My senses have never been this acute and I reached for my gun now almost instinctively. From sleep to trek was just five minutes. It was darker than the previous evening and Luc allowed me to use my torch. I was grateful for this because the forest was dense.

We made our way to our new hideout and it took us most of the night. The going was easier as we left the wood but I felt vulnerable walking in the open towards our current destination and was pleased to re-enter a forest. There were rustles in the woods and I felt the hair on my neck rise in response. It was something safer than a German Luc had said, possibly a wild boar.

We rested in the forest for a further five days. It was unpleasant as the weather turned wet and very windy for a time. Luc said that it was to our advantage as it would keep the enemy at home. I was cold most of the time and the spirit for my stove ran out. Luc managed to visit a farm in the area and he provided produce and some rough brandy for the stove, he said. The stove saw none of the brandy.

# Tuesday 16<sup>th</sup> May

# Information

Luc said he was heading for the Martin's farm and would I like to come. His eyes sparkled as he said this and his mouth twisted into a wicked grin. He did not have to ask me twice and my spirits rose at the thought of meeting Élise again. He said that he wanted to find out some news and that he was sure Monsieur Martin would have his ears to the ground.

Georges looked at me askance and smiled and made a particularly rude gesture with his arm and hand. I was pleased that this was a 21<sup>st</sup> century gesture that went over the heads of our fellow resistance fighters.

Yet again, the trip to the Martin's farm was wet and we were dripping when we arrived at the rear door of the farm having covered our advance well lest anyone should see us. It was Élise who met us this time.

"Oh yes, you are wet again," she said beaming. She was pleased to see us, despite our dishevelled appearance.

She pulled us through the door and kissed Luc on the cheeks and hugged him warmly. She then did the same to me and her hug was warm and genuine.

"I was so worried about you," she said, "I heard that two were killed. I did not know, none of us did, who it was that was killed. I just hoped it was not you. Oh it is so good to see you both."

Élise was excited, really excited to see us and I savoured her use of 'both' and was happy that she was pleased to see me too.

"Get out of those wet clothes. I will get some of father's clothes. You'll catch your death of cold."

She left the room and returned with some clothes. We were both standing in our underclothes and I swear that she gave me one of those approving looks again. I saw Luc peering at me and he was smiling and nodding.

Monsieur Martin is a bigger man than I am so his clothes were loose on me but it did not matter. I was dry and warm again in the Martin's farmhouse kitchen. Élise hung our clothes to dry above the range and I heard the hiss of steam as the clothes dripped water onto the range. Élise stoked the range and added more wood.

"Claire will be so sad that she missed you. She is visiting grandmother and taking her some produce. Alain is with her. Father is on the land somewhere, I'm not sure where."

"Tell me what has happened please Élise," said Luc.

"No, you tell me first, I want to know how you all are."

We explained to Élise what had happened and that Henri, Luc, George and I were safe. Luc explained who had been killed and how it had happened. He was sparing with the details of our encounter with the German and the tart but explained about our escape from the dogs. He did not mention to Élise where we were currently staying and I learnt later that this was to protect her and us; what she did not know, she could not tell. Élise knew the two who had died and was saddened. One of them had a wife and a small child and the other was single with a girlfriend. Élise said that she would visit the families of the dead maquisards when it was safe to do so.

"We are so proud of you," Élise said, addressing her comment to both of us but looking at me. I beamed back and I felt good, really good.

"Let me tell you what has happened in the last few days," Élise continued, "There have been no reprisals and that is unusual. The Gestapo have been active and there have been roadblocks but nobody has been arrested and there have been no atrocities."

She paused before the word 'atrocities' and again afterwards before continuing, "but the real delight is that Fritz does not have a crane that can be used to clear the track, even if they can get to it, so the main line is closed. There have been crowds of people who have been to see the wreckage. It is quite an attraction. The boche has cleared the crowds away but they don't seem to be as aggressive as they are normally, almost like they have bigger problems."

"What about the security situation?" asked Luc.

"You mean has it changed?"

Luc nodded.

"It is tighter for sure. There's a curfew at nine o'clock each evening and there are more roadblocks. It would not be a good idea for you to be roaming around the roads, even without weapons."

Élise knew we had no weapons because she had seen us practically naked.

"What about Henri?" asked Élise, "you said he has a wound. Is it bad?"

"You know Henri," I said, "he says it is fine. I dressed it yesterday and it does seem to be healing well and no sign of infection. I am nearly out of bandage though so if you have any we could do with some. He will have a scar as it's quite a deep wound."

Luc then told Élise about my role in the incident with the German and I could sense the value of my capital rise with her. I was bashful but secretly very pleased that Luc had told her.

There was some noise outside and Élise went over to the door.

"Ah, it is *papa*," she said and opened the door. She looked around.

"We have visitors *papa*," she said to him.

Monsieur Martin walked through the door. He was dirty from the fields as it was a wet day. Luc went over to him and I followed.

"I have dirty hands," Monsieur Martin said.

"It is of no matter," said Luc and he kissed Monsieur Martin's cheeks and shook his hands warmly. I did the same and Monsieur Martin seemed genuinely pleased to see us.

"You both look like you could do with a bath," he said, "and, if you don't mind me saying this, you smell like you could do with one too."

He laughed as he said this and Élise mock scolded him. He was right though, we must have looked a mess and I had not shaved for days. We both took him up on his offer and half an hour later we returned washed, shaved and refreshed. This was the second bonus of the day after seeing Élise.

The third bonus was some real food and some wine followed by coffee and a cognac. Over the meal we told Monsieur Martin what we had told Élise. He was impressed by what we had achieved.

I did not feel that I could tell the Martin's about the D-day landings though. I felt that it was important to have secrecy on this subject. The Germans must not have advance notice of this. I also knew from my history that Hitler's troops were busy in Russia, though I was less sure of the important dates here. I had a feeling that the Soviet's relieved Leningrad early in 1944 and that they had already advanced into Poland but I was not sure. What I do remember is that the Soviet soldiers were no better than the Germans and that Eastern Europe would swap one kind of oppression for another for a whole generation. It made me shudder.

"How long before we return?" asked Luc of Monsieur Martin, meaning a return to the maquis.

"I think another week yet. Things are settling by the day but the Gestapo are still crawling round. Better to let them complete their investigations before you surface again," replied Monsieur Martin.

"Visit us again, when you can of course, you are always welcome here. Now, I must return to my work. There are the hens to see to and then the cows."

He took his leave of us, hugging both of us and shaking us by the hand warmly. The Martin family had accepted me and it was a good feeling.

"One thing before you leave," said Élise, "I have some news for you. There was another drop whilst you were away playing terrorist."

She smiled as she said this and looked at me again and bowed her head slightly and leaned it to one side. It was intoxicating.

"There are jeeps and we are to use them after liberation. That means it is near, doesn't it?"

Luc looked at me and, ever the professional, knew that he could not reveal what he knew so he replied, "I don't know Élise, but I hope with all of my heart that it will be soon."

"I think there's a part of you," Élise replied, smiling again, "that quite likes playing the soldier. But be careful Luc because this isn't a game and the stakes are high. You are like a brother to me and I don't want to lose you. War is an awful business and I would like to return to a normal life and clear our beautiful country of this vermin, for ever."

Luc looked at me and grinned. I knew what he was thinking. He was the brother but what was I?

We changed into our maquis clothes again ready for our departure. It was late afternoon and the rain had stopped but the sky was still charged and menacing. There was a stiff breeze which would remove any residual dampness from the clothes but would chill the bones.

Élise said goodbye to Luc first and he left by the rear door furtively, checking that nobody could see him leave. I paused in the doorway and looked at Élise who looked back. I paused and she waited for me to say something.

"I'd, I mean, well," I fumbled.

"Yes," she teased.

Luc had crossed the farmyard and was sheltering at the other side, out of view, waiting for me. He looked at over and gave me one of his grins. He then repeated the very rude sign that Georges had given me. Luc obviously did not know what it meant and, thankfully, nor did Élise. I gave him as stern a look as I could manage and then ignored him.

"I'd very much like to see you again," I spurted out.

"You will," she said, "and I would very much like to see more of you Jacques."

She kissed me on the lips and I left, beaming.

I could not repeat what Luc said to me when I caught up with him but it was obscene. I felt good and it seemed wrong to feel this good with all of the things that were happening around me.

I knew that D-day was coming and I knew that it was going to be better. I was wrong.

# Wednesday 17<sup>th</sup> May
# Return to the Maquis

We spent five uncomfortable days in our forest hide out. We dare not light a fire for fear of being discovered and we had no spirit for my stove. We managed to obtain produce from local farms so we were well fed.

I found the five days tedious. Georges and I spoke often and Luc and Henri joined us more often than not. Luc added to the conversations and Henri contributed occasionally. I came to realise that Henri spoke only when he had something to say and was not good at small talk. I learnt not to ignore his input for it was always worth considering. I became quite close to Henri during those days and he would seek me out and sit besides me, usually in silence. These sessions were uncomfortable at first as I babbled incessantly wanting to fill the void left by Henri. I started to understand that Henri needed company but not conversation and we often sat or stood, with the inevitable cigarette, without speaking. It became no longer uncomfortable being with Henri and I knew he would speak when he wished. Georges found this easy because, like Henri, he was a man of few words and he made each of them count. With Georges, however, most of the words he used were expletives or obscene.

I was pleased when we left our self-imposed exile to return to the maquis and we did this on the 17<sup>th</sup> May. We left early because we had a several hour trek before we would reach the maquis. Some of the route was in the open and I had inherited Luc's dislike for the open space. We walked along the side of a field near the hedgerow whenever we found ourselves exposed. Luc said that we could throw ourselves under the hedge if we heard a spotter plane.

The journey back to the maquis was uneventful and we were greeted first by the guards who treated us like the prodigal sons returning after a long break. Bernard greeted us next and he kissed us on both cheeks and shook our hands for a long time. He beamed at us.

"Gabriel wants to see you. He and Pierre are back and they have some news for you."

For the first time since our arrival I felt part of the maquis; Georges and I had been accepted and the atmosphere was much more cordial that it had been previously. Wherever we went maquisards shook our hands and welcomed us back. Georges and I made for our tent and I threw my bag, but not my gun, into the tent.

"Watch it mate," said Georges as he watched my bag hit the ground, "you've got three grenades in there."

I smiled at him and replied, "Four!"

He grinned back but placed his bag down slowly.

We went to find Bernard again as he told us that he would find Gabriel. As we arrived at the communal part of the camp, André handed us his signature coffee substitute with a beaming friendly smile. It was the first hot drink we had had for days and was very welcome.

After André had handed us the drinks, with his hands now free, he shook ours and said, "Great work, my friends."

Then he looked sad, or as sad as André can look, "We lost Albert and Louis and that is always bad. They died for the honour of France and such a death is not a death in vain. We will always remember their sacrifice."

From André this was unexpected as he was rarely serious and his delivery was just a little pompous.

After he had finished he paused and then added, "And yours."

With that he disappeared to his cook station again and reappeared a few seconds later with a couple of platters of bread and brie. I smiled appreciatively at André and scoffed the contents of the platter briskly, as did Georges. Luc was nowhere to be seen and I had not seen Henri since our arrival.

We sat for a while chatting with other maquisards. The atmosphere had visibly lightened and I liked it. I felt like I was part of this team. I heard Bernard's voice in the distance and then he appeared through the trees finishing an order to an unseen maquisard. He smiled as he saw us.

"Georges, Jacques, there you are. Fed and watered too, I see. Good. Luc and Henri have met with Gabriel already. They told me about you Jacques. Brilliant work, well done."

Realising that he was leaving Georges out of the praise he followed with, "and Georges, your first campaign is to your credit."

It sounded like an afterthought and George just shrugged. I knew that shrug and I felt Georges' pique.

"Gabriel has some time now," he added in a way that sounded more like an order than a request so we made our way to Gabriel's quarters without Bernard this time. He greeted us warmly and spoke to us in English. It was strange to be speaking English again though it had been only a few days in reality that they had spoken French exclusively.

Gabriel did not waste much time and I could see that he was busy. He expressed his gratitude for what we had achieved but did this in a professional and brusque way like it was his duty to do. He seemed to be going through the motions rather than speaking from the heart.

Gabriel was English at heart and his Anglo-Saxon coolness was a surprise to us after the flow of Gallic emotions since our return.

"I wanted to tell you about the effects of your sabotage," he said, "and its effect on Fritz."

He gave us a shallow smile and continued, "The main line into Brittany is now jammed solid. The boche have insufficient cranes to clear the lines and the execution was perfect. The crash occurred within a hundred metres of where we planned and in the cutting. The collision on its own would have blocked the line but the coal train running into the wreckage has made it a most difficult task to clear the line. Without cranes it is almost impossible and I am not sure how Fritz would even get a crane to the wreck site in any case."

He paused for our reaction. When there was none he continued.

"The Gestapo scum has slithered around since the campaign." The distaste for this organisation was clear from his intonation.

"It has been difficult to move around and you were wise to lie low. I was expecting you back a little earlier and we were not sure who had been killed; most unfortunate, of course. Then we heard from Monsieur Martin that four of you were safe but that Henri had been wounded. Again, we were not sure how serious was Henri's injury. Actually, he looks fine and his wound is healing well. I believe you may have had something to do with that Jacques."

Again, I felt Georges' resentment next to me. I knew him too well and I could sense when he was unhappy, as could he with me. I said something complimentary about Georges' role in all of this. Gabriel understood my action but did not add anything. Georges merely shrugged again.

"The net effect of your action," Gabriel said looking at Georges first this time, "is that the boche have to move troops and supplies by road and that will slow them."

He now looked at me, "I have asked from my commanding officers at home for clarification about the invasion, the liberation."

Gabriel now paused but was not expecting anyone to fill the gap and nobody did.

"They are secretive, of course. But I think you may be right Jacques, the invasion is imminent. Do you know how long it is before we are liberated here after the invasion?"

I was coy. I had not exposed the location of the Normandy landings to anyone, as I did not want to increase the risk of the Germans discovering this information. I was not sure if this knowledge could change the outcome of the war and change history. I felt that the risk was not worth taking and that I had said too much already in telling Gabriel the invasion dates. Georges had said nothing at all about the future.

It was not that I was suspicious of Gabriel; I would have entrusted my life to him. In fact, I thought I had done this already. I just felt that the more information that I uncovered the more was the likelihood of it ending up in the wrong hands.

"No, no more than I have told you already," I replied. Georges looked at me and knew I was hedging but he said nothing.

"You told me that we would be liberated this year, yes?"

I nodded, as did Georges.

"That will have to do."

Gabriel scratched his head and shuffled though some papers before saying, "I have to leave for central command soon. I have another target for you. Are your ready for another?"

Georges answered first, "Too right."

"I'll take that as a yes, then, shall I?"

I smiled and said, "Affirmative."

Gabriel smiled back and said, "I have explained to Bernard what we want to achieve and he will brief you. The action happens in the next few days. Not sure when yet as we have to do a bit more intelligence. Get some rest whilst you can. By the way, Luc and Henri want to be part of this and they both want you in their team. Henri wants you too. That is pretty surprising because I think he wanted your blood just a few days ago. Whatever you've done, keep up the good work. Look, I need to make tracks. Bernard will seek you out."

We left Gabriel's quarters at the same time as he left. I saw Pierre heading towards us and he waved at us before scurrying off with Gabriel. We made our way back to the camp centre and found Luc and Henri sitting on a log drinking coffee. Luc stood as we arrived and beamed as he stepped towards us. Henri followed his lead.

# Monday 22th May
## Preparations

Bernard did seek us out the following day. He had not been seen again since he told us that Gabriel wanted us. Georges and I had a good night's sleep and I managed to sleep through Georges' nightmare. He thrashes around when he has a nightmare and usually manages to hit me but this time, if he did, I missed it or he missed me.

Luc joined us for breakfast and he asked us, for the first time, about our future. Georges told him about some of the things we had taken for granted just a short time earlier. Luc soaked up knowledge and he was intrigued when we told him about the advances in motor vehicles, aviation and electronics. My mobile had some charge left still so I showed him some of the games. When I told him that it was a telephone he simply did not believe me. I was quite relieved when Bernard joined us with Henri because I found Luc's interest a little tedious. Georges was more tolerant and I found that it was like watching two children playing together.

It made me think of my grandfather for I had always been surprised at how quickly he had adapted to changes in technology. He was keenly aware of the internet well before I was, though I was around nine or ten years of age at the time, and he shared the same fascination for the latest electronic gadgets as did I. It made me think that grandfather, right now and in this time, would be the same age as myself. I remembered from my grandfather's war time tales that he had been in Brittany and roughly where we are now. I mused that it would be good to seek him out and that rumination became a challenge.

We finished breakfast and retired again to Gabriel's quarters as Gabriel was away again. We sat around his table and Bernard began to explain what we were to do. He had a map of the area and he unrolled it onto the table.

"This is our target," he said pointing to an area near the river and on the edge of town. I studied the map and I could see that Bernard was indicating an area near a bend in the road and what looked like an airstrip. There was no shelter nearby that I could see and it looked like a built-up area.

Luc knew immediately the location that Bernard had highlighted and said, "That's the airbase. Surely we are not going to attack the airbase."

"You're right Luc, it is the airbase and we are not going to attack it. We are going to do a stealth raid and blow their fuel supply. That should slow them down a bit."

"That place is well guarded," Luc continued, "how are we going to get in and where are the fuel tanks?"

"I know where they are," it was Henri who spoke, "they are opposite the river, here."

Henri prodded the map with his stubby muscular fingers. He pointed just up from a bend in the river where it looked like it widened.

"There are three cylindrical fuel tanks mounted on short legs. I've reconnoitred them for a previous mission. We didn't go ahead with that one because it was too dangerous."

Georges looked at me and I looked at Luc. Bernard could see Henri's concern.

"You're right Henri. We called it off last time because we thought that it would be difficult to retreat after the job."

"So what's changed," Luc asked.

"A few things," said Bernard, "but mostly these."

He rummaged in his bag and pulled out a charge. It was quite large and looked heavy. It was conical in shape with short legs shaped like an upside down 'u'. At the top of the cone was a screw top and whatever screwed into the top was missing.

"They look cumbersome," said Georges, "what are they?"

"They are charges, explosives," said Bernard, "they are magnetic and are borrowed from the boche. We can attach one to each fuel tank. They are intended for real tanks so they should make a real mess for Fritz to clean up."

Bernard always used the word 'borrowed' when talking about material taken from the Germans and I never understood why he did this because, clearly, the items would not be returned.

"How are they detonated?" asked Luc.

"The detonators attach here," Bernard said and pointed to the top of the cone, "and we can attach long wires to them so that you can be across the river when they blow. Don't connect the detonators until you are ready; they are very sensitive."

"So how do we get into the camp?" It was Henri who spoke and he followed with, "It is heavily guarded. Coming in from the front would be suicide."

"We've looked at that and you are right. There are searchlight towers here," he pointed to the map, "here, and here, three in all. There are patrols along here."

Bernard pointed to the perimeter fences. It looked to me like the fence went right around the air base and Bernard was indicating that the Germans patrol the whole of the boundary.

"I see where you are heading," said Henri, "the fuel tanks are close to the perimeter fence and the fence is constrained by the river."

"Brilliant!" exclaimed Luc, "We're going by river, yes?"

Bernard was visibly impressed. I, on the other hand, was somewhat behind. Georges spoke next and it was clear from his comment that he was understanding the plot.

"Just point out the location of the fuel tanks again will you Bernard."

Bernard identified the location and Henri then showed Georges the perimeter. I was starting to follow too.

"So the fence here is very close to the fuel tanks and to the river?"

"Within a metre of the fence and a couple of metres from the river I would guess. That so Bernard?"

"You are correct Henri."

"So we cross the river here, plant the charges, get back to the other side and blow the charges," Luc said succinctly and indicated a point across the river from the fuel tanks.

"That's right Luc but there is a complication," answered Bernard, "the river is too wide at that point to allow us to be sure that we can pull the charges safely so we have to rig a pulley in the middle of the river to hold the wire and stop it being dragged by the water. We can't leave the pulley behind or it will tell the boche our escape route. We want to keep that as quiet as we can."

Bernard pulled another piece of paper from a pile and placed it on top of the map. It was a rough sketch of the target site. I could see better from the drawing what was expected of us. Bernard explained that a canoe would be hidden on the opposite side of the river. He went on to say that Gabriel's team were collecting more information about the patrols and particularly their timings.

"We are worried that the Germans may send patrols to this side of the river," Bernard was pointing at the rough plan at this point, "and that would scupper our plans. This side is lightly wooded but quite overgrown. It isn't ideal and it would be better if the cover was heavier. You'll need camouflaging, for sure. Back here is a path through dense wood."

Bernard was pointing back at the map now and his hand waved over an area of forest about a kilometre and a half from the target. It looked to me like we had a difficult escape route.

"Can we have a look, for real I mean before the mission, is that possible?" I asked.

"I have spoken to Gabriel about this already. It's a reasonable request but we must not alert Fritz so Gabriel has said no. I am sure that we can do some training close to the camp. Let me finish though."

Bernard continued with the plan. It looked simple on paper. A canoe would be left for us at the opposite side of the river to the base. We would take three charges and three detonators. The detonators would have pull rings on them and we would attach a wire to each. The far end of the wires would be left with a person on the other side of the river. The wires would be suspended in the river with a pulley structure that would be prodded into the river at the centre. Two of us would take the other end of the wire with us on the canoe. One would go ashore and cut through the fence. The person left in the canoe would pass the magnetic charges to the one ashore followed by the detonators. He would place the charges, attach detonators and wires and then they would both skedaddle back across the river in the canoe. Once over the other side we would jettison the canoe to make it look like we were escaping downstream in it. Then three of us would start to make our escape whilst the remaining maquisard would set off all of the charges with a single tug. He would then make his escape.

I was sure that it would not be that easy and I was right.

Georges made a play for the main part this time and he and Luc were chosen to cross the river and set the charges. I was to go into the river and help thread the wires and be the look-out. Henri was to pull the charges as he was the strongest. I asked him if his arm was well enough and he smiled and said that he was fine. I was amazed at Henri's recovery. He must have suffered pain from the wound but it did not seem to stop him doing anything that he would not normally have done. I caught him wincing only once and that was when Luc applied the iodine solution.

Bernard dismissed us and said that there would be a training session later in the day when Gabriel and Pierre were back. He said that there was a section of river close to the maquis that we could use.

"It isn't exactly the same but there are similarities," Bernard said, "I think you should practice threading the wires and the canoeing. The current here is slightly stronger so it should be harder for you. If you can manage it here you should manage it there. We'll do it in the light first and then, probably tomorrow, we'll do a dress rehearsal in the dark"

We made our way back to the camp, each with our own thoughts. When we arrived Luc left with Henri and I was alone with Georges. I told him about the thoughts I had had about my grandfather.

"You mean your grandfather is the same age as us now?"

"Yes," I had replied, "and he should be around here somewhere. There can't be too many maquis. What do you think about trying to find him?"

"Cool," Georges replied and then added, "and what is his name? I've only ever referred to him as Jacques' granddad."

"That's simple, I was named after him.  His name is the same as mine."

"That should make it easier.  Got to ask though, how many Jacques Richard's do we want?  One's enough for me."

# Tuesday 23rd May

# Change of Plan

Later in the day Gabriel returned with Pierre. I learnt that they had been for a reconnoitre at the target site. They had been disguised as fishermen and had joined a number of others who fish just down the river from the air base. The Germans watched them but did not interfere with their fishing. It gave Gabriel plenty of scope to watch the guards. He was close enough to our proposed strike point that he was able to gauge the water depth and current strength. This was a variable, of course, and would be affected by rain and we had had plenty of that though the weather was improving now and today had been pleasant and warm with much sunshine.

Pierre shook our hands warmly, as did Gabriel though his handshake was more sententious. Pierre addressed Georges and myself first, though Luc and Henri were with us.

"I have not seen you since you returned, except briefly," Pierre said, "I hear all went well. Congratulations."

Pierre then looked at Luc and Henri and continued with, "You've won over Henri too. I am pleased about that. He is a good man."

Henri looked down at his feet whilst Luc beamed at Pierre and went through the French welcoming protocol. Pierre was carrying what I took to be the pulley for the wires. It was made of steel and had three upright poles each with small pulley wheels at the top. At the bottom of each pole was a long sharp spike which we were told was for prodding into the mud at the bottom of the river. There was a stabilising mechanism at right angles to each pole to prevent the pulley contraption from falling over in the water when it was carrying the wires. Pierre said that he had asked a local blacksmith to make it up from a drawing and had told the blacksmith that it was for fishing.

"We've made it a little proud in case the river is higher. If the river is in flood we will call off the operation in any case as you will not be able to hold your course in the current. We'd like you to try this out this afternoon. Here's the wire too."

Pierre pulled a length of wire from his bag. It was braided and made of copper. Georges took hold of the coil of wire from Pierre and unwound a small length.

"That could be a bit awkward to unwind," Georges said handing the coil to me.

I had to agree with Georges and handed the wire to Luc. What we would have given for a length of a strong and light synthetic rope at this point. I knew that nylon had been invented already, in 1935, but I also knew that it was still in short supply and had not really made it into mass production. I remember my grandma saying that girls would kill for nylon stockings. I hoped that she was exaggerating.

"There are three of these are they?" Luc asked Pierre.

"Yes, is that a problem?"

"I think it may be," said Georges, "can we not have a single wire and then three ends, like a cat of nine tails, but just three tails?"

"That's a good idea Georges," said Gabriel, "and it would mean we could have just one pulley."

Pierre looked dejected as he had now had the pulleys manufactured. He looked thoughtful for a moment and then said, "OK, I take your point and I confess I had not thought of the logistics of threading three wires and keeping them untangled across the river. Georges does have a point. I'll need to re-think the pulley though. I can't take this back to the blacksmith today but I'll tell him that I had some problems fishing with it and ask him to modify it. He was bemused by my idea anyway."

"It will make it easier for Henri too, he'll need to pull only one wire. Can we have some kind of loop at the end and bind it with tape of something to make it easier to pull?"

Gabriel looked studious and I could see that he was impressed by Georges suggestions. Pierre looked a little dejected so Luc tried to lighten the mood by saying, "I can't see a problem with leaving the pulley as it is. So what's the problem in it having three wheels? It'll be more stable anyway. The only issue I can see is that if we have a cat of three tails on one end of the wire and a loop at the other will need to be pre-load the wire into the pulley. That sounds like it makes our job a bit simpler as we won't need to do any threading in the dark."

The term 'cat of three tails' stuck and Pierre agreed that leaving the three pulleys in place would be a satisfactory solution. Henri said nothing but I could tell from his demeanour that he was comfortable with the outcome.

"OK then," said Gabriel, "we want to do some training this afternoon so we will have to manage with what we have for now. I suggest that we thread the wire through the pulley to make it a bit more realistic. When can we have the cat of three tails and loop ready Pierre?"

"Tomorrow afternoon. Can I talk to you about the length of the tails too Gabriel?"

"That would be good Pierre. Sure, soon as we are done here. Can I ask the four of you to use the bend in the river, near the blasted oak tree, you know where that is?"

Gabriel paused and Luc nodded and said, "I know it, Gabriel."

"The current is stronger there than our objective but it is a reasonable spot for practice and the bend in the river is very similar. The depth is almost the same too."

Gabriel gave us a short briefing on what we were to do in training but it amounted to testing the plan we had discussed with Bernard earlier in the day. We would not have the explosive charge but Pierre had provided some pieces of metal for the training. He said that they were the same weight as the charges and had a mock detonator pin that would act in a similar manner to the real one. He also told us that the canoe was in position for us.

Dismissed again we left Gabriel and Pierre discussing the design of the cat of three tails. We took the kit we would need for the mission and decided between us to mimic, as best we could, the manoeuvre. We went to fetch our kit bags and packed the pulley, wire and mock explosives as if we were doing the job for real. The pulley was a problem and it was long. It would not fit in any of the bags. We tried it horizontally but felt that it would interfere with our trek through the woods. Henri suggested that it be carried and that he would carry it and that's what we did.

We made our way to the blasted oak which was a tree damaged by lightening many seasons earlier. The trunk was split open but the oak continued to grow despite its damage. The native American type canoe was made from birch bark and had two wooden paddles. I had heard about canoes made in this way but I had never seen one. It was just about big enough for two people and I was pleased that Henri was not included as crew of the canoe for he would have had difficulty manoeuvring his large frame. Both Georges and I had paddled canoes, mostly of aluminium or fibre glass and we were both expert. I preferred aluminium as I thought they were more stable but Georges preferred fibre glass or canvas as they were lighter and faster. What we both liked about canoeing was that it was possible to float through the water in almost silence and I have always felt that there is no better way of seeing wildlife. This was the reason that this type of canoe had been chosen because stealth was essential.

Luc had done some canoeing but not as much as Georges. Georges persuaded Luc that it would be a good idea to try out the canoe first before they started the practice. Luc boarded the canoe and I could see from the way that the canoe swayed that it was very light, probably as light as a fibre glass canoe though it was smaller. Luc's muscular build made him look too large for the canoe and he looked very uncomfortable. Georges clambered in next and sat down easily and they left. George rowed using the classic one sided paddle motion with the push away from the craft to keep it going in a straight line. Georges was proficient and he was soon out of sight. I heard some laughter from Luc as they went up river and I felt a pang of envy.

Henri handed me a cigarette and I took it from him and lit up. I was smoking regularly now, something I would not have done before coming here. Bernard had given Georges and I some cigarettes from the last drop so I was sharing these with maquisards too.

Henri asked me whether I had a girl back home. I was surprised by his question as he had not asked anything about my life at all.

"No," I said, "and it is just as well now, huh?"

"Luc tells me you are keen on Élise."

I reddened and Henri followed with, "Ah, I see that you are. She is a good girl from a fine family. Luc says she likes you too."

I flushed again until I was quite red. Henri smiled but he said no more about it. I was pleased to have heard independently that Élise liked me. After our last departure, I felt sure that she did like me but, with the passage of time, I had started to doubt myself .

The canoe came around the bend in the river again and we saw it before we heard it. As it came closer Georges said, "She's shit hot, nearly as good as fibre. Bit twitchy though. Can you pass the mock charges, we want to see what it's like with some weight."

"When you two talk to each other," said Luc, "you have a language of your own."

I smiled and said, "It's French Jim, but not as you know it."

Luc looked puzzled.

"Who the fuck is Jim?"

"Private joke," said Georges and grinned, "if you live long enough you might see the television programme."

Luc let the moment pass and watched as I handed the dummy explosives, one by one as they were heavy, to Georges. The canoe sank lower in the water and Luc looked ungainly.

"OK," Georges said when the bombs were loaded, "one more trial, but not as far this time."

Georges paddled the canoe away again and I could see that the water was closer to the top of the canoe. Georges manoeuvred the canoe competently and returned after a short trip round the bend of the river again.

"Yeh," he said as he pulled the canoe to, "we need to be careful when she's loaded. It handles OK but one wrong turn and we are over. We'll need to make sure those buggers are balanced too and I suggest a plank in the bottom. We balanced them on the ribs but if they move they'll puncture the skin and we can't risk that."

Georges handed the charges back to me and I put them on the bank. Luc scrambled out of the canoe followed by Georges who then pulled the canoe up the sandy bank. Henri had gone to find some wood as he had set himself the task of making a base for the canoe for the charges.

Henri returned with an axe crafted board which he then sized for the canoe and adjusted it to fit. We had Georges' plank and we were ready to start the training.

"Jacques," Luc said to me, "you are lighter built than me."

"Yes, so," I replied.

Georges looked on but said nothing.

"Would you like to go in the canoe with Georges and I'll do your job?"

I was delighted. I really had wanted to be in the canoe rather than up to my knees in cold water.

"You sure?" I said, hoping that Luc would not change his mind.

"I think it would be better," Luc replied and grinned, his face brightening.

"OK," I said, "I'd be happy too."

Georges patted me on the back and said, "OK partner, we've got to get this right."

We decided that, as Georges was a better at canoeing than was I, I would take the charges ashore and set the explosives whilst Georges manned the canoe.

"Let's get started," I said, "we need to be faultless. No fuck ups allowed."

We took our positions as we were to do for the operation. It was daylight so this made it easier. We would do the night practice later after dark. For now we just wanted to practice what we had to do. We would perfect our technique later.

Henri threaded the wire through the pulley and knotted it to keep it there. The cat of three tails would serve this purpose when it was completed. He then handed the pulley system to Luc and lay on the bank ready in his final position. I alighted the canoe first and made my way to the front. Georges climbed aboard next and positioned himself for the rowing. The board for the explosives was in position at the base of the canoe and Luc handed them, one by one, to Georges who placed them carefully on the plank. He handled them as if they were live and I guessed that he was taking the training very seriously. Finally, with the charges on-board, Luc handed Georges the pulley contraption and Georges handed that to me.

Luc leapt into the river to allow him to thread the wire that Henri was holding and prevent it from snagging.

"Bollocks, that's cold," he yelled.

"I hope you don't do that on the night," said Henri, "and quieter into the water. You want the boche to hear you."

"You guys are taking this training very seriously," Luc replied.

"And so we should," added Henri.

The rest of the rehearsal was run in this spirit and Luc changed his tack too acting as if this was the operation we were to accomplish. It gave the session a tinge of reality though no amount of training can prepare one for a real manoeuvre.

We did three runs that afternoon and improved with each by refining our approach and appraising our performance honestly and critically between sessions.

When we had completed the third and after the evaluation, Luc said, "I think the next time should be in the dark. It will make it closer to the real thing."

We all agreed and then sat on the bank of the river with a cigarette.

"Luc," I said.

"Yes, Jacques."

"Do you know of another Jacques Richard around here?"

"Jacques Richard, no I can't say that I do. Do you Henri?"

Henri thought for a few seconds and shook his head.

"Richard is your family name is it?"

"Yes Luc. My grandfather was in a maquis in Brittany during the war. He often spoke of it."

"There are not many maquis in Brittany and ours is not really a maquis of course."

I nodded and took a deep drag on my cigarette.

"I'll keep my eyes and ears open and ask around. How old would your grandfather be now?"

"Same as me, nineteen."

"That would be strange Jacques."

"What would Luc?"

"Meeting your grandfather at the same age as you are now. And even if you did, would he accept that he was your grandfather?"

I mused on what Luc had said.

# Wednesday 24<sup>th</sup> May

## Airmen

We did our last practice of the previous day in the dark and it was more difficult than I expected. There was a moon but it was covered with cloud so the night was dark. The clouds foretold of the weather to come for the 24$^{th}$ May was a wet day and that made it pretty miserable around the camp. I was pleased when Bernard, who had been discussing something with others in the maquis, asked us to join him in Gabriel's quarters. Although not completely dry, it was better than where we were sheltering.

We arrived before Bernard and were surprised to find two people already seated around the table. Georges and I did not recognise either of them and we had not seen them round the maquis before.

They looked cold and disorientated and their hands were cupping a mug of hot beverage which they were sipping slowly. They were dressed in maquis issue baggy clothes. This said nothing as any newcomer, us included, were asked to change into regular peasant dress as soon as they arrived. I was told by Luc that this was to help us blend in to the population.

As we arrived they placed their mugs on the table and stood and extended a hand. Then, in perfect English, one of them spoke.

"Well hello, and how are you? I am Clark and my colleague here is Eugene."

Their voices were rounded and polished and I had to stop myself smiling because I had not heard accents like these, except in old movies and comedy sketches. I realised that not all Royal Air Force pilots were from the upper classes and my meeting with Clerk and Eugene was a little like a parody of every bad stereotype. At this point, however, I was confronted with the archetype cinema pilot.

I understand that mimicry is a characteristic of the human and I surprised myself by answering in my best English, "We are fine, thank you. I am Jacques and my friend here is Georges."

Georges looked at me askance.

"By George," Clark said, completely missing his use of Georges' name as an exclamation, "you speak English. Thank the Lord."

"We are British airmen," said Eugene, "the bloody kraut's shot us down. We were doing a recce. Took a hit in the tail."

At that point Bernard entered and he spoke to me in French.

"You speak bally French too, marvellous," said Clark. They were beginning to irritate me so I reminded myself that one should not judge people by the way that they speak. These were brave young men who risked their lives for the defence of their country.

What Bernard said next made me uneasy. He continued in French.

"These men are British and from the Royal Air Force."

"Yes, they mentioned this," said Georges.

Bernard continued, "They were shot down and we managed to recover them. They have been sheltering in the woods but last night they managed to make it to the Martin's farm. They took shelter there and Élise alerted us last night."

"Élise, was she here?"

"No Jacques," Bernard smiled a knowing smile, "she sent a message. We have to get them back to England. It is too far to the north coast so we are seeking a route from the south. There is transport leaving for Lorient tomorrow."

I remembered Lorient from my history. It had been bombed during 1943 by the allies to disable the German u-boat base. There was much damage and Lorient was almost completely destroyed. I remember reading that around five hundred explosive bombs and a lot more incendiary bombs had been dropped leading to carnage of French civilians. I knew that the base survived and I reckoned that Lorient would be crawling with Germans.

"Lorient," I exclaimed, "is that wise?"

"Why do you say that Jacques?"

At this point the airmen heard the town's name and I could see on their faces their concern. I continued speaking in French.

"Lorient has a submarine base. It will be well guarded. How are you going to smuggle two obviously English airmen out under the noses of the Germans?"

Bernard looked annoyed but recovered his composure quickly. He gave me a Gallic shrug and said, "I know that Jacques. You think I don't know what happened to Lorient?"

I apologised to Bernard and he continued, "It is the only transport we have going anywhere near the coast for the next few weeks. We can find a fishing boat to take the airmen to Falmouth from Lorient. There are still a few fishermen operating from the harbour, even after the bombing."

"That's a long way," added Georges, "I mean from Lorient to Falmouth."

I listened to Georges and I was very worried. I knew that the submarine base at Lorient was the largest military base that the Germans had ever constructed outside of Germany and that it was bound to be well protected. I thought the plan was a bad one but I decided to stay quiet. I realised that we had been asked to Gabriel's quarters because of our command of English, not because of our military planning skills.

Bernard went on to explain what was to happen. It looked like the plan had been hatched and that there was nothing we could do to change it. I stopped trying. What was clear from listening to Bernard was that he wanted to rid the maquis of the airmen. He saw them as a threat to its security and this was his primary concern. The fate of the airmen was of secondary interest. I wondered whether Gabriel, if he were here, would have had the same attitude. He asked us to look after the welfare of the airmen until their departure which would be at six o'clock the following morning. They would have to be ferried to Lorient in three vehicles with the first being the baker's van. They would be transferred to a lorry carrying vegetables and finally on the river Blavet to the fishing port. I thought the plan was suicidal.

I was not happy that we had been asked to nursemaid the airmen for the day as I had hoped to do some more training for our operation. I wondered when we were to be asked to start our mission and I was impatient. I grumbled to George and he shrugged.

Bernard asked me to explain the plan to the airmen in English and then promptly left. He had other things on his mind that he considered more important. I explained what was to happen to Clark and Eugene and they listened without interruption. They had almost no French but had picked up the reference to Lorient and they were well aware of the significance of that town.

"So it's tomorrow at six," said Eugene, "well, we haven't much to pack, for sure."

He smiled at me and asked, "Where do you chaps come from? I don't recognise your accent and you have a strange, informal way of speaking, almost American."

"You wouldn't believe us if we told you," said Georges, unhelpfully.

I decided to continue with the training despite having to look after the airmen and despite the rain. I told them to keep as quiet as they could because their voice would attract attention. I was surprised when they did as I had asked and, when they did speak, spoke in a hushed voice. Georges and I sought out Luc and Henri.

"You want us to practice in this?" Luc said.

"It may rain on the night," replied Henri, "Jacques is right, we should train, even in this."

We made our way, with the airmen in tow, to the river again. Clark and Eugene sat by the river, sheltering under a tree and leaning against the trunk. They watched us training for our assignment with interest though I am not sure they understood fully what we were doing and I never explained it to them.

The wire coil now had the cat of three tails attached so we could test connecting the mock detonators to the ends of the tails. Young André visited us a couple of times and stopped to chat after providing us with some food and drink. He brought some food for the airmen too but they were unimpressed. I thought that they were ungrateful in complaining about the food, especially as I knew what British food was like at the time. I disliked the airmen instinctively and tried to conceal my feelings. I am not sure I succeeded.

They accepted the gauloises gratefully, however, and I watched as they savoured every draw. They looked out of place in the maquis and I felt more French at that time than I had ever felt or have felt since. My dual nationality had always been a problem to me for I was neither French nor English but something in the middle. Now I was distinctly French and the airmen in my charge looked, to me, like aliens. I was pleased when the evening came and we could retire. I determined that I would awaken early the next morning and wish them well on their journey. I did not think they would survive so I owed them that.

There was still no sign of Gabriel so the date of our operation was in the air.  As I settled down in my damp sleeping bag, for the weather had been foul most of the day, I turned to Georges who was making himself comfortable.

"I'm going to get up early tomorrow to see Clark and Eugene off. Are you coming?"

"Fuck that," he replied.

# Thursday 25<sup>th</sup> May

## Departure

At five thirty I pulled open the flap of the tent and dragged myself into a cold and damp morning. It was light and the sun was low on the horizon. It was not raining but the ground was wet from the previous day. Georges was asleep and did not stir when I pulled myself out of my sleeping bag cocoon and left the tent. I used the zip to close the flap again and put on my boots. I headed towards Gabriel's quarters because that was where Clark and Eugene were staying during their brief visit to the maquis.

The airmen were fuelling up on cheese, ham and bread and had managed to heat some water for a brew of coffee. I joined them for a mug and we sat and talked. I wished that I could say that they looked more French but they did not. Even in the peasant clothes supplied by Bernard they looked out of place. I told them to keep hidden whenever possible but if they were discovered they were to say nothing and keep their heads down.

They insisted on taking pistols with them and they wanted their air force papers to prove that they were officers. They believed that, if captured, they would be treated more leniently, as prisoners of war. I doubted it having heard of the way that the Germans had treated patriots. I was sure that they would be captured anyway so I said nothing.

At six fifteen Pierre arrived and it was time for Clark and Eugene to leave. We shook hands in a cool British way and I wished them well.

Then they were gone and I thought about the long and difficult journey ahead. I had no desire to be with them.

Feeling hungry myself I went to the mess hut to find André making preparations for breakfast. He told me that he had not managed to obtain any bread but that he had some dried crackers, some cheese and some ham. I said that I would wait for the others but that another cup of coffee would be good when he was ready. I handed André a cigarette and we smoked one together talking about life after liberation and André's dreams. André was a romantic and had many plans for his life. He believed strongly that France would be liberated and he impressed me with his vision. I liked André and particularly his optimistic character. I found it uplifting and I wondered if he ever had days where his mood was low. Then I remembered that it was Pierre who had seen off the airmen. If Pierre was here then it was likely that Gabriel was in the camp too.

"Have you seen Gabriel?"

"No," replied André.

"I've seen Pierre this morning," I said.

"You have!" answered André, "that means Gabriel will not be far behind. He must be around somewhere."

"OK André, thanks for the coffee. I just want to check something out."

I had an idea. I knew that I had a road map of Brittany in my bag and I wanted to check where exactly the location of the base we were to attack was in relation to where we are now. I had a rough idea as I knew this area reasonably well, though my version of it had changed since 1944. I particularly wanted to know where the river on which we were practising was relative to the target. I wondered whether they were tributaries of the same river. I went back to the tent and unzipped it again. Georges grumbled and turned over, sleeping bag included.  I retrieved the map as quickly as I could and left the tent. Georges slept on.

The sun was rising higher and it was to be a pleasant and warm day and this was a welcome change from the previous day.  I thought again about the airmen but put them from my mind quickly as there was little that I could have done to prevent their fate.  In situations like the one in which we found ourselves contrast is sharp: black and white, life or death.  I thought of all of the inane arguments that were to come later in the century and how the chattering classes would discuss the merits of organic production versus intensive farming and lots of other issues like it.  Right now my concentration was on simple survival and, with my reflections, I came to understand how Bernard must have felt, faced with the stark choice between two unknown British airmen and the security of the maquis housing people that he knew and loved.  It was no contest in reality and I would probably have made the same decision as Bernard.

I decided to go to Gabriel's quarters as I knew he had not been sleeping there.  I picked up the coffee that I had placed by the door before entering the tent and made my way there.  Gabriel was not in his quarters which were empty.  At six thirty, I guessed, that was not surprising.  There were a few maquisards around now and the guard was being changed so some of them were heading for their beds.  On the way I exchanged pleasantries with the guards going off duty and I saw a smiling André handing out food and drink.

I opened the map on the table and identified our current position on it.  This area had changed little being hilly, forested and rugged.  I then found the location of the air base near the small town, as it was now.  On my map the town had grown and there were new suburbs and roads.  The air base, of course, was not on my map but had been replaced by a retail park; the twentieth century obsession of my generation being shopping. The route of the river was almost identical to what it was now and I traced the two rivers, our practice river and the target river. They both emptied into a larger river flowing out towards the sea which was many miles away. I looked closer at the target river and could see that it narrowed and my guess was that this area was fast flowing with white water. Georges would have enjoyed that, I thought, in different times.

I was not sure why I was examining this in such detail but I had a fixation. I wanted to understand the topography so that I knew where the maquis was and exactly where was the site of the operation in relation to the camp. I studied everything about the route, in minute detail, as an obsessive does. I wanted to leave nothing to chance. I must have done this for over three quarters of an hour and I was engrossed. I hardly heard Gabriel enter the room and it was only when he spoke that I was aware of his presence.

"You look absorbed," Gabriel said in English. Gabriel preferred to use English if he could even though his French was good.

"Gabriel!"

I shook his hands warmly and he was surprised. I then remembered that he was English and I had given him a French welcome. I was becoming more French. I then realised that I was using Gabriel's quarters.

"I'm sorry, I thought you were away," I blurted.

"It's OK," Gabriel replied, "I have been but I'm back now and I have some news about your manoeuvre. I'll tell you about that when your cohorts are here. You are up early, what are you doing?"

Gabriel looked over my shoulder at the map and then took a good look. He looked puzzled.

"It's a map from my century," I said.

"Those things there," Gabriel said, pointing to the motorways.

"They are roads," I said.

"What, all of them. Will we need all of those roads?"

I explained that households had more than one car and people made long journeys by car.

"It's early, I don't know whether my brain can take all of that right now. I'll just accept it if you don't mind. Why are you up so early anyway, can't you sleep?"

I explained about the airmen and Gabriel was interested. I decided not to tell Gabriel about their trip to Lorient and my worries. I thought it better to leave that to Bernard.

"I'll get out of your quarters," I said.

"Only if you want to," said Gabriel but I could tell from his tone that he would prefer to have his quarters back.

"I'd like some breakfast anyway and I know that André is around," I replied and started to fold the map.

"I'll join you. I left the farmhouse this morning early before anyone was awake so I could eat."

Gabriel gave away a little more than he had intended with this as I had not realised that he slept occasionally in a safe house. I wondered where the house was but it was better that I did not know. Luc, Henri and a bleary eyed Georges were already eating when Gabriel and I arrived. Georges asked me where I had been and what I had been doing so I told him and he gave me one of his shrugs.

"Good," said Gabriel, "we have the team."

After we had eaten our fill we took our mugs back to Gabriel's quarters for his briefing.

"Let me have those cups when you've finished," said André as we left. I smiled and replied that we would. We sat around Gabriel's table and he started to tell us what he had discovered.

"We've been doing some reconnaissance," Gabriel started, "and particularly the guard's routine."

He paused for a few seconds, obviously in thought and then said, "Henri."

"Yes Gabriel."

"You remember that there are three fuel tanks."

Henri nodded.

"And they are end-on to the fence. The ends of the fuel tanks are facing the fence."

"I remember that."

"There are now four fuel tanks. Fritz has added another since we were there last. There wasn't enough room besides the other three so they have put the fourth across the others, not near the fence but the other side."

Gabriel took out the papers for the mission and drew on the plan the fourth fuel tank. The three existing tanks were like fingers at right angle to the fence. The new tank was parallel to the fence and had been placed at the end, across the other tanks just before the perimeter road.

"We had considered calling off the operation but I am told that this is important so I believe we should go ahead," added Gabriel, "but we haven't enough kit to blow all four. So we need to hope that taking out the three tanks will cause the fourth to blow and I don't like relying on luck."

"The boche alter their schedule of patrols but being Fritz they do this daily so that, on a particular day, the patrol is at the same time. They change this schedule on a rota and the next rota change is not until June so we know the schedule for this month. We've watched it for the last few months so we are pretty sure but that doesn't mean they will not change the schedule. You'll need to keep a watch."

"How close to where we'll be does the patrol go?"

"It comes along the road in front of the tanks Luc so, if you are at the tanks, they will see you and you will be foiled."

"The key thing," Gabriel continued, "is that the watchtowers are nowhere near where you'll be. They don't seem to expect an attack from the river and they have focused on the main gates and the length of road passing by the base. I see that as a positive for us."

"Is there any lighting near the tanks?"

"No Georges. Because this is an airstrip the lighting is for the benefit of the aircraft so it is mostly on the taxiways and the runways, of course. They are well away from the fuel tanks."

I asked, "So Gabriel, when is the operation to be?"

"The next new moon, tomorrow night."

I was pleased we now had a date and said so. Gabriel followed with, "Are you prepared? Do you need another training session? If you do you should do it today because we will be taking the canoe to the target tonight."

I had no idea that the canoe we were using for the exercise was the actual canoe we would use. I looked at Georges who pulled a face back and then smiled. I realised that we would not be able to do another night trial and that was of concern to me. I thought that it would be useful to do another couple of training sessions as we still had a few coordination issues. I was about to speak when I was usurped by Henri.

"We should train more today, before you take the canoe tonight."

It was agreed that we should have more practice so we said goodbye to Gabriel who wished us good luck. As we were leaving Gabriel pulled me to one side.

"I'd like you to deliver a message for me tomorrow but be sure you are back at the camp before five o'clock."

111

"OK", I replied, "who is the message for?"

"Élise," Gabriel replied and gave me a sly smile, "here it is."

He handed me a sealed envelope and I put it in a pocket inside my blouson.

"Sure," I said, nonchalantly, "does she know I am going?"

"No, It will be a nice surprise."

# Friday 26<sup>th</sup> May
# Élise

It was nearly eight o'clock and I was approaching the Martin's farm feeling excited and apprehensive at the same time. I was walking down the track leading to the farm when I heard a vehicle coming in the other direction. Thinking it was Monsieur Martin's car and conscious of the fact that I was unarmed I did not take my, now usual, precaution of hiding in the hedgerow. In any case, at my current position this would have been difficult as I was near open fields and the hedge was missing a long section.

My pulse raced when I saw a German vehicle, similar to the one we had seen after the rail mission, the *Kubelwagen*, heading towards me. It screeched to a halt just in front of my path. There were two young German soldiers; one was driving and the other was in the passenger seat. They had the top of the vehicle down and I could see sacks in the back of the car.

The passenger snapped to me in accented French, "Papers".

I was aware that I had the message from Gabriel in my blouson pocket and my papers were in the same pocket. I placed my hand slowly and deliberately into my pocket as I wanted the Germans to know I was not armed. I felt impotent and could understand what countless numbers of French citizens must have felt at times like this. How the French authorities had let their people down, I thought fleetingly. I handed the soldier my fake papers. He remained in the car but I could see that his comrade had his hand ready on his gun.

The soldier examined the papers and threw them back to me. I missed the catch and they fell to the floor. I left the papers where they had fallen.

"What is your purpose here?"

I told them that I was Monsieur Martin's farmhand and that I was here to work. This seemed to satisfy them and they sped off without a further word. I had always been ambivalent about the Germans when grandfather had told me his war tales. Right now, I hated them but I hated more the feeling of helplessness when confronted with them like that day. Yes, I could sabotage their supply lines and yes I could act as a terrorist but I realised, there and then, that most of the population had to simply endure the pain. After my fear and hate had passed, I was suddenly very proud of what my grandfather's generation had achieved with our allies from America and Britain. It was the 26$^{th}$ May and very soon would be D-day and an end to this horror. I knew that Brittany would not be liberated until August but it would be liberated. I felt like, at that moment, I was in a novel. I had a part to play and it was foretold for I was born many years from now. I felt that I could not change my destiny, but merely live it. I wondered if I was ever going home.

Stunned by the interruption I made it to the Martin's farm rear door without really remembering the walk down their track. The door opened and Monsieur Martin answered with a scowl on his face which turned to a smile as he recognised me.

"Jacques, come in! I thought it was those pigs back again."

I entered to see a young man in the kitchen.

"This is Alain," Monsieur Martin said to me, "you have not met before."

Alain was around fourteen or fifteen with a muscular physique that comes from hard work on the farm. He was fresh faced and had rosy cheeks from being outside most of the time.  He was a little bashful as he welcomed me and shook my hand.

"I have heard much about you Alain," I said, "and it is good to meet you at last."

He smiled but said little.

I was addresses by Monsieur Martin.  "You are always welcome here Jacques, but what brings you?"

"I have a message," I replied quickly and continued, "but that can wait for a minute or so.  I bumped into Fritz on your track.  Were they here?"

"Those bastards," said Alain and stopped as Monsieur Martin put his hand on his shoulder.

Monsieur Martin continued, "They were here for produce.  The don't visit us often but they seem to do the rounds of the farms.  They paid us for the produce.  Did they stop you?"

I explained what had happened and how I had explained my presence.  He laughed when I said that I was his farmhand and said that he could use some help.

"The message?" said Monsieur Martin.

"It is for Élise, from Gabriel," I said, "is she here?"

"She will be back shortly, she heard the boche arrive.  They make advances to my girls and neither I nor they like it.  Élise takes Claire to the barns when she sees or hears Fritz.  She'll have heard them go and will come back when she feels the coast is clear."

Monsieur Martin asked me if I would like to clean up before Claire and Élise returned and I took his hint for I must have looked dirty with my several days of beard growth.  I was even given my own razor and one like I had never seen before.  I was told that it was a safety razor but it had more blade showing for my comfort.  It did the job and I was shiny clean when Élise arrived.

"Jacques," she said as she saw me and smiled. I was so relieved that she was still pleased to see me. Claire bounded over to me and gave me a hug and kissed my cheeks.

Élise came over to me and kissed me gently on the lips and squeezed my hands.

"The pigs have been here," she said bitterly.

"I know," I replied, "they stopped me. I told them I worked for you."

"Then you had better," she said, "I have plenty of jobs. Have you had anything to eat?"

I was looking forward to some real food and I replied that I had not eaten.

"Before you do that," I said, "I have a message for you from Gabriel."

I reached into my pocket and handed Élise the sealed envelope that Gabriel had given to me. It was a little crumpled so Élise straightened it. She then opened it and unfolded the paper. I could see from the other side of the letter that it was written in Gabriel's hand and contained only a few sentences. Élise read the correspondence and folded it back into its envelope and placed it carefully in her pocket. We did not speak about the message again that day.

Élise prepared me a sumptuous breakfast and I ate it with gusto. She said that it looked to her like I had not eaten in weeks. André did his best in the circumstances and his food was certainly edible but his food could not compare with a farmhouse breakfast.

"When do you have to be back?"

"I need to be at the camp by five."

I did not mention the operation that we were to perform that evening as I did not want to worry Élise. She did not ask me why I needed to return and just accepted it.

"I was thinking about asking you to clean out the chicken run," she teased, "but you are far too clean for that. I have been asking *papa* to fix some fences for a while now but he does not have time. I could help you."

I said that I would do that though I had doubts about my skills. Fence mending was not something I had ever done before. Monsieur Martin and Alain left the house first and Claire started cleaning the kitchen. She smiled at me as I left with Élise and then turned away quickly. I wandered into the farmyard and Élise walked besides me. She gently placed her arm into mine and it felt so very natural. I felt as if I have known Élise forever. I realise how corny that must sound but it was true. I had never been so relaxed and easy with a person in my life. We chatted about nothing in particular but we talked easily. This was the person I wanted to be with for life; I knew that, but it was hard to square that with the fact that I had been born nearly fifty years later. When I thought about it Élise would be over eighty in my time. It was then that I realised that I was not going home, even if I knew how to. This was to be my life and I was now reconciled to it.

I did a reasonable job with the fences. Élise had not told me that there were more than one fence to mend. In fact there were over twenty that needed repair. I was happy to help and my time with Élise was enchanting. This was real courtship in the old fashioned way like I had watched in old films. Not the race to bed that had accompanied my previous relationships. Throughout the day I learned to read the signs. There was a new set of rules, new protocols that were alien to me. I learned quickly.

Élise could be funny, serious, courageous and sensual and I enjoyed every facet of her personality. We smoked cigarettes together as we travelled from field to field and simply talked. The day was bliss and, as I shared another family meal, I mused that I had been accepted quickly into the Martin's life. It was not just Élise who had accepted me, it was all of the family. I had accepted them too.

I could barely believe it when the time came for me to leave. I said goodbye to Monsieur Martin who handed me some cigarettes for the maquisards and I accepted them gratefully. Claire hugged me and Alain shook my hand gingerly. He was still a little shy of me.

Élise walked me to the footpath at the middle of the track, not far from where I had met the Germans. I could still see the tyre marks where they had stopped quickly and my impotence angered me still. This is where we had to part and I held Élise closely and kissed her. I did not want to let go of her. Finally, we parted.

As I walked away Élise said quietly, almost as if she did not want me to hear her, "Be careful tonight, be very careful."

I looked back and waved for as long as I could see Élise and then I made my way back to the maquis with haste as I was slightly late. I had a mixture of emotions. I was elated from the day but sad at the parting. I arrived back just in time and went to the tent to collect my weapons and ammunition. Georges was waiting for me and he gave me a sly smile.

"You get your leg over yet?"

I gave him an icy stare and Georges knew that he had overstepped the mark. He looked back at me, bemused.

"So, this is serious? You realise that we are not meant to be here, don't you? And, just how are we going to get back?"

I looked back at Georges and I shrugged. At that moment I did not care about going back.

# Friday 26<sup>th</sup> May

## Assignment

Dusk was later as summer advanced. The days were warmer now and the rain had subsided. This made the camp more pleasant except for the biting insects which seemed to be multiplying. Luc told me of some leaves that could help and I took his advice and rubbed them onto my exposed skin. The sap from the leaves smelt foul but seemed to work. Everyone was doing the same so we soon became used to our own odour and barely noticed it any more. I wondered what Élise would make of my new aroma.

We were readying ourselves for the mission which was scheduled for that evening. All was now set and the canoe was in place. We were given a detailed briefing which included the location of the canoe. We were then given the important explosives and, separately, the detonators.

"Be very careful," Gabriel said, "don't put the detonators in place until the very last minute. They really are twitchy and I want no mistakes. You got that?"

We all nodded and we each placed an explosive charge in our bag. They were quite heavy and, if the Germans stopped us, would be difficult to hide. As I had grenades and weapons with me that did not seem to matter. I had decided already that the Germans were not going to take me alive. In any case I knew that I would live again as I had yet to be born. Gabriel gave us some body camouflage.

"It'll take the shine out of your face," he said, "British army issue!"

Gabriel and Bernard and many of the other maquisards shook our hands as we left the maquis and wished us good luck. We were all nervous. This was the first time I had handled explosives. We had been briefed well and we had practised well. We were ready. We would hit the Germans where it hurt and I hoped I would lose my feeling of helplessness that had hung over me since being stopped on the Martin's farm track. I was not powerless now.

Dusk happened slowly and we could see our way in the greying light towards our destination. Luc, always wary of spotter planes, kept to the trees wherever possible or very near the hedgerows otherwise. He almost sniffed the air as we walked and was always alert, always guarded. This was not in a nervous way; no, he was a professional assessing the risks at all times. He was fully in control and I was proud to be with him and proud to be his friend and companion.

Luc went ahead and I followed him. Georges was behind me with Henri at the rear. Occasionally we walked in twos but more often we walked in a single line. We walked in near silence and stealth was our by-word. Georges and I had learned a lot in a short time. It was dark by the time we reached the canoe which was just where Gabriel had described. It was well hidden and I doubt if we would have found it had it not been for the briefing. It was around the bend from the target and we had not practised it this way. It made sense though as we would board the canoe away from the base. This was a lesson to us; no amount of practice is like the real thing.

I looked at my watch and I saw Luc do the same.

"We have an hour yet," he whispered.

He need not have bothered speaking softly for overhead was the drone of a *Heinkel*, or so I was told, as it approached the airfield. We saw it land and then taxi to a hanger on the far side of the base. I thought it strange that an aircraft would be flying so late in the evening. The *Heinkel* was a night fighter and was equipped for night flying. We covered our face and exposed flesh with body camouflage.

The base was quiet after the landing until later when the guard made its patrol towards the perimeter fence nearest us. I saw the searchlight beam heading towards the fuel tanks. It did not quite make it and stopped fifty metres short of the tanks. I remember counting a blessing. At least we would not have the prospect of a searchlight finding us as we were placing the explosives. I looked at my watch. Trust the Germans, I thought, the master race is efficient, if nothing else; they were right on time and would not be round for two hours if Gabriel's schedule was correct.

We watched the small squad of soldiers or airmen, I was not sure which, walk off into the distance and the searchlight followed in front of them. It was time and my heart started to race. I boarded the canoe first and Georges followed behind. Henri passed the plank for the base of the canoe and then the three charges. I already had the detonators in my pocket. He handed Georges my rifle and he passed it to me followed by my rucksack. Luc passed George his weapon and bag and then passed us some grenades. Then Luc handed George the wire cutters for the perimeter fence. Finally, Henri passed us the pulley contraption and the end of the cat of three tails. It was not threaded through the pulley as it had been in practice and I swore under my breath.

We were ready to go. George started to paddle slowly. He stroked the water gently and there was barely a sound over the normal noise of the river. We slid through the water, willing it to part in our path. We reached the centre point and I looked back to check that we were in line with where Henri was. We were a little adrift and I whispered to Georges. He understood and paddled a little further upstream until we could see Henri's position. In the half light it was difficult and it was Luc I saw first. He was standing in the river feeding the wire, on guard and looking after our safety.

We were in the middle of the river at the right location for the pulley so I threaded the cat of three tails through the pulley wheel cautiously. It was more difficult than I remembered in practice and I had to tug the last tail through. It had been much easier to do this on the bank and out of the canoe and I wondered why Henri had not done this. The canoe rocked precariously and I remember Georges telling us how the canoe was twitchy. We did not need to capsize at this stage. It took too long to position the pulley, I knew, with the cat of three tails in place and I peered at my watch. We were ten minutes behind.

George continued and I held the end of the wire. Luc was feeding it gently so that it did not snag. We drifted towards the far bank until the canoe hit and there was a jolt. I climbed up the bank leaving George in the canoe. He took hold of the end of the wire, handed me the cutters followed by the explosives. I placed the charges on the bank and then crawled forward on my stomach not wanting to be seen. I cut through the perimeter fence leaving just enough for me to scramble through. I crept back to the canoe and handed George the cutters and took two of the charges. They were too heavy to carry more than two so I had to go back and fetch the last explosive and the end of the cat of three tails. I crawled under the fence leaving the explosives handy without having to go back. I was conscious that I must not disturb the wire as I returned or I would be a sacrifice to the operation as the explosions detonated prematurely. I threaded the wire through the fence above the cut I had made and hooked it on temporarily whilst I clambered through the gap.

I was ready to place the charge. I reached back for the first charge and placed a small piece of cloth under it. I offered the base of the explosive to the first tank and, being magnetic, it accepted and the force took hold. There was a faint clink as the charge adhered to the tank. One down, I thought. I repeated this for the other two charges. Now for the difficult part, I remember thinking as I took the detonators out of my pocket. I imagined Gabriel saying that the detonators were sensitive. I swallowed and pushed back my fear.

I unhooked the wire and pulled some through the fence. I heard the whine of the wheels of the pulley in mid stream and hoped that nobody else heard it. My senses were acute. The wire was slack on my side of the fence and it had to stay that way as I did not want the detonators to fire too early. I screwed in the first of them tentatively followed by the second. I was sweating and beads of sweat were dripping down my side from my armpits. Then the third. All of the detonators were in place and all I had to do now was to connect the wires. The three tails had hooks at the end and I slipped them over the rings in the detonators. The bombs were primed and it was time to go. I checked that the wire was loose and crawled back to the canoe.

I gave Georges the thumbs up and he paddled away gently. I was shaking now as the adrenaline pulsed through my veins. I could not see Georges clearly but I was sure that he was as charged as was I. We paddled towards the far bank and I felt that we were drifting upstream too much. I thought that Georges was overcompensating for the current so I leaned forwards to tell him when we hit something and the canoe grated against an obstacle. I reached out to feel for it and was alarmed when I realised it was the wire. Then we hit the pulley and it keeled over.

The next few minutes were in slow motion to me. There was a loud explosion and the blast caught the canoe and swung us round so that we were travelling with the current. We were low in the water so most of the blast went over our heads. Luc was not so lucky and I watched him, in the light of the explosion, being thrown bodily out of the water to land on the bank. Henri was on his stomach so was sheltered from the blast.

I looked over towards the tanks as we headed downstream. One was on fire and the flames were over twenty metres high. From our distance we could feel the heat. Henri must have realised what had happened and he pulled the wire and the other two charges went off simultaneously. The sound was deafening and flames erupted into the air. The surroundings were lit up by the explosion. We were not expecting this as the plan was for us to escape, with Henri following, immediately after he had set off the explosions. We were off plan.

The last sight I had was of Henri leaning over Luc and pulling him onto his shoulder as we sped down the river. I heard the base sirens as the Germans became aware of our attack. Georges decided that we were not going back and paddled for his life down stream. This was not the operation for which we had trained.

I looked at my watch. It was after midnight.

# Saturday 27th May

# Flight

I remember from my obsessive reviewing of my map that the stream went through the town before heading back out into the country. What my map did not show was that the river coursed through a deep cutting, the banks reinforced with stone channels, through the town. The town was much smaller now than it was in 2009. The sky was still lit up from the explosion as we travelled further downstream. We were out of direct sight of the base when the final tank exploded. Gabriel had told us that an additional tank had been added. This tank was twice the volume of the others and when it detonated the sky seemed to blaze and the blast sound hit us seconds later. It was a tremendous sound and lights were illuminating throughout the town way above us. When the noise of the discharge passed we could hear voices and I looked up to see people peering out of their upstairs windows.

I wondered what had happened to Henri and Luc and I feared for their safety. Georges had a mission now and that was to make our escape down river. I knew that the river narrowed around three kilometres past the town and I guessed that this would mean rapids or, at the best, fast running water. For now though, we had to make it through the town unscathed. In the deep slow moving channel we were heading towards a bridge. The stone bridge arched over us dark and menacing far above. The sky was orange from the glow of the fire raging a couple of kilometres away. It was an eerie sight reminiscent of something from a horror movie. As we glided towards the bridge I caught sight of two trucks on the road on the left bank ahead of and above us. The lorries were difficult to make out at first but I caught sight of one of them in the headlights of the second and realised that they were German troop carriers. The Germans had mobilised and were searching for us. I saw the first lorry turn to cross the bridge, followed by the second. Georges saw them too and steered the canoe closer to the left of the channel by the steep wall that had been built to support the bank through the town. I was pleased that we were so far below the road and I motioned to Georges to position the canoe under the bridge. He understood instinctively and we slid forward towards the bridge, hugging the left bank of the river. I watched with dread as the troop carriers crossed the bridge. If they saw us we would be sitting ducks ready to be picked off. I took the safety catch off my bren and moved Georges' gun closer to him. He flashed me a glance and I saw really only the whites of his eyes. I could sense the apprehension.

We made it under the bridge as the second lorry crossed the river. I realised that we were now on the wrong side of the river and would be seen more easily from the lorries that had crossed. In the light of the rear truck I saw the troops in the back of the lorry. I caught a glimpse of the two soldiers sitting opposite each other; my senses were tuned and in that instant I could see that they were kitted for combat and had rifles at the ready. They were heading back down the river towards the site of our operation and I feared for Henri and Luc.

The moment passed and the trucks continued without spotting us in the river. I pondered our plight as I started to relax and reset the safety catch on the rifle. I realised that we had camouflage paint on our faces and a canoe full of incriminating materials. There was no way we could simply blend into the background yet. We had to escape to a place of safety and then decide the next steps. Our focus had to be on flight.

My mind was racing and I had to fight to keep my thoughts rational and not to degenerate into panic. I breathed deeply. I was being tested and I had not to fail. Georges continued his paddle downstream and with more urgency now the hated Germans had left. We were still in a deep channel and I dispatched over the side of the canoe the things we no longer needed. The wire cutters went first followed by the plank that Henri had created for the bottom of the canoe. It made very little difference to our speed and I wondered afterwards why I had done it. I needed to do something.

I am fortunate in having the ability to recall things very clearly. It was a skill that had helped me sail through school. Now it was an essential ability and I visualised the map that I had examined so thoroughly. I had it. I remembered that there were two rivers, both of which joined a main river downstream. One of rivers was the one down which we were travelling. The other led, by a circuitous route, back to the maquis. I was pretty sure that we could not navigate safely down to the main river from where we were. I remembered a number of other towns on the way and I was uncomfortable about travelling through towns in such an exposed way. In any case we needed to clean up before dawn or our goose would certainly be cooked.

I leaned forward to Georges and said into his ear, "Georges, get the fuck out of here will you. When we are in the country I've got a plan."

"What the fuck do you think I'm doing," he replied in a Georges kind of way and added, "and it had better be a good one because we are in the shit."

It was a genuine relief to see the outskirts of the town and the dark countryside beyond.  We were also out of the cutting which had sheltered us so well.  We made good progress and travelled in silence.  Canoes are good at stealth and, in the dark, it would have been difficult to see us and to hear our sound above that of the river.  It was also impossible to see obstacles and we were vigilant for the hint of white foam that suggested a rock or fallen tree.  The birch bark canoe looked fragile but it proved that it was not.  We dodged obstructions and Georges was skilful and agile.  If things had been better I would have said that he was enjoying himself.

It was difficult for me to visualise where we were compared with my recollection of the map and from the viewpoint of the river I was completely at a loss.  As it happened our decision was made for us.  We both heard it.  The sound of the river changed and we could hear rushing water.  Georges looked round at me.

"I don't like the sound of that."

It did not need saying.  There was a waterfall ahead and we could not continue.  The water became whiter and the flow strengthened.  Georges battled to control the canoe and its speed was increasing.  He brought it round and almost capsized it.  I leaned over to prevent us tipping.  It worked but it had been a close thing.  We were now heading back upstream and I watched as Georges manoeuvred the little craft skilfully away from the waterfall and rapids downstream.  It seemed like an age before he was back into calmer waters but I am sure it was merely seconds.  My heart was pounding and I was watching every move ready to throw my body in whichever direction was needed to keep us upright.  We had done this before, Georges and I, and now that skill was being put to the test.  Finally, we were on the bank and I disembarked and held the canoe steady as Georges climbed out too.  We pulled the canoe out of the water and I was surprised at how light it was.  Dawn was coming and there was a faint streak of red light showing from the east.  We chose to lie down on the bank, cold and exhausted.

.

# Saturday 27th May

# Tragedy

I surprised myself and slept for a little while and woke up with a start. I heard footsteps and was instantly awake as was Georges. We picked up our bren guns and stood set for action. We both released our safety catches and then crouched, ready for whatever was coming through the bushes. I heard the sound of boots; they were German jack boots which is an unmistakable sound. They were heading our way. It was fight or flight time and I feared that we would have to fight.

The German soldier that appeared was surprised to see us and it was clear that his intention was to relieve himself. Georges acted instinctively and gave the bren a burst of fire. I watched as the soldier was hit and blood spurted from his chest and his neck. Georges had hit the German's jugular artery and death was quick. The soldier fell. It was the first time either of us had been involved in combat like this and the first time I had seen death close up. Looking back, it was appalling that the life of a young man was taken but I did not feel like that then. What happened next has always justified the kill to me.

The soldier was not alone. Two combatants came thundering through the undergrowth after hearing the shots fired by Georges. I fired and one fell, injured but not killed. The second one fired but missed us. Georges fired back. The soldier was quick and he darted to the ground. I shot at the injured man and killed him this time.

A shot rang out and I watched as Georges fell with blood spurting from his head which was blown clean open. I looked for a moment in disbelief and then felt pure rage welling up inside. I was going to die there and then and I was going to take that bastard with me. I charged forward towards the direction from which the shot had came. The soldier sprang to his knees and raised his rifle ready to shoot. He could see that I was deranged and I could smell his fear but I cared not a jot. I was there before him and I fired in quick succession. He was dead with the first shot but I gave him several more.

I stood, shaking and looking around for more Germans. I cried out in rage and despair. There were no more soldiers to be seen. I went back to Georges but he was dead. I sobbed. I could not believe that he was dead and I embraced him even with his head torn apart. I was covered in his blood.

It seemed a long time before I could release Georges from my grip and he was turning cold by the time I did. I realised that I needed to go because the attack must have been heard by someone. Reinforcements could have been sent. I could not just leave Georges though I had no tools to bury him. I carried him to the canoe and laid him out and placed the paddle over his still body. I took the Free French armband that Gabriel had given us to identify us as combatants and placed it around Georges' arm. I wept as I pushed the canoe into the current. I hoped that a partisan would find him and give him a decent burial. I prayed that he would not be found by the Germans. I said my farewell to Georges there and then and vowed that I would never forget him.

The rest of the day is a blur to me. I spent a lot of it hiding. I did manage to clean off the camouflage paint from my face and hands but I was covered in Georges blood. I avoided everyone and I cried a lot. The day was warm though I barely noticed it. Night time came and I climbed a tree and made a bed in its bows. I slept fitfully fearful that I would fall to my death though I cared little. I re-lived the attack by the Germans many times that night and I woke up in a cold sweat. My emotions were a mixture of pure rage, disbelief, despair, self pity and hatred.

The hour before dawn I always find the worst and a panic attack hit me at that time and I could not catch my breath. I shook uncontrollably and became dizzy.

"Pull yourself together," I told myself.

I thought of Élise and that pulled me out of my malaise. My breathing steadied and my muscle spasms passed. I sobbed again. I did not know that I could cry so much. I decided that I would make for the Martin's farm. I tried to regain my composure and finally succeeded. The map, I thought, think about the map. Where are you in relation to the farm?

I brought the map to mind and tried to retrace our steps mentally. I endeavoured to visualise the waterfall's location and it came to me. I had been blind. Of course, I thought. I looked up at the sky to see where the sun was rising. I needed to head due north and I reckoned that I would hit a river. In fact it was the one that went through the maquis. I had a plan, I thought, and it was better than the despair I felt.

I listened to make sure that the coast was clear and climbed down from the tree. I took my bearings from the rising sun again and checked the trees, for they gave me an indication of direction too from the side that the moss grew most. It was tough going as it was uphill most of the way. I was sweating and I had not eaten so I was a little faint. I must have smelled awful but I was not aware of it. I recognised some of the herbs growing and I took a handful of wild rocket which I ate. There was not much sustenance but it stopped the hunger pains. Finally I reached the river at around midday. I drank for I was very thirsty. Looking back, I think this was the real reason for my dizziness. I was going to follow the river upstream so I would not be thirsty again. I needed food though and I was not skilled enough in survival techniques to find any. I thought of young André killing rabbits and wild fowl, skinning them and making our great stews. What I would have given for one of them at that time. My mind drifted back to Georges and I stopped the thought. My grief was a luxury that I could not afford, for now.

I walked on following the river and after a few hours started to recognise the countryside again. I passed the 'dropping zone' and I knew that I was not far from the farm. I strode with a single mind and forced myself on. I had a solitary goal and that was to make it to the farm; what happened after that I did not know. I did know that I must not put Élise or her family at risk and must approach the farm with stealth and not be seen by anyone.

There comes a moment when the objective is in sight when one allows oneself to relax. This almost happened to me when I saw the Martin's farm and I caught sight of Élise in the vegetable garden. I stayed hidden and decided to wait for dark. It was seven o'clock by then and darkness was not for a few more hours. I watched Élise from my hideout. I felt a mixture of emotions and seeing Élise brought back the horror of what had happened. I guess that, seeing someone you care for, allows emotions to be released and I sobbed again. This time it was deep and sorrowful and I did so quietly. I do not remember when I fell asleep but I did and I woke up again as it was becoming dark. The farm lights were on now so I stood and made my way furtively towards the farm.

I crept around the back and I saw Élise at the kitchen window. I tapped on the window.

"Élise," I said quietly and she looked in my direction. She had recognised my voice.

She opened the kitchen door and I fell in, still exhausted despite my sleep. She gave a gasp when she saw me. I must have looked a mess.

"Are you hurt Jacques?"

Élise had seen the blood. I replied, "It is Georges'."

I stopped and tried to pull myself together and said softly, "They killed him Élise, the boche, they killed him. His head was …"

I stopped because I could not live that shocking experience again. She came over to me and enveloped me for what seemed like an age.

"I'm so sorry," she said gently.

Claire and Alain came through the door and saw me. Claire put her hand to her mouth and looked at me with anguish and Alain came over to me.

"You look awful," he said, "what happened to you?"

"His friend, Georges, he's been killed."

"There will be time later to find out what's happened," said Claire, looking very shocked, "are you hurt Jacques?"

"No Claire, I'm fine. This is Georges' blood, not mine."

"Alain," said Élise and she looked at him sternly, "take Jacques upstairs and help him clean up. Find him some clothes. I'll go and find papa."

With that she left after giving me a concerned look and I followed Alain to the upper floor. He took my bag and my bren from me and placed them in the corner of the bathroom. He poured me a hot bath and I stripped and slid into it. I did not care if Alain saw me naked and he was too preoccupied to even notice.

# Saturday 27<sup>th</sup> and Sunday 28<sup>th</sup> May
# Realisation

I pulled on the oversized clothes of Monsieur Martin and started to descend the stairs. I heard voices and they were those of Élise and her father.

"It is dangerous Élise," I heard Monsieur Martin say.

"We cannot turn him away after what he's been through, and where would he go now?" Élise replied.

"I know, I know and we will not but we need to be careful with the boche like they are."

They stopped as I entered and looked embarrassed. They had not expected me to return so quickly. Élise and her father were sitting around the kitchen table and Claire was preparing some food which smelt delicious. I was hungry. Claire looked over to me and gave me a weak smile. Alain was upstairs.

"You look better Jacques," said Élise, "come, join us."

Monsieur Martin stood and came over to me and shook me firmly by the hand, held me close and then kissed me on the cheeks.

"I'm sure you heard us my boy. We mean nothing, we will discuss this later but first let me say how sorry I was to hear about your friend. Tell us how it happened. Where were you, what had you been doing?"

I told them about our operation with Luc and Henri and Monsieur Martin stood again, nearly knocking over the table. He came round to me and I stood. He shook my hand again and was beaming.

"You did that?"

I nodded.

"It was a marvellous piece of terrorism," Monsieur Martin said and savoured the final word, "and you gave Fritz a bloody nose. Things have got nasty since then though. Tell me about it. Tell me everything."

Alain had entered the room as his father spoke and he listened in awe as I told them what had happened. They listened mostly in silence as I explained what had happened. I broke down as I told them of our encounter with the German soldiers and of Georges' death. Élise came around to sit next to me and she held my hand as I continued. Élise was shocked when she heard that Luc was involved and asked me what had happened to him. I described my last sight of Luc and she gasped. It was clear that she had not seen Luc since our manoeuvre.

My stock went sky high with Alain that night and I was treated like an older brother and someone to respect from then onwards. I think the same happened with Monsieur Martin though he kept his thoughts close. On that night though I was accepted as an integral part of the Martin's family and I was happy to be a part. I finished with the tale of my wait until dark before approaching the farm and I caught Élise looking at her father.

"I do not want to put you at risk," I said as I finished my story, "and I will go back to the maquis tonight. I can see that you are worried, and I understand."

"Let us tell you first of what has happened since your daring attack," Monsieur Martin exclaimed, "but you are right, there are risks and Élise takes them all of the time. We must be wary and having an armed resistance fighter in the house is a risk too far. The first thing we have done is to emasculate you."

He smiled and I looked puzzled.

"Alain has hidden your weapons, that's all, and hidden them well. I dare the boche to find them."

"Be careful what you wish for," said Élise.

"From now on," he continued, "you are Élise's boyfriend."

He seemed pleased with his declaration and, when I looked at Élise, she did too. So was I but, with everything that had happened, I do not think I showed any emotion that evening.

"What has happened since the attack on the base?" I said this with a little too much haste and I sensed Élise's disappointment.

"The boche were none too pleased," said Alain.

"No, they were not," repeated Monsieur Martin, "but the destruction was more than you could have imagined. I know the target was the fuel tanks but you managed to take out a few planes too. The fire spread quickly and Fritz was slow to put it out. I think the last tank blowing took them by surprise."

"It took us by surprise too. It was a loud explosion."

"Heard for a few kilometres and it smashed quite a few windows. No matter though, the important thing is that there were some boche killed. I've heard rumours that five boche were killed. Just rumours though. We've had confirmation that three planes were wrecked too. Fritz was mad, really mad."

"What has he done?"

"That's the problem. The boche are ruthless and the Gestapo pigs," he almost spat the words, "have been rounding up young men, at random. Because you were from the maquis, and not near the base, the boche have rounded up local people and they don't realise that they weren't involved. There have been arrests and torture at the Gestapo headquarters. There have been some horrible stories."

Élise shuddered at this point and added, "Bodies have turned up. They were mutilated and just thrown in the street. As if that wasn't bad enough, the pigs slid in one morning, surrounded the village and rounded up all of the men, young and old. They lined them up in the square and shot one in four. They made them kneel and shot them in the head in front of their wives and their kids. You can understand why some of these people do not like what the resistance has done, can't you?"

I looked at them stunned at what I had heard.

"I never realised," I said, "what have we done?"

"It is not like that," Monsieur Martin snapped and I was taken aback by the ferocity of his retort, "What you have done was an act of bravery. I regret deeply what the boche have done to our citizens but it was the boche who did it, not you. You were defending the honour of France and for that I applaud you."

It did not make me feel better. I now had on my conscience Georges' death plus the dreadful consequences of our attack. I put my head in my hands for a moment. I felt very tired but I was also hungry. Claire interrupted with a call to eat and Monsieur Martin poured us a large cognac. Élise sipped hers but her father downed it in one and poured another, passing the bottle to me. I topped up my glass and passed around the bottle. Alain helped himself and, despite his age, nobody mentioned it.

I ate well that evening despite my anguish. The cognac helped anaesthetise me as it dulled my senses. I slept in a bed that night for the first time in what seemed like in a long time. I slept deeply waking only once just before dawn. I was hit by a pang of despair and thoughts of the finality of it all; Georges was gone and I was here, alone far from home without my family and doing things that I barely could have imagined just a few weeks ago. How I would have loved to have seen my grandfather at that moment. I drifted off to sleep and did not wake again until the door creaked and Élise crept into the room with a mug of steaming coffee.

"Are you awake Jacques?"

I stirred from the sheets and looked at her.

"I have brought you some coffee."

"What time is it?"

"It is nearly eight, you have slept well?"

I nodded and she continued, "Papa and Alain have been out with the cows but they will be back for breakfast soon. I know that he wants to talk to you more so I need to disturb you my sweet."

She kissed me on the forehead and the intimacy of the moment was not lost on me. I took the coffee from her, smiled and said, simply, "Thank you, I'll drink this and be up."

"I have some better clothes too. Some that will fit. Claire has been over to see Madame Benoit. Look."

I noticed on the chair were some clothes and Élise showed them to me. They were clean and pressed and I realised how scruffy I must have been.

"Trousers!" Élise proclaimed and held a pair of blue cotton pants. She then showed me an olive green shirt and a jacket. There were a selection of underclothes, socks and a real luxury item: boots! I looked at my motorcycle boots in the corner of the room. They had been uncomfortable and they now looked beaten. I would be pleased to see the back of them. I hoped that everything fitted, and I was to find that they did.

As I entered the kitchen, washed and shaved, Monsieur Martin and Alain entered through the rear door. They removed their boots and Alain came across to me and shook my hand.

"Wash your hands first," scolded Élise.

Alain looked at Élise but ignored her request.

"How are you this morning Jacques? Did you sleep. Will you be able to help me in the fields today?"

I had made a friend and Alain became my replacement brother.

"I will wash my hands first," said Monsieur Martin and gave a cheeky smile to Élise. Claire entered the room next.

"Good morning Jacques. Are you well?"

We sat down to breakfast and some more coffee with milk this time and I felt the tension rise as Monsieur Martin went to speak. I wondered what was coming next and I knew it must be serious for we were left alone. The rest of the family evaporated, leaving the crockery unwashed which was unusual.

"Jacques," Monsieur Martin started.

I nodded but said nothing.

"Jacques," he repeated, "the maquis."

He paused and I could see that he was pained.

"What is it Monsieur Martin? Please, just tell me."

"The maquis, it has been raided. There are many dead."

I was shocked by this news and began the route to self pity and self doubt again. Monsieur Martin was perceptive and saw my mood changing.

"No Jacques," he said, "this is nothing to do with you. Whilst you were on manoeuvre the boche were attacking the camp. Had you not been at the air base you would have been defending the maquis."

I looked at him dumbstruck. After what seemed like a long time I said, "Do you know who has been killed? How did they know where we were? Did any escape?"

The questions flooded out and Monsieur Martin simply watched as I grappled with the facts. I found out that Pierre had been killed but that Bernard and Gabriel had escaped. Young André, I was told, had been the hero of the day and had dispatched two Germans using his cooking knife and had saved Bernard's life. André had escaped and I was thankful of that. I winced when I heard what André had done for I knew that his knives were finely honed. There were many more that were killed that I knew only in passing and I found out that a third of the maquisards had been wiped out. The remainder had fled. I then understood. With the maquis raided the Germans would be systematically going around the farms looking for maquisards that had fled the attack. It was far too dangerous for me to stay here. I would put the whole family in peril. I had to retreat to the woods again and I told Monsieur Martin this and he nodded. His face took on a grave look. He did not want this, I knew. He had no alternative and I sympathised with his plight. He had to put his family first. All of them were taking huge risks and I could not let them be taken by the Germans for I knew what would become of them. These creatures that called themselves the master race showed no humanity. I wondered how I had come from relative neutrality, flavoured with some of my grandfather's prejudices, to this hatred of the German race. My feelings were not against individuals now; I hated, a strong word for sure, but I hated every German and I wanted them all dead.

"Where will you go Jacques?"

"I will see if I can find Bernard or Gabriel. Do you have any idea of where they are now?"

"There are rumours, of course," Monsieur Martin replied, "but everyone is being cautious in the current situation."

"What are the rumours?" I asked, innocently.

He told me where he thought they might head. It made sense. They were heading for more hilly terrain with high forests and rocky outcrops. It would be colder up there but they would be well away from tracks so it would be difficult for the German's to mount an attack without being seen and the use of motorised vehicles would be difficult. I visualised the location on my map again and decided that I would head that way.

Monsieur Martin stood and I shook his hand spontaneously. He looked surprised but shook it warmly back.

"Thank you for being candid," I said and I saw a shallow and uncomfortable smile come to his lips.

"Jacques, my boy," he replied, "I have respect for you. We will drink again when this horror is over."

I remembered that it was 28$^{th}$ May and only a few days to D-day.

"It will not be long," I said, "I am sure."

"Before you go," he added, "I want you to have this."

Monsieur Martin stepped across the room and out of the door. He was gone for a few moments and returned holding a small bag. He put it on the table and opened it. He took out an American colt automatic pistol and handed it to me. He showed me how it worked and then handed me an abundance of ammunition.

"It will be easier to conceal than your bren," he said, "if you are faced with the boche again."

I shook his hand again and went to fetch my bag. I loaded a round of bullets into the pistol and placed the colt in the front zipper section of my bag. I looked inside. I still had my grenades.

Élise saw me leave and tears dribbled down her face. I kissed her deeply as we reached the end of the farmyard. I told her not to come any further in case anyone was looking. Before I left she handed me something.

"Alain wants you to have this," she said.

I took the item from her hand and opened it. It was a black beret. I recognised it as a Basque beret, the sign of a maquisard. I was very proud.

I smiled at her and said, "I am honoured.  Tell Alain he will be in my thoughts."

I kissed her lightly and was gone.  I did not dare turn back.

# Sunday 28<sup>th</sup> May to Monday 5th June
# Alfonse

I had memorised my map well though I did not need it. I was heading up hill into the higher lands and I could see clearly where I must go. The day was bright, clear and warm. Élise had given me some food and water so I was well stocked. I was not sure what I was to do after this produce was gone but I gave it little thought.

My mind was preoccupied and I walked in a daze. I even forgot Luc's self survival lessons and walked in the open. It was later in the day that I started to climb the steep hills and I found the effort exhilarating. I had never felt as alive in my previous life and I did not want to return, even if I could.

The days were long as it was the end of May so I walked until dusk. I found a low tree in which to sleep. I preferred sleeping in a tree if I could, despite the insect problems that it gave me, because I was out of sight and away from the damp ground. There was always the prospect of falling from the tree in my sleep though I never did and I rationalised this as part of our simian past. I seemed to awaken and steady myself whenever there was a risk of falling. I became adept at making a nest in the tree too and was always warm and cosy. Of course, this was summer and I doubt if I would have been quite so happy surviving a winter in this way.

I walked like this through wooded areas and in the open for several days sleeping mostly in the trees but occasionally finding an abandoned hut. Generally, I preferred the trees. I came to terms with the loss of Georges during those days and although sombre I found that my tears had dried. I wondered what had happened to my friends at the maquis and where they were now. I desperately wanted news of Luc and Henri and I often thought of my last sighting of Luc being flung into the air after the explosion and Henri carrying him off. I wondered what had become of them.

It was the first of June when I came across a very small stone built cottage with a slate roof on the edge of a thick wood and set just inside its edge. With the moss covering the stone and roof it blended in well with its surroundings. I noticed a barely perceptible waft of smoke coming from the chimney. I approached the only door gingerly. I grabbed hold of the handle and went to push when the door was flung open and an old gnarled man was staring with a double barrelled shotgun aimed squarely at me.

"Please, don't shoot, I mean no harm," I said lamely.

"You are *Bretagne*," he said on hearing my accent. He then looked me up and down all of the time pointing the shotgun at my chest.

"Is that a Basque beret?"

"It is."

"You are a resistance fighter?"

"I am."

"Then you are welcome."

That was my introduction to Alfonse and he put away his gun on hearing that I was a maquisard. He was a recluse having lost his wife to another man ten years previously. He told me that he had fought in the last war though I could never reconcile the dates he gave me. He told me that he was in his forties though he looked much older; he was more late fifties or sixty but I never found out his real age. Alfonse and I hit it off immediately. He was not like my grandfather at all but I enjoyed being with him in the same way that I had with my grandfather and we enjoyed the same kind of banter.

I learnt about his way of life. Alfonse was completely self sufficient and lived off the land. He had a small vegetable plot out of the woods and he said that he spent a lot of time feeding the rabbits from it. He laughed when he told me that he did not mind because it fattened them up for the pot. He also stalked wild boar and this added to his diet. He showed the signs of a hard life and his face was lined and his body a little stooped. Alfonse did nothing in haste and he had what seemed to me an idyllic life.

The cottage had a single room and was functional and grubby rather than dirty. It had a bed and a wooden bench. I slept on the bench whilst Alfonse slept in the bed. There were some rough blankets but no sheets and we slept fully clothed. I never saw Alfonse wash at all and he was amused at my attempts and shook his head as I tried to wash using a bucket and some soapwort leaves.

Alfonse taught me a lot in a few days and I followed him around like a puppy does his master. He snared rabbits and shot game. He identified and picked wild mushrooms and we managed to catch a suckling boar and whisk it away from its mother. Alfonse also taught me the wild plants that were good to eat and those to avoid. I was grateful for his knowledge and thirsty for it. We ate well during those days and I gained some of the weight that I had lost. I helped him too doing repairs to his cottage and tendering his plot. I mastered his cantankerous range and cooked some Anglo-French dishes that I had seen my mother cook, adapted to the produce I could find locally.

Alfonse hated the Germans though he saw few. He said that he was not troubled by them here. He laughed when he told me that he had not been troubled by the French elite either and hardly noticed the difference. He told me that France had been sullied by the German presence and that they would not be missed. We talked often of my exploits with the maquis but I did not tell him how I had arrived.  I did not think he would believe me and I did not want to spoil the bond we had developed.  Alfonse liked his calvados and we would drink into the night and he would tell me of the old days.  He often repeated himself but I was happy to listen.  I was never sure from where the calvados came as he seemed to have a never ending supply.  I wondered whether he drank like this when he was alone which was more often than not.

"Do you have a girl?" Alfonse asked me one evening as dusk fell.

I told him about Élise and our parting and he nodded sagely.

"A good girl is a hard find," Alfonse said, "and a good family too. Now that is a bonus."

That was the only time we spoke about Élise and represents the totality of our conversation about her.  I asked Alfonse about his wife and all he told me was that she had left him.  I felt his reticence to talk so I did not pursue the topic again.

The days passed and I became restless.  I was learning much and I liked Alfonse and his company but I wanted to become part of the action again.  I awoke on the fifth of June and listened to Alfonse gently snoring.  It was early and the sun was making its majestic journey across the heavens to banish the stars and rise again in the east.  I could see signs of a red sky and it gave the cottage a crimson glow.  Tomorrow is a special day, I thought.  It would be the sixth of June and D-day.  From where I was now I would simply not have guessed that anything was happening, anywhere.  What I did know from my history lessons was that the allies were starting their offensive and one that would win the war.  I knew that it would take some time and that Paris would not be liberated until the twenty fifth of August.  I was not sure about Brittany but I was sure that it was liberated before Paris and early August was in my mind.  I also remembered that, after the initial invasion, the Germans regrouped and mounted a counter attack that held back the allies advance. It would be two months yet before the effects of D-day would be felt and I wanted to be a part of it. I knew that the resistance played a vital role in preventing the Germans from supplying their troops and that they virtually stopped reinforcements from being sent to Normandy from Brittany.

What happened on the fifth of June gave me the opportunity to fulfil my obligations. We rose early as usual and Alfonse lit the range. It took some time and Alfonse grumbled, as usual, about needing more draught and having problems with the damp. Finally it lit and he put a pan of water on top to boil for some coffee substitute. I was never sure how it was made but it tasted good enough. He was pouring the coffee, black and sweet when there was a sound. Alfonse reached for his shotgun and I took the safety catch off my pistol. We were ready for action and I remember having the same thought just before Georges was struck down. Another sound was heard and this one was closer to the cottage. Alfonse stood at the door pointing his shotgun at it. I saw a young person through the window. Even through the grime I could see that it was André.

"It's OK Alfonse," I said putting down my pistol, "I know him. It is André. He was the cook at the maquis."

I opened the door and André turned, startled by my sudden appearance. He stood for a few seconds barely believing what he was seeing.

"Jacques," André said quietly, "Jacques, is that you, is that really you?"

"André, André, hey it's great to see you."

We leapt towards each other and shook each others hands and I slapped him on the back.

"How did you get here? What are you doing here?" I asked.

"And you. I thought you were dead. Oh Jacques, it is good to see you. Is Georges with you?"

The mention of Georges hit me in the pit of my stomach and my torment must have shown in my face.

"What is it Jacques? Has something happened? Where is Georges?"

"He's dead," I murmured and tears welled in my eyes. These were the first tears I had shed in many days.

"The bastards killed him."

I told André what had happened and his normally cheerful face took on a sombre look. It was many seconds before we spoke again and André started the conversation.

"Have you heard about the maquis?"

I told him what Monsieur Martin had told me and he added some details. It added little to what I had been told except to express the horror from André's first hand perspective. The Germans had shown little mercy and none of the maquisards wanted to be taken alive for torture so the battle had been fierce. André did not mention his part in the raid at all so I asked him about it.

"Monsieur Martin told me that you saw off a few of the boche yourself."

"It was nothing," he said, "but I cannot use those knives for food now. German blood is very corrosive."

He smiled and his beam transformed his face. I looked at him and he looked so very young. I look back at this now and realise how absurd that was as I was only nineteen myself. He seemed, to me at that time, so vulnerable. I was very wrong about his vulnerability.

"Come, meet Alfonse," I said and dragged André to the cottage.

Alfonse welcomed André and gave him a steaming cup of his special coffee. André was appreciative and gobbled down a breakfast too. It seemed that he had not eaten for many days. Alfonse asked André why he was in these parts and André said he was heading somewhere as there was nothing much left of the maquis. André said that a major operation had been performed and another rail route was out of action. The Germans could now only transport troops and supplies by road and that was delaying their movements. André seemed pleased with the manoeuvre and it looked to me like he had been involved in it though he did not say so directly. He said also that the maquis was not very effective now as it had few arms and was far away from where it could do harm to the Germans. He also said that most of the sabotage done now was low key and less risky but surprisingly effective.

"Not like your attack Jacques," he said to me and smiled, "that was spectacular."

I was hungry for news about Luc and Henri but I was disappointed as André said that they had not been seen the missing maquisards since the explosion at the air base and the raid on the maquis. He did tell me that Gabriel and Bernard were alive and uninjured and that Gabriel seemed very preoccupied and was rarely seen. I wondered whether this was anything to do with the forthcoming invasion.

André's arrival was my signal to depart and I left with André the following day and André made the most of the food on offer from Alfonse during his day in the cottage. I felt that Alfonse enjoyed this young company and we chatted well into the night drinking Alfonse's perpetual supply of cognac. André was unusual for such a young person. He was a good listener and often joined in the conversation but rarely spoke of himself.

I was sorry to leave Alfonse the next morning. He shook my hands warmly and kissed my cheeks. Finally he hugged me and told me to be on my way.  I caught the sight of slight wetness in his eyes as I left and I never saw Alfonse again.

# Tuesday 6th June
## D-Day

André and I walked away from the cottage and I headed back in the direction that I had arrived. He handed me a cigarette and pulled one out for himself. He lit it and handed the cigarette to me so that I could light mine from his. I sucked on the cigarette and savoured its flavour. I had missed my smoke. I handed his cigarette back to him. I had not thought to ask André where he was going. I remembered him saying that he was not going back to the maquis.

"Where are we heading?"

André looked at me and said, "We? Are you coming with me Jacques?"

I was surprised at this remark. Of course I was going with André. Why else would I have left that day.

"Why yes André, that's why I left Alfonse today."

"But you don't know where I am going," this was becoming absurd.

"That's why I was asking," I replied smiling at him. André beamed back and pulled down my beret in a friendly way.

"I'm going to fuck up the Germans," he said.

"OK," I continued, "sounds like a good plan. A bit more information would be great."

André was playing with me and enjoying it.

"Jacques," said André, "is it true?"

"Is what true André?"

"That you come from the future?"

I had not talked to André in the camp about how we had arrived and André was not there when we were first met by the maquisards. There must have been talk in the camp and, when I thought about it, I had exchanged only pleasantries with André in the whole time I had been there. We had not had a real conversation at all.

"It is true," I said weakly.

André accepted this as a simple fact and asked me when I was born. I told him that I was nineteen in 2009 and that I was born in 1990, forty six years from now.

"That would make me sixty three when you were born, and eighty two when you left if I'd made it."

I thought about what André had said. André would be in the autumn of his life when I was born and potentially dead when Georges and I went through the rift in time. Now he was a mere seventeen and he looked it. His maturity was well beyond his years and I thought of the child-like seventeen year old youths of my time. There was no comparison.

"In which case," said André regaining his normal demeanour, "I'm your senior so you'd better do as you're told."

It was my turn to retaliate and I ruffled his hair and chased him for a little while. I still did not know where we were heading. When we stopped the frivolity we walked along together. The sun was higher in the sky and it was another pleasant morning though cooler in the hills. The elevated track was wooded and the scent of wild garlic was pungent, overwhelming all of the other smells. It was late flowering and I guessed that this was due to the altitude. André did not seem to notice his surroundings.

"How does it turn out?" he asked me.

"The war?"

"Yes, and everything else. Sixty three years is a long time. Do we do the same fucking thing again?"

"Well, yes and no," I replied unhelpfully and continued, "this war is won by the allies and Europe is completely reshaped. Russia, well the USSR I suppose, fucks up the rest of Europe. Right now the Russians are marching through eastern Europe and they are just as bad as the Germans. Eastern Europe is enslaved by them for a whole generation."

André was thoughtful for a moment and said, "What about France?"

"France and Germany," I started.

"Germany, what has Germany got to do with France. Do not speak of them together."

I thought about what I had said and decided that now was not the time for a post war history lesson on the European Union so I said simply, "Germany is defeated and France is liberated."

This was enough for André and he smiled at me. He stopped and pissed down the track without ceremony, unabashed.

"So André, are you going to tell me where we are going?"

"Lorient."

"Lorient!"

That city was mentioned again. I found this hard to comprehend. Why would we be going to Lorient? Firstly, it was a long way and secondly, it would be swarming with Germans. And thirdly, it was not liberated until May 1945, nearly a full year after D-day. I wondered if André knew the devastation reaped on the city by allied bombers. I asked him.

"Yes, I know. We go because it is full of Germans and where there are Germans we can fuck them. We can't fuck them here because there aren't any."

I could not fault his logic though I was not sure what he had in mind. It did not matter now. I was committed to André and, in all of this madness that was now my life, I had simply gone along with whatever was happening. I remembered Georges saying how amazing it was what we were doing. I wondered what he would have said if he had known how it would end for him. Knowing Georges, though, I think he would still have done the same. He was killed instantly I am sure and, though traumatic for me, it must have been a quick death for Georges. It gave me some comfort.

"That's a long way André."

"You've got your papers haven't you?"

"Yes."

"We're going to take a little ride, well at least part of the way, by train."

This became more bizarre by the second. Much of the sabotage done by the Free French had been targeted at the railways and many of the lines were blocked so I could not see us hopping on an inter-city train to Lorient. Lorient was a heavily fortified maritime port and the Germans would not simply let us disembark at Lorient like a couple of tourists. There was also the enforced labour regime and questions would be asked as to why we were not working in German factories. The whole plan seemed flawed. Just like when I was told of the plight of the airmen I felt severe discomfort and it must have showed in my face.

André smiled at me, "Trust me Jacques. I have a cunning plan."

"Then share it with me and I might feel better about all of this."

André was well connected and he had some friends and relatives who worked for the railway network. We were not going to be passengers on the train, we were going to work our passage. André said that we would not be able to use the train all of the way into

Lorient and in any case most of Lorient had been flattened. We would disembark at Hennebont. I knew of Hennebont and it was around ten kilometres away from Lorient. I also knew that it was on the river Blavet which flowed into the Atlantic past the infamous Keroman submarine base. Hennebont was also the location of the 'Lorient pocket' which was the last stronghold of the Germans in Brittany. I did not want to be in Hennebont in August because, if we were, we would be killed by either the allies or the Germans. Neither of these options sounded appealing.

I tried to reason with André but his mind was set. The action was in Lorient so Lorient it was to be. There was to be no shifting him.

We continued down hill until we came upon a smallholding. A scruffy middle aged woman greeted us at the gate. She was unkempt but pleasant enough. She offered us a drink and some food and we accepted it gratefully. André charmed her to give us some produce for the journey. He gave her a packet of cigarettes in return and she put it into her apron pocket.

It was early evening before we saw any further sign of life. We walked mostly through wooded areas and all down hill. I found André a strange combination. I had not spent much time with him prior to our meeting and I came to realise that I did not know him at all. He was certain in his mind about things and was a little reckless. He conversed with me and there was barely a quiet moment between us. He was also a good listener. I wasn't sure what it was that troubled me at first and then I realised. He gave nothing away about himself. In the hours that I had been with him I knew no more about him than I had when we started. The facts I did know about him or his family were utilitarian. They related to the self imposed mission we were on. I knew he had relatives in the railway because I needed to know it for our journey. I gave away much more about myself. André's reticence was not because he was shy and reserved; in fact he was very open and completely uninhibited.

I remember thinking that French society was controlled by the Roman Catholic church at this time and yet here we had a young man that would have fitted very well into my time. He was supremely confident in himself and would talk about anything and everything, except himself.

I looked at my watch as we approached a farm with several outbuildings and an open barn.

"Ideal," said André.

My watch said six thirty, probably too early to stop as we had a few hours of light left. André had different ideas.

"We could sleep in the barn. Its an easy escape if we are disturbed," said André. It looked like André had made up his mind to stop. A middle aged man walked across the farmyard, noticed us and stared. André made his way over to him and handed him a cigarette. They exchanged some words and I saw André smiling and the man and André shook hands. André beckoned for me to join them so I walked through the gate. I shook the man's hand. They were rough and deeply calloused. He was used to hard work and mine felt smooth by comparison. André passed me a cigarette too and the man lit his and handed it to me; I lit mine from his.

"André," the man said and I was puzzled.

"His name is André too," said André.

"Ah," I replied understanding at last, "Jacques."

André senior nodded. His face was grey and lined and his hair thinning and greasy. His clothes were creased and dirty.

"He lives here alone," said André, "his son is in Germany. Forced labour, where I should be if the bastards ever get hold of me. We can use the barn, yes?"

André directed his last remark to André senior and he nodded. It was clear from his demeanour that we were not welcome in the house. We were left alone as André senior walked towards the house.

"This is a farm. Bound to be food here somewhere," said André and he left me to scout around. I made my way to the open barn. The smell in the air was of a typical farmyard. It was not unpleasant. In the barn were hay bales and I moved them into position for a bed. This could end up a comfortable night, I thought to myself. André came back with fresh hens eggs and some potatoes. He disappeared again for a while and came back with two plates of omelette and boiled potatoes. André's charm again, I thought, and it even worked on André senior.

We chatted for a while and turned in as it became dark. I lay on my side on the hay bales looking out into the farmyard. We were miles from anywhere and probably had two more days before we reached civilisation and the railways. It was D-day somewhere, but here it was business as usual.

I drifted off to sleep but was woken by André who had rolled over onto my bale and was snuggled up to me with his arm around my waste. It was not unpleasant and his body heat helped keep me warm in the cool of the morning. When I awoke André was missing from our makeshift bed.

# Wednesday 7<sup>th</sup> June to Friday 9<sup>th</sup> June
# Jean and Maria

André had awoken first the next morning and was bright and breezy as usual. I did not mention the events of the night but I think that André knew that I was aware of his actions. He caught me looking at him and he stared back and smiled. I think he enjoyed my embarrassment. I did not want to speak about it because I was embarrassed and, if I was honest to myself, had enjoyed his closeness. We looked for André senior but he was nowhere around so we left him a note and started our descent into the valley.

"Were you warm enough, Jacques?" André said and smiled. He was teasing me again.

"Perfect," I said dismissively.

André had a look in his eye that I had not seen before. He came close to me and put his hand on the back of my neck and caressed it gently with the palm of his hand. He smiled at me and released his hand and the moment passed. We walked in silence for a while and I pondered on the intimacy that André had shown me. I wondered if this was what my grandfather had meant by the close bond of comrades in war. André spoke first and our previous conversation and his actions were now in the past; André had moved on.

"We've another night out here," he said, "and then we will be near the rail depot. We can stay with my uncle for a few days. My aunt cooks well so we can replenish our reserves. I have another uncle in Hennebont. He has a small house near the river. I doubt if we can stay there for too long and his wife is very prudish and of-the-church, if you understand my meaning."

André winked at me as he said this and I was not sure that I did know what the term meant.

"Their son, my cousin, lives somewhere near them. He's a good man. Just a bit older than you I think. If we can stay with him we can have a good time. He hates the boche too and he's active."

Listening to André I was beginning to think that I had lost my way. André was too confusing for me. His attitude was radically liberal for this time and even for mine. This seemed to be a big game for him and his game was not my game. I listened to him and decided that I would follow him to Hennebont and would then try to secure a passage to England, like the airmen had, or at least I hoped they had. I remembered thinking then that their attempt was suicide. I wondered whether my attempt would be the same. Whatever happened I did not want to remain with André. I had money. Gabriel had given me some and I even had Euros though they would, of course, have been useless. Would anybody here believe that the whole of Europe, well almost all of it, would use a single currency one day? I doubted it. I wondered to what dark recess André was leading me and whether I would exit unscathed. I was to find out.

The day passed and I thought of the allies in Normandy building their bridgehead and shoring up their defences. I knew that the Germans would mount a counter attack and also that men were being killed that day. We slept in the open that night and walked on the next day until we finally approached the railway depot just short of the town. We sought out André's uncle's house.

When we found it I was surprised at how young was André's uncle. I placed him in his mid thirties along with his wife who was probably a couple of years younger. They lived in a small, terraced three story stone built house very near to the railway depot. The house shook when the huge steam driven beasts thundered by. They greeted André as if he was the prodigal son and fussed him. As a friend of André's, I was also a friend of theirs and I immersed myself in their gracious hospitality.

André's uncle was called Jean. He was a tall and solidly built person and it was evident that he loved his food for he was quite rotund. Maria was his wife and she was of Italian origin with long, almost black hair and olive skin. She contrasted starkly with Jean, as she was petite in frame and height. She was stunningly beautiful and had a reserve about her. She looked down slightly as she spoke and, had she been wearing spectacles, which she was not, she would have been peering over the top of them. She spoke French well with the hint of an Italian accent. I thought how difficult must have been their marriage since the war with the Italians siding with the Germans and, until their humiliating defeat, the enemy. They had no children and I wondered why this might be.

As I entered Jean and Maria's home I pulled off my beret and held it in my hand. When Élise had given me the beret I had not realised how recognisable it would be to people. The difference between a Basque beret and the normal French beret is slight. I knew the German's would not recognise the distinction but I wondered whether the Milice would know better. I saw Jean look at the beret as I removed it and again when I held it in my hand. He said nothing to me then about it.

It was around five in the afternoon and I was very hungry. We had eaten little that day as we had not passed many farms and those that we had passed were devoid of life. I used some of the skill that Alfonse had taught me and had managed to find some fungus for us to eat. I hoped that I had learned well from Alfonse for I knew that the consequences of an identification error could be dire. André concurred with my classification so I felt confident.

Jean opened a bottle of Beaujolais and we sat in his small lounge having been chased out of the kitchen by Maria who wanted to prepare us a meal. I was grateful for this. The bottle was opened and small glasses poured for each of us. I sipped mine and Jean took a single swig and drank the whole glass. He refilled his and topped up my and André's glasses. André had also finished most of his glass. This glass Jean drank more slowly. He asked questions of André, about André's father and mother and of his family. Jean asked questions about me politely and I told him about my grandfather, as he was the only link to this time.

Finally Jean asked, "So what brings you here?"

André looked furtively at me and said, simply, "We want to get to Hennebont."

"Why would you want to do that? It stinks of pigs."

By this, of course, he meant the Germans.

"That's the point, I want to fuck-up the Germans."

André used the first person, rather than including me here and Jean picked this up. He frowned at André's expletive and shook his head. André understood and did not swear again in Jean's presence.

"And you Jacques, what do you want to do?"

This simple question took me aback and I realised that I had not my own agenda. I said simply that I was with André and this sounded very lame. It was clear from Jean's questioning style that Jean had depth. He also commanded a quiet authority. I was to learn soon that he was a very important person in the local community and he was a person who could make things happen. The wine went to my head quickly and I was pleased when the food arrived. I hoped that I did not gobble my food too quickly but I finished well ahead of the others.  Maria was delighted and filled my plate again.  I finished this at the same time as everyone else completed their first helping.

"My," Maria said, I must make more next time, "young men have good appetites for sure."

"I don't think they have eaten properly," said Jean and smiled to Maria.  They were a very close couple and I wondered again about their lack of offspring.  This was unusual for this time and I guessed that there must have been a problem.

After we had eaten André was dismissed with Maria.  Jean did this pleasantly but it was clear to all of us that Jean wanted to talk alone with me.

"Your beret," he commenced, "do you know what it means?"

"I do," I replied.

"Tell me then."

"It is a sign of the Free French, the resistance."

"And what qualifies you to wear this?"

This was like an interrogation and I felt myself becoming irritated.  I suppressed the irritation but Jean was perceptive and he noticed my discomfort.  He did nothing to relieve it and looked at me, awaiting a reply, in a hostile silence.

I told him about the maquis, the drop, the operation where we blocked the railway track and the attack at the air base.  I told him about Georges and I told him about Élise and how she had presented me with the beret and how I wore it with pride.  I felt like a cockerel puffing out my chest as I was telling this and it did the trick.

"I think that may qualify you," he said, "and I am sorry about your friend.  We have all lost someone dear."

Despite the cross-examination from Jean, I liked his directness and I warmed to him.  His authority was something he wore lightly but it was unmistakable.  Here was a confident man who knew his place in the world.

"The allies have mounted an offensive," he said to me.  I thought it best to profess surprise so I did.

"I hope the end is in sight to this madness.  We will see."

"Do you also want to go to Hennebont?"

"I have tagged along with André," I said, "after I lost Georges."

Jean nodded and sipped at his wine.

"He is a wayward boy," Jean said, "are you sure you want to tie your flags to his mast?"

This remark astonished me.  Here was his uncle telling me that his nephew was rebellious.  I hardly knew Jean and yet he was confiding in me so quickly.

I did not have a chance to answer his question as Maria and André re-entered the room carrying espresso coffees.  Jean smiled at them and leaned back into his chair.  He simply nodded to me and I knew from his demeanour that we would return to this subject.

The coffee was real and delicious, a rare luxury.  Jean balanced the saucer on his ample stomach as Maria perched elegantly on the arm of the chair besides him.  I caught sight of her long legs and I looked away, embarrassed lest I be caught looking.  We chatted mostly small talk and I noticed that Jean was not particularly good at this and he took a back seat.  Maria did a lot of the talking and, at the end of the conversation, I realised that we had spoken a lot but passed on very little real information.

After the coffee there was another luxury and that was a room of my own, away from André.  I was delighted and I hoped that this did not show too much.  Maria showed us up to the top floor where there were two rooms with a small toilet between them.  As I said goodnight to Jean and Maria I asked Jean what time he started the following morning. He told me and it was early. I was determined to be awake and up before him so that we could talk over breakfast, hopefully alone.

I turned in and sat awake for a while going over in my mind the conversation with Jean. I think I knew then that he was a special man though I did not realise at that time just how extraordinary he was and how lucky we were to be in his home.

# Saturday 10<sup>th</sup> June to Monday 12<sup>th</sup> June
# The Railway

I was in the kitchen making a cup of coffee at five o'clock. Maria came down first and was surprised to see me.

"Couldn't you sleep Jacques?"

"I'm an early riser," I pretended and realised that I would have to live that lie.

Maria looked very attractive even with her dishevelled hair and in her dressing gown. She pulled it close on seeing me. Jean arrived next.

"Jacques," he exclaimed, "is the bed uncomfortable?"

I repeated my untruth to Jean but I could see he was not convinced. Jean then surprised me and switched to English.

"I am glad you are awake," he said, "I wanted to finish our conversation and wondered when I would have the time."

Maria looked at us and, realising that Jean wanted to talk to me in private, continued making the breakfast. She did not appear to mind. Jean continued almost at the point he had left the conversation the previous evening. He spoke in strongly French accented English but I could understand him easily. Occasionally he used a word of French where his vocabulary deserted him.

"I know of the raid on the air base," he said, "and you have my admiration for that. I understand that the two who were missing have turned up at a patriot's house. One is badly injured and is being cared for."

"Luc and Henri," I said, "they are safe?"

"If that is who they are, then yes. One of them was in a poor state. I have no more news so I do not know about his recovery."

I was pleased to hear this news and I smiled and said, "Thank God."

"Praise indeed," continued Jean.

"Let us return to my André for a moment," he said. Maria turned on hearing André's name.

"He is a difficult child."

Somehow the term child did not seem to fit the André that I knew. He was young, for sure, but I never thought of him as anything but a man. Jean must have seen the astonishment on my face.

"Maybe you don't see him as a child," he said, "and I guess he is no longer. His behaviour is anarchic though and he has been a trouble for his parents and for us whenever he has stayed here. He is erratic and uncontrollable. We love him, of course, but we would prefer him to behave differently."

I felt protective of André though I did not know why. I told Jean about André's exemplary behaviour when the maquis was attacked. Jean was pleasantly surprised but not convinced.

"Yes, he can do this," Jean said, "and I have no doubt he would be a good partner to have in a scrap. But it would be better not to follow him into the scrap. He has some strange bedfellows too."

I did not understand his last remark but I let it pass.

"OK, Jacques. I must let you make up your own mind but think on what I have said. If you have to travel with him then take care of him and keep him out of trouble."

Jean switched back to French and said, "Jacques, what do you know of two British airmen who were sent from here by your maquis?"

"There were two airmen," I said, "Eugene and Clark were their names. Bernard sent them to Lorient for transport to England."

"Was he mad?"

I told him that I thought the plan was a bad one and that the airmen were more likely to be killed. I also told Jean that Gabriel was not at the maquis at the time. Jean seemed to know the commanders of the maquis and I guessed that this would have come from André. I was wrong about this for Jean was intimately involved in the resistance movement and he told me so that morning. He was an important commander and he had his finger on the pulse. Jean impressed me immensely and I was beginning to like him. I think he liked me too.

"Jacques, if you are determined to go then I want you to do something for me."

"I'll be happy to."

"You do not yet know what it is I want."

I looked at him but said nothing. He continued, "OK, I will tell you. I would like you to look up a friend of mine. He is like you and he wears the beret of the Basque. His name is René or at least that is how he is known. You must go into the *Chez Maurice* on *Rue St Caradec* and ask for René's special cognac, recommended by Jean. Wear your beret, as it will help. It is about the airmen and that is all I will say. René will handle the rest. He is a good man and can be trusted. I would trust him with my life. Be careful, Jacques, around Lorient is very dangerous. It is not like around here."

"I need to go," Jean said.

"Can I come with you?"

"Not today Jacques," Jean replied, "but I will make arrangements for your training. You and André are about to be firemen on the train to Hennebont. It is a hard and unpleasant job but will not arouse suspicion with the boche. I need to get you permits today. You can come with me tomorrow."

Jean left me alone with Maria who handed me some breakfast and sat across the table from me with a coffee.

"Are you not eating?"

"I will eat later with André. This is too early for me."

I ate my omelette and Maria talked to me of Jean. She adored him, I could tell, and greatly admired him. There was a fear for his safety too and I could tell that in the way that she spoke of him. She was proud of his stature in the community. I remember thinking that there were a large number of ways of resisting and living in the forest and performing acts of sabotage was just one. In many ways Jean, living among the enemy, was braver than were we as he was in continual risk of being detected or, worse, somebody informing on him. The consequences of exposure were grave and the thought of this courageous family at the hands of the Gestapo appalled me. I hoped it would never happen. Jean's job at the railway gave him access to valuable information. It also meant he was watched by the Milice and he knew it. Jean was very careful but this surveillance meant that our stay with Jean and Maria was recorded carefully in the files of the Milice. A consequence of Jean's marriage to Maria, however, was that he was trusted more. After all he was married to a German ally, or so they thought.

It was seven o'clock when André surfaced and appeared at the door in his shirt and underclothes. Maria went over to him and kissed him on the cheeks.

"Come, sit down, I will cook you something. Jacques, would you like some more?"

I declined, except for a coffee, and sat with André and Maria as they ate their eggs. I mused that Maria fussed André as if he was a child and I realised that this was how both Jean and Maria saw André. This was quite different to how I saw him. André finished his meal and burped loudly. Maria reprimanded him and André smiled one of his charming smiles and he was soon forgiven. I felt a little like an outsider when Maria and André were together. This was Maria's missing child, I thought. It seemed to me that Maria wanted a child and needed to be a mother. My conclusion was that there must have been some problem preventing them from conceiving. To me this was a great shame for both Jean and Maria would have made perfect parents.

That evening Jean arrived home from work. He kissed Maria, ruffled André's hair and shook my hand warmly.

"I have your permits," Jean said, "tomorrow you start work as trainee firemen. You'll do a short trip to get the hang of it for a couple of days and then you can make the trip to Hennebont if you still want to do that."

André beamed and made an obscene gesture. Jean cuffed him around the ear and Maria pretended not to have seen.

"Why do you want to go there André," Maria said, "the town is full of the boche. Stay here a while. We will look after you."

"That's the point," said André, "we can …"

He stopped, realising that he was about to swear in front of his aunt. Jean was about to speak to block the expletive and stopped when he realised that André had behaved himself.

The next day we rose early. I knocked on André's door to wake him but he was already downstairs. He was eager for the start of his adventure. We left with Jean and arrived at the rail yard shortly afterwards. We were assigned a freight train and found ourselves on the footplate of a steam locomotive. These things are magnificent. They are barely under control and one can feel the enormous pent up energy waiting to be released. It was very hot work and I found myself sweating profusely, as did André. We stripped to the waist and shovelled coal into the firebox what seemed like all of the day. The beast had an appetite for the black fuel and it took two of us to feed it. Whenever the furnace like door was open the heat struck like a hammer and I swear that it singed the hair on my chest. André was luckier in that he had no chest hair. We made several journeys with barely a break, except for regular drinks of water that were a necessity in that heat. We were soon black with coal dust and it made its way into every crevice. Even my pockets were coated with grime on the inside.

We finished at around four o'clock and made our way to the showers to wash away the dirt. The communal showers were hot and welcome and other firemen and engine drivers joined us in there. I left to dry myself before André and waited for him to arrive. He was the last to leave the shower and I was fully dressed when he turned up naked and beaming. He was last to dress too. I felt uncomfortable in the changing room so I went into the locker room and spoke with some of the others.

The next day was a repeat of that day. When we arrived back at Jean and Maria's, Jean said that we were ready and would be leaving the next day. Maria's look of anguish spoke volumes and I could tell that she did not want her child to leave. I slept very well that night after half a bottle of Bordeaux wine and a couple of large cognacs. I learned that André could not hold his liquor that evening and he was loud and coarse. Maria left us and went to bed and I was embarrassed for André though he did not seem to notice.

# Tuesday 13th June

## Hennebont

We left early with Jean. Maria was sad to see us go and I was sad to leave. I had enjoyed my time with Jean and Maria and, as André had said, Maria was an excellent cook and that was a real bonus. It was Jean who had made my stay so pleasant for he had accepted me completely and, for that, I will always be grateful. I had written a letter to Élise the previous evening and I asked Maria to try and send it to her. Maria said that she may have to rewrite it to avoid the German censor and I told her to do whatever she felt she needed. I desperately wanted Élise to know I was safe and thinking of her.

We were on the footplate again shovelling coal. The locomotive was hurtling towards Hennebont and we were being buffeted around. I imagined what it must have been like when the locomotives that we set free hit each other and the boilers blew. It would have been frightening from the vantage point we had now. We were stripped to the waist again in the searing heat of the firebox. I looked at André and he was glowing red. I must have looked the same and sweat was pouring down my chest and sides. The grime stuck to us again and I saw André change from pink to grey and then to almost black as the coal dust stuck to his wet body. Finally, we were in Hennebont and it was the longest stint we had done on the footplate. André looked as tired as I felt and I took the water that the driver passed me gratefully. I slurped the whole mug in one go and André did the same. The locomotive squealed and squeaked to a halt at the station groaning and grumbling. The safety valve opened and the deafening sound of escaping steam filled the air. We had arrived. The passengers disembarked and the driver told us to leave as he was going to shunt the train into a siding. He patted me on the back as I left and said well done to us.

The shower was heaven and it soothed my aching bones. This time it was only André and I in the shower and I noticed how he enjoyed it. Most houses had baths so this was a rare luxury. It was at times like this that I noticed the difference between us. Although I was only two years older than André I found him child like in the shower. He would throw the soap at me and generally lark around. I would push him away but he would come back for more. In the end, I would become annoyed and I would leave the shower and I wondered whether this was what he wanted. He was always last out and I was in the mess room and drinking coffee before his smiling face appeared around the door.

We were in Hennebont and it was time to leave the rail depot. I knew that our railway permit would prevent awkward questions from the Germans. This was a restricted zone and travel through it was strictly controlled. Jean had been correct and this place was crawling with Germans. I saw patrols and heard their jackboots marching the streets. I realised that my bag contained a pistol and grenades. If I were caught with these I would have been in serious trouble. I whispered to André, explaining what I had in my bag. He said an expletive and motioned me to follow him away from the main street. We headed for his other aunt and uncle's home. André told me that his uncle was called Dominique and his wife was Martine. He also said that Dominique was the older brother of his mother whereas Jean had been the younger brother of his father. A consequence of this was that Dominique was in his fifties and Martine was about the same age. They lived at the top of a steep hill in a small house set back from the path. It had a steep roof and the chimney was smoking as we arrived.

André knocked on the door and Martine opened it. I could see immediately that she was not happy to see André. Martine was short and plump and wore a loose fitting dark grey dress. Her hair was grey and lank.

"André," she said, "and a friend I see."

"Hello Aunt Martine," said André and he smiled, trying to charm his aunt. She was having none of this.

"Why are you here? What do you want?"

"Who is it," said a voice from indoors.

"André!" replied Martine, looking back towards the hidden voice, "Trouble, that means."

A red faced, tall and very fat man came to the door. He was dressed in loose fitting trousers, a collarless shirt and a grubby cardigan.

"André," he said upon seeing André.

"Yes," said André, still trying his charm but failing.

"And who is this?"

"Jacques," I said and put out my hand.

Dominique shook it limply and Martine kissed me on one cheek more out of duty than desire. I hoped we were not going to stay here because I knew I would not like it.

"You had better come in. At least you look clean. Have you eaten?"

We entered the house. It was small and very spartan in its décor. Where Jean and Maria's house had been small and homely this was austere and unwelcoming. I looked at my watch and it was six o'clock. I thought that we were probably going to have to stay the night, if they would let us, but I was not happy about it. My fears were grounded and we spent an uncomfortable evening trying to converse but ending up with periods of painful silence. Martine would not leave André and I alone either and she followed us everywhere and then finally to our bedrooms. She led André to a room on one side of their bedroom and myself to another on the opposite side. She watched us both as we closed the door. The bed was decked with coarse blankets; the room had no furniture and a single small rug covered a rough wooden floor. I was pleased that it was summer for I thought that the room would be cold and disagreeable in the winter. I threw open the window to rid the room of its musty smell. I so wanted to tell André that we could not stay another night but we were not allowed a moment together by Martine. I left the room to use the toilet and Martine appeared in the hallway. I did not understand her problem.

I slept in my clothes that night for I did not wish to touch the grubby grey blankets. I was not sure if they were clean or not but I did not wish to take the chance. I find this strange, looking back, because I had slept in muddy forests, in the open, in shacks and in the trees. I found all of those preferable to this bed. I looked out of the window when I returned to my room, my return being chaperoned by Martine. André was looking out of his room too. I peered at him and frowned and gave him the thumbs down. He looked back at me and gave me his signature smile and repeated the thumbs down sign. He knew what I meant. I really could not wait to leave this awful place.

# Wednesday 14<sup>th</sup> June

## René

I woke early and went to the bathroom to wash. Martine was missing so my guess was that she was asleep. I wondered whether she thought that I was going to steal something. When I looked around I reckoned that there was little to steal even if I was inclined.

The water was cold but that was not a problem. I had become hardened since my rough life in the open. On reflection, I think I came to prefer my time in the wild and away from people. This madness in which I was immersed was caused by the power struggle between the rich and powerful. In Christianity, of course, Jesus had said that the meek will inherit the world. Even in the future I had yet to see this happen. To me it seemed that the meek were the ones doing the suffering.

I descended the stairs into the parlour and then into the kitchen. I was going to make a coffee but I realised that the only way of heating anything was via the range which was unlit. There was a pile of logs besides it but I did not know if I had the knowledge or daring to try to light it. I poured a cup of water and gazed out of the kitchen window. It was a pleasant garden and, in the French style, semi-wild rather than manicured like the English prefer. One section of it was packed with vegetables and it looked to me like André's relatives were self sufficient. There was also a hut and I could hear the sound of a cockerel so I guessed that that there were hens too and I was right about that. I wondered why his aunt and uncle disliked André so much. I thought back to Jean's warning. It was clear that Jean and

Maria were fond of André but that their affection was not blind. They knew of André's weaknesses, whatever they were, and accepted them whereas Dominique and Martine did not. André could be irritating, for sure, but I had found him full of juvenile impulses rather than bad intent. I just thought that he needed to grow up and in some ways he had done this but in others he had a long way to go.

Martine entered the room dressed in the same clothes as she had on the previous day. I said good morning to her and she replied curtly. I tried a little small talk but found it pointless so I asked her if I could do anything to help. She asked me to fetch some eggs and I was pleased to be out of her company. I walked down the garden and over to the hen house. Martine had also asked me to open the door to the hut so that the hens were clear to roam the garden. I did this and the hens sought their freedom and were quickly herded by the strutting cockerel. The madness of the male again I thought to myself.

It was a warm morning again and there was a light dew on the ground. The scents of the herbs reminded me of my time in the wild and I longed to be back there. I was never sure why I had come with André. I think, now, that it was a reaction to Georges' death in that I needed to be with someone. I had found being alone after Georges was shot to be intolerable. Here, I did not like being in the proximity of so many of the enemy. I was used to having my weapons to hand and I felt vulnerable without them. Now, however, I felt vulnerable with them. I decided to do as Jean had asked me today and seek out René.

I took the eggs back to Martine and she put them on the table. The range was roaring when I returned to the kitchen and I could smell the smoke.

"Do you know where *Chez Maurice* is?", I asked and then added, "It is on *Rue St Caradec*."

Martine looked at me for a few moments and there was a perceptible change in her demeanour for a second or so.

"How do you know of *Chez Maurice*? Have you been here before?"

"No, Jean mentioned it to me," I said innocently.

"Jean did," Martine said, "and what did he ask you to do there."

This was becoming uncomfortable as I did not wish to break Jean's confidence. I could tell that Martine knew of Jean and probably of his importance in the resistance.

"Sit down Jacques," she said to me and beckoned towards the solid kitchen table. I pulled out a heavy chair and looked at the surface of the table. It was well worn and deeply marked.

I waited for Martine to continue. She sat opposite me so that she could look into my eyes which she did. She looked very fierce but I held her gaze.

"Tell me about your relationship with André," she started.

I explained and told her about the maquis and how André had been the cook. I told her about what we had done at the maquis and I told her about Georges. My eyes welled up as I relived the German attack but I held back the tears. I think Martine was quite moved by the tale as her attitude towards me changed.

"Why do you dislike André so?"

"We do not dislike him. He is the son of my husband's sister after all. We have a duty to protect him. He is a difficult child and he has vices that I cannot accept. It is against God."

I wondered what these could be and remembered some of his vices myself. This was 1944 though and the taboos of this time were discussed more openly and accepted more in my time. I did not pursue the issue further.

"So, you are not close to André?"

"He is my friend."

"Just a friend?"

I did not like this line of questioning and was not sure where it was leading. I replied brusquely.

"Not like Georges," I said, "I have known Georges all of my life. I hardly know André at all, except for this last week or so."

That seemed to satisfy Martine and she switched track.

"So, why are you here? This is a dangerous place. I would not decide to be here if I had a choice. There are boche everywhere. You know about the submarine base in Lorient? You know about the devastation in Lorient and around?"

I nodded and Martine continued.

"Tell me then, why are you here?"

Put so directly it was a difficult question to answer. Until Jean had given me a mission I had no idea why I was heading for the worst place in Brittany to be during the allied invasion. I leaned on Jean's mission as a reason for my presence. I did not want to give too much away.

"Jean has asked me to do something for him."

Martine nodded but remained silence.

"And I was hoping to get a boat back to England."

"Back?"

"Yes, I am English."

"You do not sound it. That is a *Brettagne* accent is it not?"

I was in difficult water now as it would be challenging to reconcile my childhood and the events happening in the forties in Europe.

"My father is English," I said simply, hoping this would suffice and it did. I breathed easy again.

"You will not get a passage anywhere from here," Martine said, "the boche have tightened their grip. It isn't possible to travel and even the fishermen are confined to their berths."

I must have looked disappointed and Martine's mood lightened further. She rose and filled a kettle with water from the tap and placed it on the range. She added more wood and came back to the table.

"What does Jean want you to do?"

Before I could reply Martine added, "Jean is very important to the Free French. He is a very brave man. If he has entrusted you with a task then he trusts you and who am I to doubt Jean."

Martine's remark made up my mind; I would tell her about the airmen.

"Jean has asked me to make contact with René. Some airmen were sent to Lorient by Bernard."

I stopped, realising that Martine would not know Bernard.

"He is the French commander of the maquis. The English special operations commander has a code name of Gabriel."

"I know of Gabriel, but not Bernard. Why were they sent here? This is the last place they should be. What were you thinking of?"

"I thought it unwise at the time," I said.

"Unwise? You choose your words badly young man. It was not unwise it was madness."

"Well, I thought suicidal at the time and I said so. I am not the commander, Martine."

She nodded. She understood military discipline. This was a different Martine to the one with which I had interacted only yesterday.

"Jean said that René would know of the airmen's whereabouts and that I was to help them. I don't know what I am to do and Jean said that René would tell me."

"I know of the airmen," said Martine, "they are being hidden and were to be smuggled out of town. The invasion has changed all of that. They speak no French and we have nobody who speaks English. It is difficult. They stand out like a sore thumb. They have to be kept hidden all of the time. They are pretty frustrated, I've heard."

I told Martine that I spoke English well and she nodded again.

"I will help you," she said quickly, "but first some breakfast. I hear father rising and maybe even André."

She walked towards the range wiping her hands on a grubby cloth. As she did so she said, "Jacques, just be careful of André. He can lead you into trouble and here, trouble is easy to find. My advice would be to go to *Chez Maurice* on your own. Leave André here."

I was surprised at this conversation with Martine. I looked at her; it was difficult to believe that she could have had the knowledge that she had just portrayed. Maybe that was the point, I thought to myself. She was probably beyond suspicion by the Germans. I decided to take her advice and listened carefully to Martine's directions. My ability to recall information came in useful again. I left the house before André came down for breakfast and decided to forgo breakfast at Martine's. She understood and wished me well. Her attitude towards me had softened and with it my attitude towards her.

I left and kept to the back roads that Martine had described to me. Within half an hour I was at *Chez Maurice* and sat at the bar with an espresso coffee and a croissant. I wore my beret indoors and leaned forward to the bartender and said to him, rather ridiculously as it was before eight o'clock, "Jean said that I was to ask for René's special cognac."

I looked at the waiter expectantly and, feeling foolish added, "I know it is early, but ..."

I did not have a chance to finish my conversation when a man in his twenties, I guessed, came through the curtain from the back room and into the café. He had heard me and came around to my side of the bar and sat on the stool besides me. He handed me a cigarette which I took. He lit a match and used it to ignite my cigarette. He then lit his own. I looked at the newcomer. He was very good looking. Dark, tall and slim with deep set eyes and an intense stare. He was intelligent too and this was very evident the moment he spoke. He was in a class apart from me and I was somewhat wary of him.

"How do you know Jean?"

I looked around lest anyone might hear and I told René about our trip on the footplate as firemen. It seemed to make a difference to him and he motioned to a table in the corner. The café was not particularly full so we would not be overheard. There was something different about René. His speech pattern was unusual and he phrased things in a different way to others. As we were talking, I realised what was different. René's conversational style was like mine. It was less formal. It was from my century.

"You are not from this time," I said to him.

"No, and nor are you," he replied.

# Wednesday 14<sup>th</sup> June

## A Dangerous Plan

"When did you arrive?" René asked me.

"Fifth of May," I replied.

"Where?"

I told him and he replied, "Why are you here, I mean so close to Lorient? You must know how dangerous it is here?"

I thought about what had happened to me since I arrived and I told René all of it. He barely had chance to say anything at all during the telling of my tale. He listened mostly in silence and it was difficult to read anything in his face. Only when I mentioned Jean did his demeanour change. When I told him about the death of Georges I noticed barely a flicker in his eyes. I guessed René had seen some awful things too and it had hardened him.

"Why did Jean ask you to find me?"

"The airmen," I replied.

René looked around furtively and I could see that he did not want to discuss this in the open. So far, I had found out nothing at all about René and he had discovered everything about me.

"How long have you been here?" I asked him so that I could change the subject.

"Just over a year. I arrived here, in Hennebont" he said dismissively.

"Alone?" I continued.

"You mean, did I arrive alone?" René asked.

"Yes," I countered.

"Yes, there was a mist and I was here. It was bloody frightening. " René said and continued, "There'll be time for that later, for now, you need to go."

"What?" I said.

"I'm sorry Jacques," René said, "but we have Germans who frequent the café and they usually arrive soon. It would not be safe. I've so many questions but now is not the time. I will be finished at one this afternoon. Meet me here then and we can go somewhere more private and talk some more. You must go now, or you will regret it."

I was bundled out of the café and found myself on the street near the harbour. Hennebont is not a place to loiter. The Germans sweep the street of people and continually ask for papers. I had the railway permit but questions would be asked as to why I had not returned. At least I was not armed. I had left my pistol and grenades at Dominique and Martine's. There were times when I felt more insecure with arms than without them. I had discovered that being able to react quickly and use one's wits were just as important as being armed. However, I was not accustomed to having so many of the enemy in my proximity.

I made for the back streets again and looked at my watch. It was not yet nine so I had a long wait. I could not face going back to the house so I headed for the railway yard. I felt secure there. There were Germans but they were the lazy type. They were there to guard a strategic resource and they did it from the comfort of an office. The work was done by the French and many of them were not sympathisers.

I made my way to the mess and helped myself to a cup of coffee. There was nobody there that I knew so I picked up a newspaper. There were large parts of it that had been obliterated by the censor.

Presumably this was news about the invasion. I was not sure how it would be going on the fourteenth of June. I remembered a counter attack from the Germans but I thought this was later. I had a mild attack of hysteria when I started thinking of the allied offensive. I needed to leave Hennebont and leave soon because I knew that German troops would amass near here and maintain a last bridgehead in Brittany before their defeat. I wondered if René knew this.

I thought about René. He was French and from further south. I would have placed him around Nice and I was close as he was actually from Toulon. I had assumed that he was from my time and I was almost correct about this. I was not sure how the rift in time worked. Was there just one rift? Was it at the same time in my time? René was transported to a time nearly a year before my arrival. Did that mean his starting time was a year before mine? I just did not have any answers. The big question though was: Could we go back? With Élise in my mind, did I want to go back?

I tried to recall my history lessons. Something awful had happened in June, I seemed to remember. I sat back trying to think and was interrupted by a young train driver fetching a cup of coffee. He asked me whether I knew what had happened in *Oradour-sur-Glane*. I told him that I did not though I was starting to remember some of my teaching. He filled in the details for me. The SS had ordered all of the villagers to assemble in the square on some trumped up charge of hoarding explosives. The cowardly master race had separated the men from the women and children and locked the men in barns and the women in the church. The SS had set alight to the village, including the barns and the church and had machine gunned anyone trying to escape. In total over 200 children, nearly 250 women and nearly 200 men were killed. Their charred remains were found in a heap days later by a Bishop. The young driver, being able to travel quite easily, was party to news that the censor would not allow everyone to know.

I shivered in disgust when I was told this. I then started to recall the other thing that I knew happened around that time. This was the time that the first *Vergeltungswaffen* or V-1 bombs were dropped on London in reprisal for the D-Day landings. I had always thought of D-Day as the end of the war. It was not; it was the beginning of the end and the Germans continued their atrocities even using their barbaric gas chambers until nearly November.

I looked at my watch and it was almost time to meet René again. I said goodbye to my new acquaintance and made my way via the back streets to *Chez Maurice*. The café was bulging but I did not make it inside as René was waiting by the door. He looked impatient and whisked me away without ceremony. We went to his small second floor apartment which was in a road behind the café and a short walk away. He made me an espresso coffee without asking and I sat down in a low chair and one of only two chairs in the room. René lived alone. The austerity of the place showed that this was a bachelor flat. It was clean and tidy but it was clear that René spent little time here and did not think of his home as having any importance in his life. I noticed that René's apartment had a balcony and I was looking at it when René came back with the coffees.

"It offers a quick escape if the boche arrive," he said and smiled. This was the first time I had seen René smile at all. He had quite a stern face and a smile did not sit easy with him. I looked at him. He was stunningly good looking and would not have looked out of place in a film set. He had natural poise about him and an airy confidence. I wondered how, in a year, René had managed to command so much respect.

"I have spoken to Jean," he said and this surprised me. I knew that communication was difficult though obviously not impossible.

"And?" I replied more curtly than I meant.

"He has told me that you are with André."

"I am."

"Where is André?"

I told René that André was with his aunt and uncle.

"You know of André?"

"Everyone knows André, well everyone that matters. He is a loose canon. Do not trust him with anything important."

There it was again. People who had come into contact with André warned me of him. Whilst I could not pretend that life with André had been ideal I had never had any reason to mistrust him. I found him erratic and juvenile rather than malevolent. At the maquis André had been optimistic and fun loving and, mostly, a joy to be around. He had not disgraced himself during the raid at the maquis. I told René all of this but he was disinterested.

"Does anyone know you are here?"

I thought about this. I had told only Martine of my plans. I had not told André.

"Only Martine," I replied.

"Martine Desmarais?"

I did not know Martine's surname so I answered, "I only know her as Martine. She is André's aunt by marriage on his mother's side I think."

René mused for a moment, asked me where they lived and then said, "Yes, that is Madam Desmarais. I had no idea that they were André's relatives. I know of André only through Jean."

"Martine and Dominique are partisans.  I am confident that Martine will have said nothing, even to Dominique.  She tells him little of what she does."

I remembered Martine's change of heart during my conversation with her but I would never have guessed that she was active in the resistance.  Here was all of the proof I needed.

"OK," René said, "to business, but first, some explanations."

René asked me lots of questions and I told him of everything that I had done and what had happened.  I went over again some of the things I had told him at *Chez Maurice* and he listened intensely.  Again, he told me nothing and I was beginning to feel cheated.

"I still don't understand what brings you here, to Hennebont I mean."

"André."

"André?"

"I did not question enough," I stated, "I had just lost Georges and I needed some company.  I just tagged along with André."

"That may have been a mistake.  No matter though.  Jean has a task for you and he wants me to help you."

René stood and walked to his small kitchen.  I watched him go.  He was enigmatic and infuriating with it.  I was not quite sure what he would say or do next.  René returned with two plates containing some cold meat, cheese and a baguette.

"Sorry," he said, "all I can muster up at the moment."

"It looks great to me.  I am pretty hungry."

René watched me start to eat but did not touch his own.

He told me of his arrival.  He had left nearly a year earlier than I did.  This meant that my rift was not the only one and that time rifts seemed to transport a person back the same number of years.  I wondered if there was a reverse rift.  If someone was to be transported from 1944 would they end up in 2009?   It was a rhetorical thought.   René was visiting friends in Hennebont and was walking down a country lane towards his friend's house when he came through a mist.   When he came out of the other side he was in 1943.   He did not realise it at first until he came to his friend's house.   It looked different but he had ignored that and knocked on the door.   Two familiar and yet unfamiliar people opened the door.   It turned out that these people were the grandparents of his friend.   René had a difficult time understanding what was happening at first so he stayed with the grandparents for a few days.   He was gradually assimilated into the local community and had the good fortune to meet Jean who encouraged him to join the resistance.   René was another person who seemed to idolise Jean.

René said that he hated the Germans though he said it in an automatic manner, like it was something he had to say.   He knew some history so he knew of the heinous crimes they had committed. Like me, he had done sabotage missions and like me he told me that he had lost a good friend, this time a girl friend who had been brutally raped, tortured and then killed by the Gestapo.   She had been found with a message intended for the resistance and the Germans had shown no mercy.   It seemed to me that René felt personally responsible for her death but I did not pry.   René's had a coldness about him and, even whilst he was telling me of this tragedy, his real personality was absent.

I had finished my snack by the time that René had completed his story.   He had not touched his meal.   I told him to eat and he started to consume his food as I explained to him a little more about my life since I had arrived and elaborated, telling him things I had glossed over when we met in the café.   I did this more to give him time to eat than because it was important to René. René completed his platter and put the plate, and mine in the kitchen sink.

"The airmen," he said.

"Yes," I replied, simply.

"They are safe but I don't know for how much longer. I think we both know that it was lunacy bringing them here but that is done now."

René lit a cigarette and handed it to me and I took it. He lit one for himself and we savoured the nicotine rush as we smoked them.

He continued, "Jean wants you to take them away from here, into the countryside, maybe near the maquis?"

I pondered his request and he looked at me thoughtfully.

"I know the place," I replied, "you remember me telling you of Alfonse?"

René nodded.

"Well his place is well hidden and I'm sure he would not mind the company. He has an unending supply of calvados too," I said.

René smiled and said, "Something we would all like, I'm sure."

René asked, "Perfect, where is it in relation to Jean?"

"A couple of days by foot," I said, "if they are fit."

René stood and looked out of the window of his apartment. I could see that he was thinking so I did not interrupt. Finally he turned around.

"Jacques," he said in a low voice. I said nothing so he continued.

"Can you arrange a locomotive heading back to Jean's yard for tomorrow?"

"I can try."

"A freight train?"

"I don't know René, maybe."

"Broad daylight if possible. The boche will be less suspicious."

"What do you have in mind?"

"The airmen are very conspicuous the moment they open their mouths. When they speak they can be heard for a long distance."

I remembered Eugene and Clark at the camp and I knew that René's comment was justified.

"We can dress them to look like railway workers but neither of them speak much French and when they do their accent is shocking. You said you speak English, don't you?"

I said that I did and René apologised and said that he did not speak any English. He tried to say 'good day' but sounded ridiculous.

"How are you going to get them on and off the train?" I asked. I was concerned as the Hennebont railway depot was guarded and the depot at the destination was also manned by a few German soldiers. These were idle soldiers, I knew, but they were soldiers never the less.

"I had in mind a delivery to be loaded on the train. These things must happen all of the time."

I had an idea. If we timed it right we could catch the mail train. I suggested this to René.

"I'm not sure Jacques," he said, "mail trains usually carry Fritz protection."

It was true, they did and this was a risk. The advantage of the mail train, however, was that a lot of bags were loaded in the wagons and there was a great deal of coming and going. It would not be unusual for there to be movement of personnel on a train like that. That would not be the case for a regular freight train.

"You are right René," I replied, "but where would the airmen go on a freight train?"

"Depends on the train Jacques. If there were doored wagons there would be places to hide. This is speculation though. Can you find out the trains that are leaving tomorrow so that we can decide. How long will it take?"

I looked at my watch. It was two thirty. I thought that could be back by four and I told René that. I left him in his flat and he said that he would be there when I returned. In the event, I was back by three thirty with some news. There were two freight trains leaving Hennebont the following day. One was a German arms train and the other was the mail train. The mail train left at four in the afternoon.

"The mail train it is," said René reluctantly. He was then thoughtful for a few minutes.

"I think we should arrange for some spare bags," he said finally.

I looked puzzled so he added, "The airmen can climb inside once they are on the train. That way they will not be seen or heard."

That was how the plan was hatched. It was not a great plan but it was the only one we had. I agreed to make the arrangements at the rail yard and the airmen would arrive by postal van just before four o'clock the following afternoon. They would be dressed as postal workers and would carry bags onto the train. I hoped that we would not be watched by the guards. This was a very risky plan.

I called into the rail yard on the way back to Dominique and Martine's and met Jean who was about to commence a return trip. He greeted me warmly and I told him what was planned. He shook his head and I could see that he considered the operation to be perilous. He took some convincing but concluded that it had sufficient chance of working to be worth the risk. I was not so sure but did not argue with Jean.

I saw Jean's prowess as he organised the airmen's return. He kissed me on both cheeks and shook my hand again before he leapt onto the footplate of his now moving train on his return journey.

I watched Jean's train leave and turned to go myself. As I did I saw one of the idle guards coming towards me. He was bored and with little else to do asked me to show him my papers.

"Why are you still here?" He said in bad French.

"I leave tomorrow. I have had some repair work to do on a loco," I lied.

He passed me back my papers, seemingly happy with the railway permit and my explanation and sauntered back to the wooden hut. I breathed a sigh of relief.

I left the yard and made my way back to my temporary lodging. I knew that I would be spending another night in the house for there was nowhere else to go now. I looked at my watch and it was seven o'clock; two hours before the curfew. I had been out all day and had not told André where I was going.

# Wednesday 14<sup>th</sup> June

## Truth

I arrived back at Dominique and Martine's to find that André was missing. Dominique was indifferent but Martine was concerned in her low key way. She told me that there had been an argument and André had stormed out. It was eight o'clock by now and André had an hour to return before the curfew or remain out all night.

I asked Martine if she knew where he was.

"You are not his nursemaid," she said curtly and then softened her tone, "he will be in that bar. The one behind the harbour. It is a cellar bar frequented by people like André."

"I'll go and get him," I said. The harbour was not far and I thought that I could be there and back before the curfew.

"That is not a place for the likes of you," Martine said, "let him stew in the bed that he makes."

I was surprised by the venom in Martine's voice. I wanted to ask her lots of questions but, if I did not leave soon, I would fail to return before the curfew. I was not looking forward to extracting a drunken André from the bar and bringing him back here.

"I'll be back soon," I said and picked up my beret.

"Be very careful," was Martine's parting comment, "and get out of that bar as quickly as you can."

"It is best he knows," I heard Martine say to Dominique as I closed the door.

I made haste to the bar, following Martine's approximate directions. Roughly translated the bar was called "The Sailor's Rest" and to enter it required a climb down a set of steep steps and entry through a solid black door. It was dark inside and it took a few seconds for my eyes to become accustomed to the lack of light. It was dingy and I panned around the room trying to find André. There was something odd about the bar. There were women here and I guessed that they were prostitutes as they were gaudily painted and wore bright clothes. It struck me then; these were men dressed up as women. Their posture, height and build gave them away.

I then spotted André and he spotted me. Thankfully he was not dressed as a girl but he had one of the boy-girls sitting on one knee and had his hand in a compromising position between the boy-girl's legs. He was clearly enjoying himself at least he was until he saw me and I understandably spoiled his experience. He jumped up spilling the boy-girl off his lap and stood facing me. His trousers were bulging and he looked comic standing there with an embarrassed look on his face and the evidence of his pleasure visible for all to see.

I was shocked for I had not suspected at all that André had been gay. I turned to leave and I heard André behind me scramble through the bar. He reached me as I was opening the door and put his hand on my shoulder to stop me leaving. I struggled free, exited the bar and stepped into the fresh air. The smoke from the bar followed me and a cloud of it dissipated into the breeze. André followed me out into the street. He looked at me straight in the eyes and gave me one of his disarming smiles.

"Don't you dare try to charm me," I said. I looked at my watch and it was eight forty five. I had to leave and I no longer cared whether André came back or not.

"Why didn't you tell me you were gay," I barked at him, almost hysterically.

"Gay?" he said. I was so upset I did not realise that I had used a twenty first century term.

"Homosexual!" I shouted, "Fucking gay. That's my term."

I was not sure why I was so upset. I did not care whether André was gay or not. I was not homophobic but I was certainly acting as if I was.

"I've got to get back," I said to him dismissively, "Fuck off and leave me alone."

"Jacques," André said and then stopped and started to listen. I thought he was trying to distract me. Then I heard it. There was the unmistakable sound of a squad of German soldiers and their jackboots heading our way.

"Let's get the fuck out of here," André said and dragged me down an alley way. We ran until we were well away from the bar. I was out of breath so I stopped at the top of the hill. Those damn cigarettes, I thought. I needed to give them up.

The run had calmed my temper.

"We need to get back before the curfew," I said to André.

"OK," he said.

He looked bashful and this was not a look I had encountered on André's face before. We made it back to Dominique and Martine's without further conversation. We entered by the back door and Martine threw us a look. Her displeasure with André was clear but she looked at me in a questioning way.

"Are you hungry?" she asked me.

I shook my head and asked her if I could talk to André alone. She leaned down and handed me a bottle of red wine from under the sink, dried two glasses on a grimy tea towel and handed them to me.

"See if you can talk some sense into his head."

She then came towards me and kissed me on both cheeks. I was surprised by her gesture but it was clear that I had made my mark with Martine.

We headed for the room at the front of the house. It would have been a dining room but it was not used as that. It was a cold room, despite the summer warmth and it was obvious that it was not used very often.

We sat at the table opposite each other and I took the cork out of the bottle. I poured us both a drink, downed mine in one and refilled it. André sipped at his.

"Why didn't you tell me?" I said to André.

"What could I tell you Jacques? That I like men and that I want to suck your cock?"

André shocked me again and I could feel my anger welling. I paused to let the shock subside. Anger is such an unhelpful emotion sometimes.

"Look André," I replied, "can we keep this civilised."

"Queers like me," he said, "and that's what they call us, are misfits. Do you know what the fucking boche do to us. They don't even consider us human."

"You are only seventeen André," I said, "how do you know you're gay? Have you tried being with a woman?"

There I was again. Confronted with rampant homosexuality I turned into someone who wanted to cure André of his affliction, like it was some kind of disease. I thought I was so liberal; then and there I acted more like a fascist and I hated myself for it.

"There's that word again," said André, "is that what you call queers? Anyway, I'm nearly eighteen."

"Yes," I said, trying to reconcile myself to André's homosexuality, "It is what they call themselves too. Homosexuality is tolerated more where I come from."

"The way you are acting," he replied, "you wouldn't know it."

I remembered what the Germans had done to homosexuals. They had been rounded up and gassed and in many cases they had been tortured too. I looked at André and he looked very vulnerable suddenly. André was a master at deflecting criticism and I wondered whether he was doing it again. I paused to think. This time it was not André. It was me who was being intolerant. His sexuality was his business. He was hurting nobody and what he was doing with other guys was consensual. It seemed to me that the problem was with me and not him.

"Look Jacques," he said, "this isn't some kind of illness. I am attracted to men. I always have been since before I reached puberty. It is the way I am. Take it or leave it."

I looked down at my drink and poured another and topped up André's glass. It was a little time before I spoke again.

"OK," I said, "I'll take it but the next time you mention sucking my cock I'll beat you to a pulp you little pervert."

André smiled and raised his glass towards me and took a long swig.

"So you aren't gay, then?" he said and grinned.

# Thursday15<sup>th</sup> June

## British Airmen

"You talk any sense into him?" asked Martine as we sat at the kitchen table the next morning.  I had woken early again and I was having breakfast.  André was still in his room.  He was going to leave Dominique and Martine's today though he had not told them yet.  André was not coming back with me.  I think I now realised why he wanted to be in Hennebont.  He was attracted to the gay scene; I had simply followed him without asking too many questions.  If André had given me any clues about him being gay, I had missed them.  I was not looking for them, of course.

"I don't think that's possible," I said but did not elaborate.  I knew that there was no reconciling Martine's views with those of André.  Liberal attitudes to homosexuality would be a long time coming.  I realised in myself that these attitudes can sometimes be only skin deep.

I explained to Martine that I would be leaving today.  She surprised me by saying that she knew that I was going and I suspected that she knew of my mission too; she did not tell me this.  We talked of little things until it was time for me to go.  I came to like Martine in this short period.  She had hidden depths but she did not suffer fools gladly.  Somehow, I had managed to endear myself to her.  Had it been the other way around I think Martine would have been intolerable.  With Martine things were very clear and were either black or white.  There was no room in Martine's life for any other colour.  With what was going on around her I could understand her stance.

I did not say goodbye to André that morning and it is something that I regret. I should have taken the trouble to go to his room and bid him well. To this day, I do not know why I did not do this.

I arrived at the rail yard early; too early really because the postal van was not scheduled to arrive with the airmen until four o'clock in the afternoon. The lazy guards were not around so I made my way to the mess. I asked if anyone wanted any work doing and, as a result, helped one of the firemen ready a train for its journey. This involved loading the coal, topping up the water and stoking the boiler to achieve a head of steam. I was surprised how long this took. I was pretty dirty by the time I had finished but, as I was working on the footplate on the way back, this did not really matter. I really enjoyed my railway job and wondered if this was something that I could do permanently after the war.

My mind then drifted to Élise. I hoped that she would figure in my life after all of this was finished and I wondered what she was doing at that moment. I thought about Jean and Maria and how happy they were together. I wanted it to be like that with  Élise and I andI wondered what a farmer's daughter would make of a railway worker.

The train was ready to go and the fireman had been joined by the driver. It left on time with its load of munitions and I waved to the driver and fireman. I was becoming hungry so I made my way back to the mess where I conversed with a very animated character who was staunchly communist. I had heard that communism was rife among the proletariat in France during the war. In fact, the maquis were split and there was an independent command chain for the communist and non-communist maquis. The communists took their steer from Moscow and I found this difficult to accept given that I knew of the atrocities done by the advancing Soviets and of the damage done to a generation of Europeans by the Soviet empire.

There was no shifting this man. He would not listen to reason and I did not want to put myself into the limelight today, of all days, so I let others take up the baton.

The time passed slowly and I found things to do to occupy myself. I saw none of the idle soldiers during this time and I hoped that my luck would hold. Finally it was time to prepare the mail train and I helped load the coal into the tender and top up the water. The locomotive had been on a journey already that day so there was a good head of steam. We shunted the train into position ready for the arrival of the postal van. It arrived on time at four and I saw the two airmen in the back of the van. One of them, Eugene I think, spotted me and gave me a shallow smile. He recognised me despite our short time together. I hoped that he would not speak to me. René was driving the van and he was dressed as a postal worker. Another person was with him and I guessed that this worker was also a member of the resistance. I was right and wrong in that he was both a member of the postal service and a partisan. We started to load the mail wagon and René threw in the two empty sacks first. The airmen took a sack each and jumped into the wagon. They then did as they had been told and climbed into the sacks, placing them in the corner of the wagon. It would be uncomfortable for them but not as uncomfortable as the Gestapo could make it. I helped them load the remaining sacks and we placed them carefully around Eugene and Clark. How they were going to remain like this for the two hours of the journey I was not sure.

There were two sacks left when the lazy guard arrived. He was the guard who had stopped me yesterday and he looked at me and spoke to me in poor French.

"You are here still, are you leaving now?"

René looked at me and I read his unspoken message. I was to keep the guard occupied. The guard yawned and repositioned his genitals.

"I had some work here but this is my train. I'm leaving on it."

"You look like you have already done much working," he said.

I knew what he meant but I pretended that I did not.

"Sorry," I said, "I don't understand you."

"It is my French. It is not so good."

I could see René out of the corner of my eye but I dared not look. I saw him slam the wagon door and jump into the postal van. His colleague went around the van and opened the passenger door.

"All done Jacques," he shouted, "you have a good trip."

With that he slammed the van door and they drove slowly away from the yard.

"You have loaded the wagon. That is good. How long before you go?"

I had finished with the guard now and I was keen for him to leave. I did not want him to open the wagon door and start snooping around so I kept up the pretence. I also did not want a German guard on the train though I was powerless to stop that if the Germans wanted one. I was also concious that, hidden at the corner of the footplate, was my bag complete with pistol and grenades. If that was found I was a dead man. I had to resist the temptation to glance at my twentieth century watch and I hoped that lazy would not see it too.

"In fifteen minutes," I guessed, and added, "or so."

The guard stood there looking at me and I wondered what was going through his mind. He yawned again, adjusted his belt and scratched his backside this time. He was truly revolting. I tried hard not to show my disgust.

"You have a girl?"

202

I remember groaning internally as he started to make conversation with me.

"Yes," I said tentatively.

"Is she pretty?"

This was painful but I persevered. This was the longest conversation I had ever had with a German. He seemed to be trying to be friendly but all of my senses were screaming 'trap, be careful'.

"I think so," I answered.

"I have a French girlfriend," he said.

"You do?" I said not hiding my surprise.

"You are surprised, yes?"

"Yes," I said as I had expressed my amazement already.

"She is pretty also. She fucks me very well."

Now it was shock I felt and, despite my efforts, it showed on my face.

He laughed, a hollow raucous laugh.

"I bet yours fucks you well too," he said and winked. Now I felt the red mist of anger welling up. I told myself to control it. I knew that I could not win in this situation. I wanted to wipe that supercilious grin of his ugly Nazi face. I swallowed hard and tried a little humour.

"She fucks me up," I said, weakly, "don't all women?"

He laughed, scratched his backside again and slapped me on my back.

"You get back to that girl of yours. You give her one tonight." With his coarse comment he winked and walked away. I heard the sound of his jackboots recede into the distance. I felt soiled by his presence. My hate was now absolute and almost out of control.

I breathed easy again though my heart was racing and the driver peered out of the cab.

"That was close," he said quietly, "I think it's time we left before we chance our luck any further."

I now looked at my watch and we were past our scheduled departure time. The signal was on green and we had managed to load without attracting an on-train guard. I jumped onto the footplate and started shovelling coal. I was on my own this time and I had a lot of shovelling to do to keep the furnace going. We pulled away and I heard the characteristic sound of a steam engine as the pistons pulled, groaned and huffed. These creatures had personality.

In a rare rest period I managed a cigarette with the driver and we had a shouted conversation over the deafening sound of the locomotive. Then it was back to shovelling until we pulled into the rail yard at just after six. The postal van was there already and so was a German guard of two armed men. They had the ridiculous hair style preferred by the Germans. It was short at the sides and long at the front, overhanging their faces. They looked like they may be efficient unlike lazy guard at Hennebont. How were we to unload the airmen was my thought. I then spotted Jean talking to one of the postal workers. I hoped that he had a plan.

Jean went over to the soldiers and I saw him say something to them. He and they walked over to the wagon holding the mail. I wondered what he was doing. Jean nodded to the postal workers and they opened the door of the wagon. Jean spoke to the guards in German and they continued along the train. He walked past the wagon and the soldiers followed him. He was three wagons away from the mail wagon when he opened the wagon door and the guards climbed onto the train. As they disappeared one of the postal workers jumped into the mail wagon and released the airmen who leapt out and were shoved into the back of the postal van and covered with sacks. The space where the airmen had been was replaced by two sacks of mail. The postal workers then went back to their original positions. Had I not known better I would have said that they had never moved.

The soldiers reappeared and one jumped out of the wagon. A wooden box appeared in the doorway, pushed by the other guard. He leapt out of the wagon next and they manhandled the box along the train. Whatever was in the box it was very heavy and the guards carried it with some difficulty. As they walked by me Jean winked. Jean said something to the soldiers in German and then he turned to us.

"OK, lads," he said in French, "you can unload the mail now and take it away."

My heart rate was high during this manoeuvre and it felt like my heart wanted to leave my chest. I tried not to hold my breath but it was difficult and I really did not realise how tense I had been until I relaxed. At one point I thought I might wet myself. I saw the postal van leave the yard. I had to stay behind but I had passed my bag with its incriminating contents to Jean before he left. I was filthy so I made my way to the shower. I met up with some of my erstwhile colleagues and we shared a cognac before I showered. The experience was bliss and it eased my aching bones.

I had another cognac before I left the rail yard and headed for Jean and Maria's home. I hoped they were expecting me and I hoped that they had housed the airmen somewhere.

# Friday 16<sup>th</sup> June
## A New Plan

Jean and Maria were expecting me and had been worried that I had taken so long to arrive. Their hospitality was superb, as usual, and I was treated to more cognac before I retired, slightly inebriated, to my bed.

The airmen had been sent to a safe house and I felt a little sorry for them. They were in a country that was not their home, among enemy combatants and unable to understand very much. They were being well cared for and they were now, at least, out of the extreme danger zone.

I awoke the next morning later than I had for days. I had a sore head and needed water, badly. I looked at my clothes. These were the same clothes that Élise had given me. I had given up on underclothes some time earlier as I could not face wearing the same pair any more. I had managed to wash my clothes a few times but the railway work had not been kind to them. I pulled on my trousers and looked down. A pile of coal dust lay where they had been. I made my way downstairs. Maria was in the small kitchen.

"Jacques," she said and came over to kiss me, "good morning and how did you sleep. Well by the look of you."

"I slept very well Maria," I answered, "the best for days."

It was Jean's rest day so he was at home and he entered the kitchen as he had heard my voice. He slapped me on my bare back.

"Jacques, my boy," he said, "I am very proud of you."

I smiled at him and I was beaming inside. To be praised by Jean was like being praised by one's father.

"But you are grubby. Or at least your clothes are filthy. What have you been doing?"

It was a rhetorical question, I knew, so I did not reply. Jean continued.

"There are some clothes on the side there," he pointed to the table, "Maria will wash yours but I think they will disintegrate in the wash. Have you been wearing them for months?"

I said that I had, that I had grown quite accustomed to them and that they were moulded to me. The clothes that Jean gave me were from a colleague of his. He must have been slightly taller than me but we were of the same build so they fitted reasonably well once I had rolled up the trousers. I thanked them both. I noticed that I now had more than one set of clothes so that I could at least change them and have them washed. This was my new measure of opulence.

We sat together for breakfast. I enjoyed their company and it felt like home. I knew that I could not stay for long as I had airmen to transport. For now, the pressure was off and Jean did not press the matter until later. After breakfast Jean asked me about André.

"I know about André now," I said to him.

"How did you find out? Did Martine tell you?"

I told him about the Sailor's Rest but omitted the detail.

"He is not a bad boy," said Jean, "just misguided."

There was such prejudice in this time that I did not pursue the subject further. It was a comfort to me that Jean and Maria still cared for André. I said simply, "He is young yet."

I knew that age had nothing to do with André's sexuality. It must have been difficult to be homosexual at this time. France, I seemed to remember, was a more tolerant country than was England in the thirties and forties. I let the moment pass and we did not discuss the subject again.

"I have something for you," Maria said to me, grinning.

"For me?" I asked.

"Yes, Jacques, for you." Maria was teasing me.

She handed me a pink envelope addressed to Maria. The letter had neat small handwriting on the front and had been opened. The ink was blue and it had been written with a fine nibbed fountain pen.

"Can I look?"

"It is for you."

I opened the envelope and pulled out the letter and read it.

*My Dear Maria,*

*How long it is since we have spoken. Can you convey to my dear brother Jacques how I miss him so. I await his safe return and my heart will be empty until I see him again.*

*I was so thrilled to receive your letter and your news that my dear brother had stayed with you and is safe. I know that his railway job takes him distances but I so would like to be with him again and I hope we can soon.*

*The love I feel for dear Jacques makes my heart ache and I long to be with him again.*

*Please let me know of any news you may have and I remain your friend.*

*Élise*

Maria looked at me and smiled, "It is in code, to fool the censor."

I understood. Maria had rewritten my letter so that it appeared to be from her. Élise had understood and replied in the same manner. I reddened to think that Maria had read my letter.

Maria simply smiled. I looked at the letter again and felt so very alone. I wanted to be with Élise so much that it hurt.

"She is a clever girl Jacques and you are a very lucky man."

Later, Jean and I sat and talked and Maria left the house to meet with a friend.

"What's the plan?" I asked Jean, "I mean about the airmen."

"Tell me about Hennebont first. Not the André bit but tell me what you found out from René."

I thought about this and I realised that I had found out very little from René. I told Jean about my meeting with him and that he had told me that he had talked to Jean.

"Not exactly 'talked'," said Jean, "but we communicated."

I realised that Jean was fishing. I had not mentioned the obvious thing about René . I had taken it as red that René was from my time. To me it was just a factor. To Jean, it was everything.

"You know about me, don't you?" I said to him.

"That you come from the future, like René, Yes. René informed me."

I wondered how they had communicated. There were telephones, of course, and telegraph but these were primitive and heavily controlled by the Germans. There were messengers too. The way that Jean was describing his interaction with René sounded too immediate for René to have sent a messenger. In any case how could the messenger have met up with Jean and then back to René in the time I was away? I considered this completely impossible. René and Jean must have used something from my century and something that the Germans did not have the technology to intercept. I was correct. Jean had a small laptop computer with a built in modem. René must have had the same. They connected to each other and did the equivalent of an internet chat over an encrypted channel. There were lots of questions in my mind but I left them there and accepted the facts for what they were. I wondered what the Germans would make of this piece of technology and, if they managed to capture it, whether it would make a difference to the outcome of the war. Had the Germans had a sophisticated computer like this they would have been able to crack all of the allied cyphers and they would have been able to create scrambled messages of much greater complexity than the famous enigma.

"The Germans must not get that," I said, "that could change the outcome of the war."

Jean looked puzzled. I decided not to elaborate as it was just too complicated. Yet again, though, Jean had shown hidden depths. Managing the intricacies of Microsoft's windows operating system and interfacing with the telephone system of the 1940's was no mean feat.

"Tell me," said Jean, "when will it be over?"

"When the fat lady sings." I said flippantly and then added, "It isn't over in one go. If you mean here I think it is about August. Right now, Normandy is being liberated and the soviets are marching across eastern Europe. They will not retreat, not for a generation."

Jean considered this but said nothing.

"Paris will be liberated around the 24th August and Brittany is freed around the same time, maybe a little later. Lorient holds out for nearly a year. That includes Hennebont, where René is."

"You know more of your history than does René," Jean said to me, "that means that René is in grave danger. We must recover him from Hennebont. Leave that to me."

"A lot of people will die during this battle," I said, "and the Nazis counter attack viciously. They are overcome though, in the end. Hitler is never caught."

"He goes free?"

"No, he commits suicide."

"Coward to the end," spat Jean.

I had never thought of that before. The way Jean looked and the way he spoke left me with the image of Hitler and his mangy team skulking in their bunker and finally taking the easy way out rather than facing justice.

"How do you know so much?"

"It was my grandfather. That is why I speak such good French. We lived here when I was a boy, not far from where I arrived. My grandfather was a member of the resistance."

"What is his name? I know most of the resistance members."

"The same as mine, Jacques Richard."

The last time I had said that had been in front of Georges and he had joked that one Jacques Richard was enough. It made me maudlin.

"No, I do not know that name. I will ask around. It would be strange meeting your own grandfather, no? How old would he be now?"

"Same as I am, nineteen."

"Even stranger. He wouldn't believe you would he?"

I shook my head.

"We need to talk about the airmen. We need to get them out of here. I need to lean on you to do this. You are the only one of my fighters we have that speaks good English."

I was proud again that Jean had called me a fighter and 'his fighter' at that.

"I will take them to Alfonse's place, Jean."

"Alfonse?"

"I met him on the way here. He is a patriot and he lives very remotely. It will be ideal but they will probably have to stay there until liberation. As it is only a month away ..."

Jean stopped me, "No, I don't think that will do."

I looked at Jean and said, "Why?"

"We are talking pilots here Jacques."

I still did not understand.

"They will be required for the war effort. Pilots are in short supply. We need to get them back to England. You need to travel to the north coast, maybe through the front line."

"The front line? With those guys. Not a chance Jean. They will be killed. I will be killed."

Jean was thoughtful for a few moments and then he said, "You are right Jacques. There has to be another way. Skulking in the woods is not the answer. If we are to win this we all need to pull together."

I felt like I had been scolded, like I had let down my teacher with the wrong answer.

"We will win this Jean," I snapped.

"I wonder if we could arrange an aircraft to collect them?" Jean was talking to himself, thinking aloud so I did not interrupt him. He went over to the wall and pulled back the corner of a rug. He then lifted a floorboard and pulled out a wad of papers. He searched through them and pulled out a map. He put the rest of the papers back and replaced the floorboard, leaving the corner of the rug pulled back.

Jean spread the map out on the table and I glanced at it trying to pinpoint where we were. It was quite a large scale and I spotted Lorient and Hennebont and then the railway track until finally our current position. It was a hilly area and Jean made a sweeping gesture with his hand indicating north of our location.

"An aircraft cannot land here, nor here and there is the issue of range. I think we need to be further north. I agree with you Jacques, the coast will be well defended so we need to avoid the coast."

Jean was going over the possibilities rather than stating a plan at this stage. I decided to express my opinion.

"Here?" I pointed to a lowland area on the map north and east of where we where, "It is away from the coast but close to northern Brittany and away from the populated areas further east. What about the aircraft range from England? I have little knowledge of this. Falmouth is just over there."

I indicated the location of Falmouth and Jean scratched his chin. I could hear the sound of day old whiskers being disturbed.

"The terrain is good there," he admitted, "but I would prefer a little further east if we can. It will make seventy kilometres difference and that could be significant. It would be more dangerous, of course."

"Danger, I can cope with," I said, "suicide, not."

Jean smiled and ruffled my hair. I felt superb being so close to my father figure and my mentor.

"How about here?" Jean said, indicating an area further east and slightly further north. It was a smaller section of lowland and was completely surrounded by forest. I thought about it. It would certainly have offered more cover and would not have presented too much of a problem for a good pilot.

"It is smaller," I said, "but the wood will help to hide us."

"I will talk to my English contacts," said Jean, "see what they think. How long will it take you to get there, do you think?"

"That's quite a long way. What shape are the pilots in?"

I looked at the map whilst Jean was speaking, mentally plotting a safe route. It was a long way and we were bound to meet Germans on the route.

213

"They have been idle for a while so they will be out of condition. They're young so they should shape up pretty quickly," answered Jean.

"Two weeks, I think," I said finally.

"That gets us to early July. We'll be out of touch during that time so I will not know whether you have arrived on time. I think we should allow another week because your estimate seems optimistic to me," said Jean and he looked at the map intensely.

"It is a bit out of your way but I don't think we have a choice," said Jean. He pointed to a small village west of where we were heading and probably half a days walk away.

"There is a bar," Jean smiled, "always a bar! I think you know the ropes. Ask him about the special cognac again. I will make sure that they know you will be arriving and they will let me know that you have arrived safely. Keep the airmen out of sight. Fritz is everywhere around there. The bar is the only one in the village. It changed its name recently at the request of the local Gestapo officer who was offended by the previous name. I'm sure you know what I mean by 'request'. I cannot remember the new name but people will know it by its old name of Café Porc, pig café, I think you would say."

Jean spoke the last part in English and I preferred his French.

"I think we have a plan," I said, "I will have to memorise the route. Can I have a few minutes before you put away the map?"

"Take as long as you like. Can you work from memory Jacques? Do you not need to write out the map?"

I explained that I had good recall but that I needed to study the map for a while before the route registered. I asked him if he could supply a compass as I felt, with the distance we needed to cover, I would need one. Jean said that he could and then left me to study the map.

# Sunday 18<sup>th</sup> June

## Reunion

I had a normal weekend, well reasonably normal. I helped Jean at the railway yard and helped Maria tidy the garden. Generally though, it was uneventful compared with the whirlwind of things that had happened to me since I arrived. I knew that much was happening in Normandy and that it would be a week or so before the allies captured Cherbourg and started their push south. I listened to the news on the radio but most of it was propaganda. Only the BBC gave any real news and I was aware that some of this was propaganda too. Listening to the BBC was a crime, of course, so it had to be done surreptitiously and I did not want to put Jean and Maria at any more risk than they were due to Jean's undercover work. I shivered at the thought of what would happen to this remarkable couple if the Gestapo thugs found out of their work.

Monday came and I found out that my surrogate family life was to be cut short. I knew I had to leave but I was sad because I really liked living at Jean and Maria's. I found life relaxed and easy. I learned that Jean and Maria were moving on too. I mentioned that fear of discovery of Jean's resistance work haunted me. It did Jean too and they moved on regularly. Jean's job in the railway allowed him to do this and he moved from railway house to railway house roughly every six months. It was time for their move again and it was time for mine too.

Jean had organised an aircraft to pick up the airmen. It was tentatively scheduled for three weeks time.

"I don't want you to travel alone," Jean said to me at breakfast, "I have arranged for some people to accompany you. They'll be here soon."

We talked about the plan as Jean wanted to be sure that we had the same understanding. He went through it several times until he forced me to repeat it back to him so that he could be sure. He wanted nothing to be left to chance. When I had finished the recitation I looked at my watch. It was early at six o'clock and I was to meet the airmen at the edge of town at eight. I wondered who was to accompany me on the journey. After my experience of André I think I had a preference for travelling with the airmen alone. There was a knock on the door and it opened gently with a groan. A head looked around the door and I recognised the face immediately. I leapt to my feet.

"Luc, Luc," I yelled, and dashed towards him shaking his hand vigorously and slapping him on the back, "is that really you. I thought you were dead."

My next surprise came through the door and it was Henri.

I greeted him warmly too and I could see in his face that he was pleased to see me too though he was not as demonstrative as was I.

"You have no idea how difficult it has been to track down these men," said Jean and it was clear that Jean had orchestrated what he called the return of the three musketeers.

Luc came forward to me and held my shoulders and said, solemnly, "I heard about Georges, I am very sorry."

Henri came forward too and tapped my back.

"Yes," I said, "it has been difficult. I do not think he suffered Luc. We took out some boche too."

"Catch up a little," said Jean, "I have some things to do. You need to leave at seven and you need to leave separately and then regroup. Luc and Henri know the plan too. I have been through it with them."

Jean smiled as he said this and I knew what he meant. I was sure that Luc and Henri had to recite the plan in the same way as I had until Jean was comfortable.

I had so many questions but mostly I wanted to ask about what happened after Georges and I had our forced retreat by canoe. I heard that Luc had been blown off his feet by the blast. That much I had guessed from my last sight of him. Henri had picked him up and carried him until Luc came round. That must have been difficult for Luc was sturdily built and must have been a dead weight.

The Germans had reacted quickly to the blast and had sent out two trucks full of soldiers to where they thought the attack had taken place, on the other side of the river. Once Luc had gained his conciousness he and Henri had taken a route perpendicular to the river and this had probably saved their skin. The Germans had scoured the river and found the wire we had used. Most of the rest of the evidence was down river with us or was at the bottom of the stream. Henri had covered their tracks well and they had escaped and hidden for several days. Luc had been injured by the blast and they could not move on again until he had recovered.

"I heard late," said Henri, "that they had massacred the innocents again due to our action."

His voice was sad when he said this. Henri was very sensitive to German atrocities and his anger rose quickly. I could see him redden and then regain control. Henri was a good companion to have. He was disciplined but his anger simmered just under his skin. He would fight to the end in any conflict with a German and he would show no mercy.

I noticed that Luc had a new scar on his forehead. I asked him about it and Henri answered.

"Don't let him tell you his tale," said Henri, "he had a brawl in a bar over a girl. He was drunk."

"Yes, OK, I did and I was," said Luc.

"Did you get the girl?" I asked.

"Yes and no," he replied obtusely and grinned.

"What he means by that is that the girl gave him the scar with a broken glass," said Henri.

"I like your mating style," I said, "I bet you score often like that."

Luc laughed and then said, "The official line is that I got it in action with the boche, OK! Makes me look tougher, don't you think."

I thought Luc was tough enough anyway but I did not say so. Instead I said, "Makes you look like a girl Luc."

I grinned, lest I be misunderstood and Luc said, "You piss taker. Good to see you Jacques. Looks like we are a team again."

I looked at my watch again. It was nearly time to go. I went to my room and picked up my bag. It was a little heavier because I now had a change of clothes but it was manageable.

Jean arrived back before we left and Maria packed us some food for the journey. It was a sad goodbye and I asked Maria to let Élise know that I had left. She said that she would. I wondered when and where I would see this wonderful couple again.

I left the house first and made my way to the edge of town where we had agreed to rendezvous. Luc was going to leave next and then Henri. We all took different routes and met an hour later at the agreed point. We hid in the woods and awaited the arrival of the airmen who were late. This was not going according to plan.

# Sunday 18<sup>th</sup> June

## Treachery

Half an hour came and went and then a further half an hour. We were becoming concerned. We had a long way to go and, although the nights were light and we could walk late into the evening, we wanted to be away from the town with its incumbent risks.

Finally the airmen arrived from an unexpected direction and from behind our hidden location. We kept ourselves concealed until we were sure that there was no trap. We could see the two airmen; I recognised them and they were accompanied by a partisan. He looked anxious and was fidgeting as he looked around for us.

Luc stood first and I heard him release the safety catch of his bren gun. I wondered what he feared. As a response to Luc's action I put my hand on the pistol in my pocket, ready to use it if I had to.

"Identify yourself," Luc hissed. His rifle was pointing at the newcomers.

The partisan turned around to face Luc.

"I am Daniel, Luc, you know me. Stop being such an arse."

I recognised him too. Daniel had been at the maquis and had been in the group of maquisards who had discovered Georges and I initially. I relaxed and so did Luc and he reset the safety catch on his bren. Henri had been covering us from his hidden position and he stood now. We shook Daniel's hand and then shook the hands of the airmen.

"I hope you are fit," I said to them in English, "because we have a few weeks of walking to do. Then, maybe, we can get you home."

"That would be jolly good," said Eugene who seemed to be the spokesman. I smiled. I had forgotten how upper class was their English accent.

"Where the fuck have you been?" said Luc to Daniel.

Our introductions did not seem to put Daniel at ease so I asked him if there had been a problem. His reply was a thunderbolt.

"It is Jean," he said abruptly, "he's been taken."

"Taken?" I said, startled and fearing the worse.

"Not long after you left," continued Daniel, "the Gestapo came and took Jean. They are searching his house now."

I knew what 'taken' meant and I feared for Jean. He would be tortured, I knew and he may even be killed. The risks to Jean and Maria, Jean knew, were great. We did not talk about it very much when we were together but I knew that he was concerned that he would be caught. I was worried about Jean but I was equally worried about Maria.

"Maria," I said, "was she taken too?"

Daniel's answer was reassuring but not absolute. He said, "She is with others and is safe for now. She is distraught about Jean. She knows what will happen."

I was distressed at this news and it dragged down my mood. I wanted to stage a daring rescue and release Jean and kill the Gestapo pigs. I was angry, very angry. I knew it was a fantasy though. Daniel was more realistic.

"If Jean talks we are all in trouble," he said simply.

He was right of course but I did not like him saying it. The thought of Jean being tortured was unbearable but I knew that it was going to happen. My hate of the Germans was never to subside; I never forgave the whole nation for the rest of my life.

"Look, Jacques," Daniel said, "you need to go. This place is crawling with the boche and the worst kind of boche."

"All boche are bastards," I said venomously.

Daniel ignored me and continued, "You need to put some distance between you and here and quickly. Getting the airmen to this point has been difficult enough. We have had to skirt the town from the east. Why do you think we were so late? I was worried that you'd be gone, we couldn't find you or that we were going to be caught. Now fuck off will you and now."

Daniel's logic was unquestionable. We said goodbye quickly and my parting question to Daniel was, "Where are you going now? Come with us."

"No, I'm going back to the hills," was all he said and he left us heading into the forest.

We marched through the wood and up the hill all of the day, stopping only for a brief snack and to drink. We put thirty kilometres between the town and us that day on difficult terrain. When I look back on that feat I realise how disturbed we had been. I was morose all of the day and I feared for Jean and worried that Maria would be caught. Even if Maria had not been caught I knew that she would be distressed and that upset me too.

As instructed, the airmen spoke little that day. They had been given food and water so we did not have to share out our meagre rations that Maria had supplied. I knew that the next day we would have to replenish our supplies from farms that we met on the way. This is a task I would leave to Luc. He was good at it.

The day had been warm and dry and we slept in the open under the canopy. I had a fitful night with nightmares about what was happening to Jean.

# Sunday 9<sup>th</sup> July
## The Pig's Café

We took three weeks to reach the village Jean had told me about. We had some torrential summer rain and thunder storms during our trip that slowed us down and made our journey miserable. We managed to find accommodation out of the rain in barns and deserted huts. Most of the time we kept out of the way of habitation for fear of discovery as Eugene and Clark were too obviously non-French to take any risk at all. None of us knew the route we were using and we knew nobody and that meant we did not know who to trust.

When we saw main roads they were packed with German vehicles moving armaments and soldiers to the front line ahead of us. They were shifting massive amounts of equipment and it was obvious that they were fighting to win; there was no sign of contrition, yet.

I tried to talk to the airmen as much as I could. They had had a pretty ghastly time in France since they ditched. The journey to Hennebont was a mistake and, of course, I knew that. They made the outskirts of Lorient by boat and told me that the town was wrecked with barely any buildings left standing. They had been told that the submarine base was intact but the supply routes had been destroyed so preventing the submarines from doing their damage in the Atlantic. Most of the time Eugene and Clark had been separated and placed in safe or semi-safe houses and were moved regularly. They had not been spotted thanks to the vigilance of the Free French and of Jean's meticulous planning. It had not been pleasant for them and Eugene described it as being in solitary confinement most of the time.

"Better than a Gestapo prison," I remember saying to them and they tacitly agreed.

I left the airmen with Luc and Henri when we finally arrived in the countryside a few kilometres from our first rendezvous point at the pigs café. Luc wanted to come with me to the village and I persuaded him not to take the risk. I said that it would attract more attention with more people. He was alarmed when I changed into fresh clothes and gave him my bag for safe keeping. This meant that I was going into the village unarmed. I could see no other option. There were Germans on the move and they were bound to be jittery so close to the front line. I was not to know that the front line was many kilometres from where we were now but was going to become much closer.

I walked into the village and sought out the café which was very easy to find. It had been renamed the café of capitulation by someone who had scrawled the new name above the window. The window had been daubed with the old name of 'pigs café'. The words 'death to Fritz' adorned the wall next to the café. The locals were evidently not happy.

I looked inside and there were groups of shabbily dressed men occupying most of the tables. The air hung with tobacco smoke. A young, greasy haired man cleaned the bar with a dirty cloth and then wiped it with the tea cloth he used to dry the glasses and cups. A cigarette hung from the corner of his mouth. I opened the door and a cloud of smoke blew into my face and dissipated into the air. I looked around. Something felt wrong though I could not put my finger on exactly what it was that was wrong.

I strolled over to the bar trying to look confident and not sure whether I had achieved it. I sat at one of the spare stools at the bar next to a wizened man of late middle age. He wore a beret and his shoulders stooped.  His face was deeply lined and he had the pallor of a man addicted to nicotine.  He nodded as I sat down and I said good day to him.  His eyes spoke to me but I did not know what they were saying.

I asked for a coffee from the greasy haired barman.  I noticed how pock marked was his face now that I was closer.  He scratched an itch between his legs and I could see his tackle moving around in his trousers as he did so.  He lifted my cup with the same hand and wiped it with the tea cloth.  He then moved the cigarette in his mouth, flicked the ash into a glass and then replaced the cigarette between his lips.  He poured the black coffee and I sipped it, trying not to think of where his hands had been.

I wondered whether I should ask for Jean's special brandy with all of these people around.  I felt uneasy so I decided to wait.  I asked for a cognac anyway and sipped it slowly.  I swung around on my chair so that I could look into the street.  The wizened man looked at me but said nothing.  His eyes were talking again but not anything that I could comprehend.

I sipped on my cognac, finished it and asked for another.  I was hungry as we had needed to ration our supplies on the journey.  I was not going to eat in this café though.  I needed to keep a clear head so I limited myself to two cognacs and followed with a further coffee.  The café remained full.  Nobody left.  I was not going to be able to ask for Jean's cognac if this continued.  I looked across the room, through the nicotine fog and out of the window.  The window was grimy with the stain of countless cigarettes as were the walls.  The sun was shining today but it was not visible from within the café.

A young man walked in front of the café and I blinked.  I was sure I knew him from the way he walked.  I saw him walk across the square.  I knew who it was.

I turned around and paid the bill and left. I strolled across the quadrangle towards a point opposite for this is where I thought the man was heading. I turned into the road and past a small arched passageway. As I passed the man hissed to me.

"Jacques, Jacques, this way."

I turned around to face André who was grinning at me.

"I've been looking for you," he said, "what kept you?"

"André, what the fuck are you doing here?"

"You could have said goodbye Jacques," he replied, "you miserable sod. It's because I'm gay isn't it?"

"I felt bad about that," I said, "but it just happened."

"What are you doing here?" I asked as I looked into André's smiling face.

"Look, there'll be time for that later. Tell me, did you say anything in that café?" André snapped.

"You mean?" I asked.

"You know what I mean Jacques. Stop pissing around, we don't have much time and it's fucking dangerous around here."

"No. It felt wrong. There was something I didn't like. My senses were tingling. There was this old guy too. He was trying to tell me something but I couldn't work out what."

"Your senses did you proud Jacques. That café is full of *Milice*. They were waiting for you. Come. We'll have time to talk. I have a room just out of the village. It isn't much but it is safe."

André took me through some narrow streets and then down a steep set of stairs to his room. He was well underground and, even in the summer, the room was dank and dark. It smelt musty.

"This has been home for a few days," he said, "I was waiting for you."

"For me?"

"I heard about Jean," André said, "from Martine. I was very shocked. I went straight back to see if I could find Maria."

"Did you find her? Is she OK?"

"This is a long story, lets get some wine and some food. I don't have much."

André opened a bottle of red wine and ripped apart some crusty bread and then handed me a portion of soft cheese that I did not recognise. It had a slightly harder consistency than brie but had a similar rind. I was ravenous and ate it quickly.

"You haven't eaten?"

"Not properly," I replied.

"Jean was taken Jacques. He's in a pretty bad way but he is away from the pigs now. We organised an attack on the Gestapo jail and managed to free Jean and a few others. We had to use explosives so we killed a few of ours too. I was worried that we may have harmed Jean but he was in the lower cells. The bastards had tortured him pretty badly. One of his knees is shot and he's lost the sight in an eye. They used a sledgehammer on his knee and his eye was damaged from the beating he took. They are savages."

I reeled at this news. I was incensed that Jean could have been treated in this way and yet relieved that he was away from the Gestapo.

"You said 'we' André. Were you involved in this?"

"Of course," he said without emotion and with a shrug, "it was the least I could do. We took out some of the pigs and I slit the throats of two of them myself. The commander was killed too by the explosion. It is a pity he couldn't have died a slower death. He didn't deserve to go that quickly."

"How is Jean now?"

"When I left," André replied, "and I have been here a week, he was poorly. He was being cared for by a doctor and is well hidden. He did not want Maria to see him but I don't think a steam train could have stopped her. She screamed in anguish when she first saw him and I have not ever seen someone so distraught and despairing. I felt so helpless. How I hate these animals."

"It will soon be over," I said, "the nightmare has about a month to last for us here, maybe a little longer."

"Despite all of that Jacques, Jean wanted me to warn you. He didn't talk Jacques, you must know that, despite the brutality. The Germans knew something of your trip. Not all of it, but some. Someone told them, we don't know who. Jean told me where you were heading and told me to stop you going to the café. That was tricky, believe me. Loitering around these streets is not good for your health. Not many good looking guys around either!"

With that he grinned at me.

"Pervert," I said.

"Except for you Jacques," he said.

I pushed him off his stool and he laughed.

"You are late Jacques. I expected you around the same time as me. I was worried I was going to miss you, or had already missed you."

"Yes, it was a rotten trip. It's pissed down most of the way. We've been miserable."

"How are your charges?"

"They'll be glad to be home, I think."

"Well, they have their chance. Tomorrow night at ten o'clock is when the pick up is arranged. You are just in time. Thank God you are here. I'm coming with you. Give me a chance to clear up and I'll come back with you. We need to be careful. This place is crawling with *Milice*."

André gave me a bag of food for the others and I left first. I kept to the back streets, hiding in doorways and pretending to look in shop windows whenever there were people around.

We met in a wooded area on the outskirts of town and our route took a wide loop to where I had left the others. In a strange way it was good to be back with André. He seemed to sense that his sexuality was not an issue to me. That must have been rare for him in 1944. I wondered how Luc and Henri would have reacted to André being homosexual. It was something that I would never discuss with them.

# Monday 10<sup>th</sup> July

# Goodbye

André had another piece of surprise news for me. We had to deliver some aviation fuel to the landing strip. The aircraft could not make the return flight without refuelling. He told me that he had managed to secure some fuel and we were going to borrow a tractor from a local farm and transport the fuel to the makeshift aerodrome.

"When you say 'borrow', André do you mean with or without the owner's permission?" Luc said.

André smiled and I knew instantly that André had done his magic.

"I persuaded them," he said.

"Like only you can," Henri added.

"We need to go this morning. I'll need some help. You want to come Jacques?"

"It would be better if I came," said Luc, "Jacques is the only one who can speak to the airmen. My English isn't good enough."

André looked disappointed so he said, "It's time they knew a bit of French, why don't you teach them when we are gone?"

There was no shifting André. He wanted to go with me and that was how it was to be. Half an hour later we were walking towards the farm. The ground was damp after the rain that we had had but it was a pleasant and sunny day. The insects were a menace and I spent much of the time on the walk swatting them as they tried to drain me of my blood.

André was comfortable in my company and I in his. Our difficulties seemed to be behind us and we talked of many things, easily, like friends do. He was very worried about Jean and Maria; Jean because of his injuries and Maria because she was so upset as he left them. He was concerned about what might have happened to Jean in the intervening week.

André had a real empathy with people. I should have known this from our time in the maquis. After all, he was chief cook and general dogsbody at the camp and he took on this role willingly. He had always been there with a hot drink, food and a welcoming smile. It cannot have been easy for him looking after the maquisards in those primitive conditions. He had turned out to be a formidable fighter too. On both of the occasions that I had heard of his involvement in a skirmish he had done himself proud. He never bragged about it and, when the subject arose he described what he did in a factual but graphic way; it was often too graphic for me. He carried two knives at all times and they were perfectly honed.

He spoke a little about himself on our journey to collect the tractor and fuel and this was the first time that I have learnt anything of André's past. André had a pretty normal childhood and a loving home. His parents had two children: André and his younger sister Marianne. The family home was modest and his father was a shopkeeper and his mother still ran the shop with his sister. André's father was killed at the start of the war unsuccessfully defending France against the German invasion. André had not wanted to leave his family but did not want to, indeed would not be, part of the hated German slavery programme which had young people working in factories in Germany as part of the third Reich's war machine. That was how André ended up in the maquis. Luc had taught André to fight and to defend himself. He had been a good learner and Luc, as I knew, the consummate teacher.

André spoke a little of his sexuality and I felt that he was pleased to have a sympathetic ear for his thoughts which, I'm sure, were aired rarely. I asked him if he had fought his homosexuality originally and he surprised me and said that he had not.

"Since I became aware of my own body," he told me, "I have been attracted to men. I was conscious also that I'm not the only one."

André continued, "You know the feelings you have for Élise, Jacques."

I was surprised at the question and I replied simply, "Yes?"

"Be honest Jacques. Tell me what you really think and what you really want to do?"

I reddened at my own thoughts but did answer André as honestly as I could.

"The feelings are very intense. I want to be with her, be close to her and I love her."

It was the first time I had admitted that I loved Élise to myself, let alone anyone else.

"Physically?" he probed.

I looked at him askance, "You mean sex?"

"Yes, if you like. Do you want to make love to her?"

"Of course," I said.

"And have you?"

"Not yet," I said, "but we have been close. We have not had time enough together."

I was not sure why I was telling André this but I did. André was very disarming.

"All of that is very natural," he said with wisdom above his years, "is it not?"

"Yes," I said and I wondered where this was heading.

"And have you had sex with someone you didn't love?"

I looked at André, unsure whether I should commit more confidences to him. I noticed that he used the phrase 'had sex' in this context whereas he had used the phrase 'make love' when referring to Élise.

"Well yes," I said, "it is part of growing up, isn't it? That's more lust than love, I think."

"Well, that's what it is like with me. I have lust to satisfy and the feelings you have for a woman I have for a man. They are just as intense, Jacques, and, to me they feel just as natural as yours do. It is other people who think they are unnatural."

I was starting to understand. Here was a young man with the sex drive of any young man and the only difference between me, at his age, and him was our sexual preference. I also realised that I could be friends with André without his sexuality being a barrier to our friendship.

Our arrival at the farm cut our conversation short. I did not mind this as I was in the metaphorical water out of my depth. It was only later that I was able to rationalise our conversation without emotion clouding my judgement.

André went to find the farmer leaving me beside the machine that we would use to transport the precious fuel. André asked me to hitch up the trailer whilst he was gone and I did this easily. I noticed two drums in the barn and assumed that these were full of aviation fuel. I wondered how André had managed to supply it but, with André it was best not to ask and I was sure he had charmed it from the hands of someone. André returned with the farmer who shook my hand vigorously. His hands were rough and calloused from hard work and mine were becoming similar.

André introduced the farmer as Monsieur Dupont and I never learned of his first name. He was pleased to see us and even more pleased to help us.

"They are advancing," said Monsieur Dupont furtively, "the Americans. They will be here soon and we will be free again."

Monsieur Dupont was a patriot and ashamed of the fall of France. I did not have the heart to tell him that the Germans were counter attacking and that it would be around two months before he would be truly free. No matter though, he would be free and that was the point. He treated us like heroes and I wondered what André had told him. André winked at me at one point and I realised that Monsieur Dupont had been spun a yarn.

French hospitality being what it was, we shared a cognac with Monsieur Dupont before we loaded the aviation fuel onto the trailer and strapped it on using ropes. We then started the precarious journey to the landing zone and we stopped several times to tighten the ropes. I was anxious that we should not lose our load which bounced onto its supporting ties and I irritated André by forcing him to stop more regularly than he would have done.

"Who's the puff now?" André said to me at one point. I gave him a black look but André barely noticed.

We unloaded the drums at the edge of the landing area André had selected from Jean's instructions. He had brought over lamps previously to mark the strip for the aircraft landing and he stacked them next to the drums. These he had placed into the shrubbery and he then covered them with branches. I jumped back on the trailer and André backed the vehicle out to a clearing. He then turned around and we made our way back to the farm. André went back to thank the farmer and handed him a packet of cigarettes which the farmer accepted gratefully. Monsieur Dupont stood leaning on the gate as he watched us walk back to the others. He watched us until we could no longer see him.

"You've been jolly kind to us," said Clark as we stood by the landing zone later.

"Don't mention it," I said in English, "I hope you make it home OK."

The civility of our interchange disguised the underlying tension. I was very nervous and I could tell that so were Eugene and Clark The aeroplane had to make it from Falmouth through the German defence lines and then land here successfully. We had to refuel without being detected by the Germans and the plane had to make it back through the same lines safely. It seemed a tall order. We had taken the precaution of being far from the roads and, if we were to be detected then the Nazi's would have had to have been forewarned. This was always possible as the Milice had spies and many had infiltrated the resistance. Many brave young men had met their deaths because of these spies. I hoped we were not going to join their numbers.

It was becoming darker now and the night sounds were starting to replace those of the day. I heard the screech of an owl and the tee-wit of a male searching for a mate but no return call. We stood silently listening for the aircraft. The tension rose and nobody said a word. I thought I could hear the low drone of the light aircraft. I cocked my head so that my ears faced the sky. It was faint but it was unmistakable. The aircraft was approaching.

"It's time," Luc said and he and André ran out to light the lamps. The drone became louder until we could hear it overhead. The pilot circled the landing zone twice to get the lie of the land and then we heard him making his approach. I saw the wings of the plane close to us but the pilot misjudged the landing, piled on the power and climbed swiftly back into the sky. The aeroplane looked flimsy to my untrained eye. It was a single propeller light aircraft. I asked Eugene what it was and he said it was a Lysander.

"Bloody small," he whispered, "not much room to swing a bloody cat."

The plane circled the landing zone again and I looked at the marked area. One of the lamps had been extinguished by the breeze but there was still sufficient light to identify where the pilot was to land. The plane circled again and I heard it descend and the engine changed its note. The noise became closer and I saw the wings again, a little further away this time. I heard the screech of its tyres on the grass and the brakes being applied. The plane was down. The pilot cut the engine and I heard the feathering of the propeller. Finally the plane was silent except for the tapping sound as the engine cooled.

The relative inaction came to an end as I helped Luc drag the fuel tanks over to plane for the refuelling. The pilot jumped out of the cockpit and shook the hands of the airmen. André helped to recharge the fuel supply of the plane which took a short time. I had a panicky feeling and hoped that the aviation fuel was of sufficient quality for the plane. Henri brought over a further drum by himself and we filled the other tank. They were ready to go.

Eugene came over to me and put his hands on my shoulders.

"Thanks for everything, old man," he said, "good luck."

He released his grip and shook my hand. Clark said goodbye to me in much the same manner. They then went over to André and Eugene said his thanks and farewell in dreadful French. Clark did not try to speak French but spoke in English to André. André responded in French and kissed their cheeks. I think he did it to embarrass the 'stuffies' as he referred to the English.

Finally they said goodbye to Luc and Henri and they crammed themselves into the small plane.

"Good luck," I said as they leapt aboard, "I hope you make it home safely."

They waved from their cabin and the pilot climbed into the cockpit and beckoned for us to step back. They were jammed in to the little plane and I hoped that it had enough power to take off.

The pilot cranked the engine and it fired first time. He revved it and the plane turned to the end of the makeshift runway. He opened the throttle and the plane veered towards us and the trees behind. It took off with plenty of room to spare and the pilot climbed sharply. Within seconds the sound of the plane was a low drone and shortly after that we could hear it no more.

There was an eerie silence and I felt empty. André put his hand on my shoulder and asked if I was OK. I told him that I was fine but I did not feel it.

# Tuesday 11<sup>th</sup> July

## A Welcome Break

It was late so we went back to the farm and slept in the barn. Monsieur Dupont joined us and brought some calvados and Madame Dupont supplied us with cheese, cold meats, potatoes and bread. We devoured the food as if we had not eaten for days. I think it was the early hours before we turned in.

My mood was black and I knew that it was important not to let depression take hold. If it did it was difficult to drag oneself out of the deep well of self pity and despair. I knew what it was like and I did not want to enter that place. I was determined to fight it.

I was not sure why this depression should happen now with everything that had happened to me but I could feel all of the bad things starting to close in on me: Georges death, my experiences with André, Jean and now the loss of the airmen. I was not sleeping and the sun was up so I decided to take myself off and do what I always do and try to talk myself out of my black mood. It sometimes worked. Henri must have seen me go.

I sat on the edge of the trailer we had used to transport the aviation fuel and lit a cigarette. I took a long, slow drag and thought of the things that had happened since I came through the time rift. As I was pondering my fate I heard a voice.

"Can I join you," Henri said in his deep low tone.

I beckoned for Henri to join me on the trailer and said, "You want a cigarette."

Henri nodded, took a cigarette and lit it from mine.

We sat there for a few moments in silence and then Henri said, "We are very proud of you Jacques."

Typically a man of few words, Henri surprised me with his candour. I put my head in my hand and wept. These sobs came from deep inside and Henri let me cry. He did not say the usual things that men say to each other when they are embarrassed. He was simply there. I could feel his support and it was tangible to me.

"I'm sorry, Henri," I said finally.

"You do not need to be sorry Jacques. I know that place and I have been there."

I looked at Henri. The strong, solid and reliable Henri. He was so dependable that it was difficult to imagine him having any weaknesses, let alone crying.

"That's why I am sorry, Henri," I replied, "you have been through much too. Nobody ever asks how you are."

"I have had support," he said, "when I needed it. I don't forget Jacques, just like you don't forget. It just becomes easier to bear. It will for you too Jacques. You have Élise and a life in front of you. Live it. Don't waste it."

I wanted to hug Henri at that moment but he was not that kind of man. I held out my hand and he shook it warmly. It was like a hug. Henri broke the descent into the blackness of my mood. I had felt a depression come close and then move away. I had escaped it this time. I knew the dark ghost would be back but, for now, it had gone.

"What are you going to do now Jacques?"

"It is not over yet, Henri."

"I know that Jacques. But you deserve some rest. You have been running for months."

"You too Henri. I am not the only one."

Henri smiled. He could see that his line of questioning was not achieving any results. In reality, I did not know what I was going to do next.

"I would like to see Jean," I said, "to see how he is doing. Maybe I can be some comfort to Maria too?"

Henri nodded and became thoughtful.

"Maybe you could go via the Martin's farm?"

Élise was someone that I really wanted to see. I thought about it and I did not need to think for long. It sounded like a good idea and it lifted my mood further.

"I don't think it would be a good idea for us all to go," added Henri, "with the way the boche are now. Maybe we could arrange a meet up in a few days somewhere near to Jean?"

"I'd like that," I said, "and I would like to see Jean. Let's see what the others say."

I finished my cigarette and stubbed it out on the trailer. Henri and I sat in a comfortable silence for a few minutes watching the swallows raising their broods oblivious to the lunacy of mankind  The silence was broken by the sound of Luc and André discussing something as they came over to the trailer. They greeted us and I offered them cigarettes which they took. Henri and I lit another and we talked a little of the previous evening. I told Luc and André of my discussion with Henri and Luc nodded in approval.

"You could do with some R&R," he said and winked at me. I knew what he meant and it made me think of Georges. He would have done more than winked at me; I was sure of that and I missed him.

"Jacques," said André, "I have been thinking about Jean."

"Me too," said Luc, "that's what we were discussing just now."

André looked at Luc and smiled one of his charming smiles. He was putting Luc in his place.

"Don't you think it was strange," André continued, "that Jean should be taken the day we left with the airmen."

I hadn't really thought about why Jean had been taken. I had only concerned myself with the fact that he had been taken and what the Germans were likely to be doing to him.

"Now you mention it," I said looking at both André and Luc, "it does seem too much of a coincidence. Are you suggesting that they meant to get us too? Plus the airmen, of course."

"It had crossed our mind," interjected Luc, before André could respond.

"Who knew of the plan?" André asked.

I remembered that I had left André at Dominique and Martine's and not told him that I was leaving nor where I was going. I had spoken to nobody about the plan. I had not known, at that time, that Luc and Henri were alive so I did not know that they were part of it either.

"How did you come to be involved?" I said, addressing my comment to Luc.

"Jean told us. He didn't tell us that you were coming with us. I didn't really know that we were to be together until we met up with you Jacques."

I took a drag of my cigarette and let the smoke hang in the air as I exhaled. Who could have known that we were transporting the airmen? Maria knew and Jean, of course. I did not know who Jean had told but I did know that he was very discrete and guarded. Maria was beyond suspicion. The more I thought about it though, it looked like a trap. I thought about the café in the village. Whilst I was inside the café I was being snared and I had felt the wire tightening around my neck. The old man tried to tell me something. He was trying to tell me that it was an ambush. Thankfully, I smelled a rat but it was a close shave.

"The café!"

"The café Jacques?" said André.

"The fucking café. I was given the same code word as the café in Hennebont."

"I'm not following you Jacques," said Luc.

"That's because you don't know Luc and nor do you André or Henri because I haven't told a soul about this. That's my point."

André looked at Luc and Henri and shrugged. It was Henri who spoke next.

"You met someone in a café?"

"Not quite Henri," I replied, "I was asked by Jean to meet a guy called René in a café in Hennebont. I used the same code words that I was supposed to use in the café here."

"You met up with him?" André asked.

"Yes. I met him in his apartment. Jean trusted him so I can't believe that René would betray us."

"So what are you saying Jacques?" Luc questioned.

"I'm not sure Luc," I replied, "we met in the bar initially. We didn't speak of the airmen, at least I'm pretty sure we didn't. Maybe someone overheard us."

"Tell me about this René," said Henri.

"He is from my time," I said and this seemed to surprise Henri.

"Not exactly my time but he came through a time rift a year or so before me. He seemed to hate the Germans and he told me that his girlfriend had been raped, tortured and then killed by them. He seemed genuine."

Luc looked at Henri and then at André. I knew what was in their thoughts.

"Are you suggesting that I've been duped?"

"I don't know," replied André, "I didn't meet him.  What was he like?"

I explained what I knew of René and, as I was telling it, I realised that I hardly knew the man at all.  I had taken everything he had said at face value and I had entrusted a lot of information to him.  Then I remembered the laptops.  Jean had trusted René; of that I was sure.  I tried to explain the computerised communication between Jean and René but it was too difficult for any of them to comprehend.  I could not understand why René would betray Jean and I did not believe that he would.  However, there was now doubt in my mind.  It was a doubt that was to remain and I realised that, at best, I had been gullible.

It was decided unanimously that I was due some rest and recuperation and we hatched a plan for me to visit the Martin's farm and then rendezvous near the old maquis before heading back towards Jean and Maria's.  Only André knew where Jean was hiding so it was important for me to keep to our meeting schedule for I did want to see Jean.

We walked together for most of the way.  It took a week and early on the seventh day I peeled away for my two day break with Élise.  I was very excited at the prospect of our reunion and I was not disappointed.

# Tuesday 18<sup>th</sup> July

## Élise

I walked toward the Martin's farm with a spring in my step. The sun was warm and the day dry and I was very nervous. I walked over the crest of the hill and I could see the farm in front of me. There was smoke coming from the range flue and cattle in the meadow. I climbed the fence into one of the fields, missing the track so that I could take the more direct route. There was a small coppice of trees with a path that I knew from my last visit. Élise and I had walked through it and chatted and kissed. She laughed in a girlish way and those moments and sounds had been precious memories to me in my dark moments in the preceding weeks.

I entered the coppice of trees and took the path. I heard a sound on the path ahead. I blinked to allow my eyes to become accustomed to the lower light and hid myself behind a tree. The newcomer had seen me and it was too late to hide.

"Jacques," the newcomer said, "is that you, Jacques?"

It was Élise of course, taking an early morning walk. I stepped out from behind the tree and she stifled a shriek. Élise stood there for a few moments and then started running towards me. We flung our arms around each other and kissed both passionately and tenderly. I held her close and I did not want to let her go ever again. I knew that she felt the same. Her hands explored my body and mine hers. I am not sure how our embrace became intimate but it did and we made love for the first time in that coppice exploring our bodies together. It seemed so natural and simply an expression of our love for one another. I told her that I loved her and she told me that she loved me. It was bliss and I wanted it never to end.

What I did not know at the time was that I had planted my seed that day. This was the seed that was to become our first son who we were to name Georges after my fallen friend.

I had two extraordinary days at the Martin's farm. I am sure that Monsieur Martin knew of my intimacy with Élise for he left us alone, keeping Alain and Claire out of the way. He was also raucous when he arrived back making a lot more noise than was necessary. I was grateful to be allowed this privilege. Monsieur Martin had accepted me as the suitor of his daughter and, after the loss of his wife, that must have been difficult for him.

I did not want to leave after my two days. Élise accepted my departure because she knew that I had to go. This was one parting that was more difficult than any other. Before I left the Martin's farm I asked Élise if she would marry me and she said that she would. I asked Monsieur Martin formally for the hand of Élise and he acquiesced willingly and then wept openly.

I left Élise with a heavy heart but much hope for the future. Even if I could go home I no longer wanted to go. I had every reason to remain alive and realised that within the month the war for most of France would be over.

# Wednesday 19<sup>th</sup> July

## Stark Realisation

I reached the rendezvous place in good time and before Henri, Luc and André had arrived. We were close to the caves where we had hidden after our first sabotage mission. The sun was warm and I sat on a rock waiting for my crew enjoying the moment. The closeness and intimacy with Élise had left me feeling elated and I felt as if I could achieve anything. I had a whole life to live and I wanted to live it with Élise. Georges had once said, in a way that only Georges could, how amazing had been our experience. That was how I felt then. Except for the obvious issues with France being occupied by a bunch of Nazi thugs, I liked this time. It was a simpler time and I was beginning to feel that society in my time had become too possession orientated and too complex. I missed none of my toys and had not used any of them since their batteries expired. I did miss some things like a well made cappuccino, junk food and rock music. I realised that I was about to live through one of the most explosive times in music with the arrival of the fifties and then the sixties. My grandfather often said that he wished he had been my age and I was then eighteen, during the sixties. If I stayed in this time, I would be in my forties during the 1960's.

I heard the sound of boots on the path. They were not German boots which had a distinct sound to them. These were well worn boots and their wearers had walked many miles in them.

"Jacques," Luc shouted to me when he saw me, "and a clean and tidy Jaques, too."

Luc came over to me and stroked my chin, "and clean shaven too. And you smell nice."

"Piss off," I said and smiled and shook Luc's hand.

I then shook Henri and André's hands.

"Did you have a good R&R, Jacques?" said André, beaming. He was fishing and I was not about to reveal anything to him.

"Great," I said simply.

Henri butted in, "You look more relaxed, Jacques. You needed the break."

"Thanks, Henri," I said and turned to him for I wanted to tell Henri my news first.

"You look like the cat who got the cream," Henri said.

"Henri, I've some terrific news," I said. I was smiling inside and out.

"He got his leg over," said André and Henri clipped him around the head.

"That's Jacques business, not yours," Henri scolded, rather more seriously than was necessary. André took little notice and winked at me. I ignored him and continued addressing Henri.

"I've asked Élise to marry me," I exclaimed, "and she has said that she will. Isn't that great?"

"You did what?" André said, "You want to be tied down so early. Are you mad?"

Henri could not contain himself now and he struck André viciously on his cheek. André retaliated and Luc came between them. I had been surprised by the ferocity of Henri's attack, as was André.

"Hey," I said, "quit fighting. I'm happy about this. André, keep your infantile views to yourself. When you love someone, you'll understand. Don't spoil my moment, fuck you!"

The mood lightened with my expletive and Henri apologised to André who accepted it grudgingly. I remember being on the other side of Henri's temper and he was quick to anger. Now, I respected him greatly and I'm sure that, in time, André would come to see him as I saw him.

Henri held out his hand and I took it willingly. He put his other hand to the left of my shoulder.

"Congratulations Jacques. Élise is a fine woman and the Martins are a good family. I know Monsieur Martin well. Madame Martin was a splendid woman too. Élise is like her mother. You take good care of her."

Luc shook my hand next and then André.

"If you are happy, then I'm happy," André said his face lightening and he came close to my ear and whispered, "but I thought you were saving yourself for me."

I pushed his head down and tugged at his hair. He laughed like the teenager that he was. It was not often that I saw the youth in André.

I took out a packet of cigarettes and handed them around. We smoked and Luc explained what they had been doing whilst I was at the farm. They more, or less, drank the whole time and Luc had acquired another scar this time on his arm from a knife wound. This fight was over a girl again and this time he won the fight and the girl. I was not the only one playing the mating game. With Luc it was never serious and Henri commented that Luc liked the conquest but not the commitment. I think the war had affected Luc and he seemed to view everything as ephemeral.

It was still early when we left together. We knew that we could reach Jean and Maria by nightfall but we decided to camp in the hills above the town rather than risk being out after the curfew. André would venture out the next morning and seek Jean and confirm that we could see him. I realised that we could not travel together to see him and that we needed to be discreet as Jean's safety was paramount. From what André had said, Jean did not sound like he would survive recapture by the Gestapo.

We reached our chosen camp site well before nightfall. We were hidden from the town but, from out vantage point, had a good view of it. I could see the rail yard and the roads leading to it and out of the town. The rail yard was busy, busier than it had been during my journey to Hennebont, and there were German trucks loading something onto the train. I could not tell what it was that they were transporting from my distance but my guess was that it was munitions or supplies for the front line. I knew that the railway line was blocked. I mused that the Germans were using rail transport where they could and then road for the rest of the journey.

There was road traffic movement too and I could see troop carriers driving through the town taking young men to prevent the allied advance. I knew it would be futile and I knew many of them, and the allies, were yet to die and I felt helpless to stop the lunacy that was Europe at this time.

The place was crawling with Germans and I wondered how we were going to meet up with Jean without being detected. I crept back to the team and we ate some of the food that André had used his charm to obtain from a farm along the way. I told them what I had seen. André said that Jean would have been moved regularly and that he would have to find out where he was. I wondered if Jean had been moved out of the area. This looked like a dangerous place to be a fugitive. Jean, of course, was no stranger to danger.

The evening was warm and André walked off to find a toilet, as he put it. Henri was quiet and I think he was regretting his burst of temper with André though André had forgiven Henri quickly. With André things do not fester; he says what he thinks and then moves on. I envied him because I would dwell on things and I think this is what contributes to my black moods.

I sat with Luc who had a bottle of calvados; this was another of André's acquisitions. He passed me the bottle and I took a swig. It was rough and I coughed as I took a gulp.

"Is that neat spirit?" I said.

"It wards off the cold," Luc replied.

I was not sure how much Luc had drunk but his mood was mellow. Luc could hold his drink and his muscular frame absorbed the alcohol well.

"I am pleased for you Jacques," Luc said, "does this mean that you will not go home now?"

"I'm not sure I know how to," I replied and took another slurp from the bottle before passing it back to Luc. It had started to taste better.

"But no, I don't want to go back now. There are people and things that I miss, especially my grandfather and my mother, but my life is here now."

"You never mention your father," said Luc.

"My father died," I responded, "in a motorcycle accident. My grandfather sort of took his place, though I have always been close to him."

"What was his name?"

"Georges," I said and surprised myself.

"Like your friend."

It was true, my father and my friend had the same name and I had never really associated them.

"Yes," I said, "though I had never really thought of that before."

Luc took another swig and passed me the bottle. I drank and then passed the bottle back. Luc declined the offer and I put the cork stopper back into its neck.

"How old was he? I mean when he died."

"In his early thirties," I said.

"Young."

"Yes. My mother did not want me to take up motorcycling at all. Grandfather was OK, though. I was never sure why because it was his son who had died. I always thought that odd."

Luc pondered what I had said but did not reply immediately.

"I've been thinking about your grandfather. I've made some enquiries."

"Yes," I said, interested.

"I can't find another Jacques Richard in this area. You said he was here during the war, fighting for the Free French, yes?"

"That's right," I said.

"Well he isn't here, and he is," replied Luc, obtusely.

"Sorry, I'm not following you," I said, perplexed

"Well, you are here and you are Jacques Richard are you not?" Luc continued.

"You've lost me Luc. The calvados has got to your brain," I remarked.

Luc smiled and continued, "Listen me out Jacques."

"OK, I'm listening."

"How old would your grandfather be now?" Luc asked.

"Same age as me," I replied.

"Exactly," Luc said.

"You are talking in riddles Luc," I spat, "I'm not sure I understand what you are saying."

"It's fucking obvious Jacques."

"What is?" I exclaimed.

"You are your grandfather," Luc said with a flourish.

"What, are you daft?" I said.

"Think about it Jacques. Aren't there some things about your grandfather that are odd? Isn't there anything he said, anything he has done, that would substantiate this?"

My head was swimming and I could not take any more of this.

"You're wrong Luc, it just can't be. How can I be my own grandfather? It would mean that my son is my father. That's fucking crazy." I was completely confused.

"Crazy it might be Jacques but I think I'm right."

André and Henri returned at this point and stopped our conversation. Henri and André were talking together comfortably so I guessed that the animosity between them was over. I was preoccupied when they joined us on the rock. I removed the cork from the calvados and took a long drink and passed the bottle to Henri.

He took the bottle and said, "You two OK? There's a bit of tension here."

"Yes," we both said together.

André looked at Henri and shrugged. They both drank from the bottle. When it was finished we retired to our rough beds. I slept fitfully. What Luc had said disturbed me. I thought that I did not believe him but there were parts of his logic that I found uncomfortable.

# Monday 23<sup>rd</sup> July

## Acceptance

The night was cold and it took a long time for sleep to come. The conversation with Luc rotated in my mind. There were things that I thought strange about my grandfather. My parting came to mind and I remembered how distressed he and my grandmother had been when I left.

With a jolt I was awake. How could I have been so stupid, I thought. Grandfather called grandma 'El'. Though I had never asked what 'El' was short for, it was obvious now. Grandmother was Élise. Élise, for God's sake! Luc was right after all. I was my grandfather. I sat up and thought about my grandfather. My head was awash with memories.

It was not all bad. Grandfather lived to an old age and so did grandmother. They had four children and my father, who was also my son, was the first. I would call him Georges and that made sense to me considering my loss. Then there were the bad things. My son would be killed in his thirties and I would have to bear that loss. His son, me, would travel through a time rift and start the whole cycle again. Were we destined to circulate in time forever, I wondered?

I thought about my father, who was now my son. I thought hard about how old he was when he died. I worked out when he was born. It hit me like a thunderbolt. My son would be born in nine months time. The mould had already been set. This was all too much for me and I put my head in my hands.

Luc turned over and saw me.

"You OK?"

I looked at Luc and he could see that I was distraught. He stood up and beckoned me to follow him. We sat on the rock that we had used the previous evening. The empty bottle was resting against a tuft of grass. Luc plucked two cigarettes from a packet and lit them both in one go. He handed one to me and I took a deep breath and let the smoke trickle from my mouth and then down my nose. How unappealing this would have been to me in my time.

"Luc," I started.

He looked at me, his muscular frame towering over me, despite his short stature. Luc nodded but said nothing.

"I think you are right. I've been thinking about what you said. A lot of it ties together. It's confusing Luc, really confusing and it hurts my head to think about it."

"Yes, I guess it does. It isn't what you might call normal is it?"

"No," I said and paused. Luc did not fill the pause but smoked his cigarette in silence, waiting for me to compose my thoughts. Luc surprised me with his sensitivity. He was rough and could be quite coarse. He liked his drink and he liked a collection of women and was not averse to being serviced by the sex industry if the need arose. I was seeing a more sensitive and inquisitive side of his character. These were strange times and I was also discovering facets of my own personality that I did not know existed.

I told him of my thoughts during the night and of the morning.

"You see Luc," I said, "my son will be my father and that is really odd. And what's more, he will be born soon, within the year."

I did not tell Luc that I thought that Élise may already be pregnant. I doubted if Élise knew yet. I may have been wrong. My calculations may have been incorrect. I did not want to take the chance.

Luc grinned at me and added, "You'd better get back to Élise Jacques. It looks like you have a job to do."

I smiled back at him and said, "Do you think the future is set? Can I do anything to change it? Does all of this have to happen?"

These were rhetorical questions and Luc simply shrugged and said, "Fuck knows. It's all beyond me, Jacques."

He tapped me gently on the cheek and said, "Whatever will be, will be, Jacques. Let's live for the day. Tomorrow may never come. At least you know you have a tomorrow. Despite all of the odds, so does Georges."

I was not sure at this point whether he meant Georges, my friend, or Georges, my son, and I did not push the point. In any case we were disturbed by André who rushed by us and headed for the woods.

"Where's the fire?" Luc asked but André did not answer.

He arrived back five minutes later. He was very pallid.

"I've got the shits," he said.

Later that day it hit Luc, then Henri and finally me. If everyone else had felt like I did that day, and the following, then I would have felt sorry for them were I not feeling so sorry for myself. A consequence of this is that we did not seek out Jean until Monday after the malaise had passed. I lost around three kilograms in those three days and was feeling quite weak when the illness passed. Living rough is not the best place to be ill. Henri knew of plants that could help and, despite being pretty poorly himself, prepared a concoction which gave some relief from the stomach cramps.

André decided that he was strong enough on Monday to venture into town and make some enquiries about Jean. He seemed well enough so we agreed and asked him to obtain some produce as we were all feeling pretty hungry. He said he would bring back some food and some spirit, if he could find it, for my stove. We watched him leave and saw him veer off the track and into the woods for protection. I looked at his slight frame. He had lost weight too and he had less to lose than most of us. I feared for his safety.

It was evening before André returned. He returned with a girl of about eighteen years old. She had striking blue eyes, was skinny with little bust to show and long blond hair tied back. Her eyes betrayed a keen intelligence and I found out quickly that she had an obstinate streak. This was a girl who knew her own mind and knew what she wanted. It was clear very soon that she wanted Luc and Luc did not stand a chance.

"This is François," André said, "she is a partisan. She has news of Jean and I thought you should all hear it. She is very brave and can help us."

I looked at the slight frame of François and wondered how she had been brave. I did not have to wait long.

"François is a messenger. Without her the resistance would not work. She takes incredible risks." André said as if trying to convince us.

François fixed a stare on us and I knew that here was somebody not to cross. I was pleased that she was on our side. François looked at Luc and there was chemistry between them. I found this strange. François was not Luc's usual type of girl. He liked well built girls with full breasts and, as he often said, with something to hold. François was also very intelligent and dominant, which was something that did not fit well with the machismo of Luc.

"I can speak for myself," François spat.

"I work for the Free French, that's all. I want to see France free of this vermin. It looks like it might be soon. The allies are advancing and are now making some headway after Fritz made a counter attack. *Vive la France*."

"What have you to tell us of Jean," Henri interjected after we had all repeated François call to arms.

"Can I have some introductions first?"

"I'm sorry, I said," we are forgetting our manners. We have been men, alone, for too long."

We introduced ourselves to François and she replied to Henri's question.

"Jean is no longer here."

We looked at each other and I was disappointed at the news though not surprised.

"He has been moved to a safer place. You must have noticed the troop movements here. The boche are moving north to defend the front line. It wasn't safe for Jean to be here. We could not risk him being caught by the pigs again."

"How is he?" I asked.

"He is improving," François continued, "but he has difficulty walking. Those bastards smashed his knee cap. He will always have a limp now."

"Is Maria with him?" Luc asked and smiled at François. The chemistry was mutual, I thought. I had seen Luc's seduction look before and he was trying it with François. François was going to make Luc work for her affections and, if she did notice his obvious mating call, she ignored it.

"Yes, they are together. They travelled separately but they are now reunited."

"Can you tell us where they are?" Henri asked.

"That's why I wanted François to come here. I wanted her to tell you this herself," André exclaimed, obviously excited.

"OK, André, thanks but let me tell this in my own way," François rebuked.

"We have sent them a distance away and into the country. They are in a small farm north of here. You probably haven't heard of it. The farm has cows, hens and a little arable."

I looked at André who was grinning. He knew something. I guessed before François told me. Jean was at the Martin's farm. He must have arrived after I had left. I missed him by a day.

"Now that's a coincidence," said Luc, "Jacques was there a few days ago. He spent some time with his girlfriend."

"You know the Martins?" François addressed her question to me.

"Very well," I said.

"*Very* well," André repeated but with a different intonation in his voice. I ignored him.

"I do not," she continued, "but I have heard that they are good people. Jean will be safe there. There are very few people who know of this. You must repeat it to no one."

I was both delighted and concerned at the same time; delighted because Jean was with the Martins and concerned because it put them at risk. Élise was a messenger, like François, and she would bear the risk willingly, I knew. It did not stop me worrying.

"There is more," André said and François shot him a look of resignation. She was not going to quieten André.

"Jean was betrayed," François said.

"Do you know who did this?" I asked, fearing the answer.

"No, we are still looking."

"We thought it might be René," I said weakly.

"René!" François exclaimed, "are you mad? René is the backbone of our organisation. René would never betray Jean any more than I would. How could you even think that?"

François paused after her outburst and, when she had calmed said, "What made you think that René would betray Jean."

There was doubt in her voice now. I explained my reasoning; when I was talking I realised what a poor case it was and how circumstantial was the evidence. François looked thoughtful but said nothing further. What I had said had disturbed her though she did not say so. I asked François if she knew what had happened to the airmen and whether they made it to England.

"They made it," she said, "and they have been debriefed and are back in active service. You did a good job. Jean was pleased to hear that they were out of harm's way. Whoever transferred them to Hennebont?"

"That's a long story," I said, not wanting to implicate anybody. François did not pursue the issue further and I did not want to elaborate. I was not sure that I liked François much at that time.

André had brought back food and drink and we were all hungry after our forced fast brought on by our illness. I was over the stomach cramps by now but I was not able to drink the red wine that André brought. After we had sated our appetites François went for a stroll with Luc and I stayed behind and smoked a cigarette with André and Henri.

"What do you make of that?" I asked.

"Of what?" Henri replied.

"François. She is fierce, isn't she?"

"She's OK Jacques," said André, "she knows what she is doing. I think you hit a raw nerve with René. You think he is implicated here?"

"I don't know. I hope not. I don't really have any reason to suspect him. Jean trusted him so why shouldn't I?"

"What is your gut telling you, Jacques?" asked Henri.

"It is screaming that something is not quite right."

"Then listen to it. We need to find this René and find him quickly. I want to meet him and I have a few questions of my own. Jacques, let's find François and see if she knows where René is."

"I'm not going to Hennebont again," I exclaimed.

"I wouldn't mind," said André who grinned. I cut him a look of disapproval and he performed a crude gesture which I ignored.

"Pervert," I said to André who blew me a discrete kiss and then I continued, "you need to understand that the Lorient pocket holds out for longer than the rest of France. If we get stuck in Hennebont then we are stuck for nearly a year."

"We may not have to go to Hennebont," said Henri, "and all I'm suggesting is that we find out."

Henri and I left André alone and walked in the direction that Luc and François walked. I wondered if it was a good idea to try and find them; they may have wanted some time alone. We discovered Luc and François sitting by the river chatting. I breathed a sigh of relief. They looked comfortable in each other's company but were not dismayed by our intrusion. François smiled at me and I sat beside her. Henri sat next to Luc.

"Hi," she said, "Luc was just telling me about your adventures, and about your friend Georges. I'm sorry Jacques. It must have been hard for you."

"It was," I said more coolly than I intended.

"Luc also told me that you are like René," she said.

"Not exactly," I interjected, "I'm not at all like René."

"I don't mean that," she continued, "I meant that you are from our future."

"I am," I said, continuing the chill in my voice.

"René thinks we can change the future. What do you think?"

I did not like this line of questioning so I kept up my cool front and replied, "How do I know. Your future is my past. You change the future and you change my past. If my past changes then how can I be here? So, the future can't be changed. That's my reasoning."

"Can't fault that logic," she said, trying to melt the ice.

"Why does René think he can change the future? How does he want to change it?"

"He thinks that Europe became a mess after the war. He thinks it could have been different."

"He's right about the mess. Half of Europe was behind an iron curtain for a generation after the war. The soviets oppression was nearly as bad as the Nazis. That's for sure. How does he want it to change?"

"I haven't really discussed that with him," François said, "maybe you could find out yourself?"

"That's why we are here," said Henri, "we'd like to find René. Do you know where he is?"

Henri's directness stunned me. I had seen it before, usually when he was disturbed by something. I reasoned that something was troubling him at that moment.

"Yes," François said, "I will take you to him. It is late now and I need to be back before the curfew. Come to the bistro in the square at eleven tomorrow morning and I'll take you to René."

François stood and kissed Luc lightly on the lips. She then kissed us on the cheeks and rushed off to find André. When we returned to André, François was gone but, like a tornado, she had left her mark behind.

# Tuesday 24<sup>th</sup> July

## Finding René

Henri and I were outside the bistro at before eleven o'clock the next morning but François did not appear. The town was busy when we arrived and German troop carriers thundered down the main street. They did not stop and ignored our presence. There were many Germans patrolling the streets and again they disregarded us. I found this odd but was grateful. I had my papers and I had left my weapons with André so I should not have been treated with suspicion. I gestured for Henri to join me in the bistro and we drank a coffee and a cognac. I was ready for neat spirit by now and it settled my stomach.

"Where is she, I wonder?" Henri said.

There was a tone in Henri's voice that I had not heard before. Henri was distrusting of everyone and I was used to that. This tone was different. He was anxious and this was not an emotion common to Henri. He looked around the square. I was feeling the disquiet now.

"The square, have you noticed." Henri said.

I looked too. The crowds in the square had thinned. It was now nearly empty and, those that were about, had scurried to the edges.

"We need to go," Henri said, "and now Jacques."

I dropped some francs on the table to pay for the coffee and cognac and we left.

"What's up?" I whispered to Henri.

"I don't know, but I feel something is wrong and I don't like it. Come over here. I want to watch what happens next."

Henri led me to a doorway in a narrow walkway and we lit cigarettes so that we were not conspicuous. We had a good view of the bistro when the black Mercedes car full of Gestapo officials glided to a halt with the car's engine cut. They opened the car door and six of the thugs exited slowly and deliberately. Here, in front of us, were supremely confident men and I knew that many of them would slink away back to Austria or to South America to evade the justice they rightfully deserved. They entered the bistro, were inside for a few minutes and came out of the door with two men. One of them was René. He and the other man were bundled into the back of the car. The Gestapo officers alighted the vehicle, boxed in their captives and then the car sped off with a skid of tyres. Were it not so serious I would have taken it for a Hollywood movie.

I drew a breath through the lighted cigarette and savoured the noxious weed that I knew was doing my body harm. With what was going on around me it seemed a small risk and I understood the allure of the cigarette at times of stress. I tried to look nonchalant so that I would not attract the attention of the remaining Germans. They were not interested in me.

We finished our cigarettes in silence and Henri offered me another which I took. He lit it from the stub of the last one and we remained at our post. The square started to fill again with people living their lives under these impossible conditions. The action was over and life was returning to what comprised normal in these times.

François arrived at the bistro a few minutes later. She went to the entrance and looked around. She did not see us but we could see her. She attracted the attention of a German soldier and I could see by his posturing that he was flirting with her. She was having none of it and her manner was icy.  On a hunch I walked out into the square towards François.  Henri tried to stop me but I freed myself from his grip of my arm.  As I closed the gap between François and myself she saw me and smiled over the soldier's shoulder.

"Alex," she shouted, "I thought I had missed you.  The whole town was cordoned off.  Did you get caught in it?"

Her acting was good.  I nearly fell for it myself.  She oozed past the soldier giving him a look that would have turned his soul to stone and flung herself into my arms and kissed me like I was a long lost lover. I was initially stunned and then surprised at how much I enjoyed the experience.  She then put her arm through mine and she led me away across the square without looking back at the soldier.  This girl had class.

We headed away from Henri who was observing everything and he followed us at a discrete distance.  François guided me towards a narrow walkway and we were out of the square.

"Your breath smells like an old ashtray," she said, without flattery. My swelling ego had been pricked.  I gave her a pathetic look which she ignored.

"Henri is with me," I said, "I'm sure he'll follow us.  Can we wait for him here?"

"Yes, let him catch us up.  I'm sorry I was late.  The Germans put up checkpoints and they were preventing people from entering the square.  Did you get caught in them?"

"No, we were early.  Henri thought there was something wrong.  I think he saw the square emptying."

"I believe that there was something going on," François added.

"The Gestapo were here," I said.

"That was what it was," she mused, "did you see them?"

"We had a grandstand view," I replied.

Henri came round the corner at that moment and François greeted him by kissing him on the cheeks.

"I was just telling François about the raid," I said to Henri.

"I think we should get out of here. We can come back later and talk to René. It's too dangerous at the moment."

"You haven't told her?" Henri said.

"Told me what?"

"That's what I was trying to say to you," I replied, "René has been taken by the Gestapo."

François gasped and put her hand over her mouth.

"Fuck!" she exclaimed, "That is bad. René knows too much. If he talks we are in deep shit."

I immediately thought of Élise and her family. Were they in danger, I wondered? They were caring for Jean and Maria, after all, and that must have put them in the front line.

"What does he know? Does he know where Jean is?"

François looked puzzled at my question and said, "No, why do you ask? Jean's whereabouts is known only to a few people. You are among the privileged. René does not know."

Henri answered the question for me, "Jacques is engaged to Élise Martin. He speaks from his heart in this matter."

She shot me a shallow smile and then continued, "I need to go now. This news is bad. I need to talk to others. Can you pass a message to Luc for me?"

"Willingly," I said.

She passed me a small sealed white envelope and I placed it in my inside pocket of my blouson. She kissed us lightly on the cheeks and was gone in an instant.

"Time we got back," I said to Henri and we made our way via a circuitous route back to our makeshift camp.

# Friday 27<sup>th</sup> July

# Duplicity

We did little of consequence in the three days that followed René's capture. Luc read his message but did not share its contents with us. André tried to find out what François' letter had said and he was relentless in this. He stopped only when Luc became aggressive with him. André gave up reluctantly and at one point I thought that he was going to search Luc's clothes when he was washing.

I wanted desperately to return to Élise but Luc had told us that there was still work to do here. I was not sure what he meant and I wondered if the message from François formed part of his plan. Our reason for being here, after all, was to find Jean. We now knew the whereabouts of Jean so I was not sure why we were waiting. I had asked Luc but he was reluctant to tell me anything. I was puzzled by this as Luc was normally an open person. I felt as if I was being manipulated and the three days of inactivity did nothing to dispel this feeling. Tensions between us grew during those days and I did not like it. It left me with a feeling of foreboding.

We woke up to a heavy dew on Friday and I was cold. I was feeling belligerent and I was not going to put up with this any longer. Today, I thought, I would confront Luc but I did not need to as that day everything changed. I am still not sure what tipped the balance but Luc awoke that morning and he was different.

Over breakfast he spoke to us.

"I know you've been pissed off with me," he started, "but I've had a lot to think about. I wanted to make sure that I'd got it right in my head. I think I'm there now."

"OK," said Henri, "you want to share it with us?"

Luc looked at Henri. There was a real bond between them and Henri sat there looking solid and dependable. Luc smiled at him. Henri's expression did not change.

"François has asked us to remain here. Obviously, she did not know that René would be taken so this has delayed whatever she had in mind for us. I think we have waited long enough. I'd like to find François before we go, though. I want to go into town again. André?"

"Yes, Luc," André replied.

"Do you know anybody here that can accommodate some of us tonight. I would like to stay in town. If I can find François then I can find out what she wants."

"Some of us?" said Henri.

"I don't want to put all of you at risk," Luc said, "and in any case more of us will make us conspicuous."

"I'm not staying here any longer Luc," I said, "either we come into town with you or I'm heading back to the Martin's."

"I'm coming with you, like it or not," said Henri.

"And I'm going with Jacques," added André and he grinned. I gave him a shallow smile back. He was not helping.

"I think Luc is talking through his cock," commented André, unhelpfully, "he fancies François and that's what's driving this. Why can't you just be honest Luc?"

Luc took a deep breath and swelled his chest like a cockerel strutting. Testosterone was in the air and I sensed the aggression.

"Enough André," said Henri, diffusing the ensuing situation and interposing himself between Luc and André, "we don't fight amongst ourselves. It's the boche we're fighting. Never forget that."

Henri stood his ground and the tension diffused. Considering that Henri was the only person I had seen strike any of us, his comment was full of hypocrisy. Not one of us noticed it then.

"What are you hoping to achieve from this visit to town?" Henri asked Luc.

"I don't know," answered Luc, candidly, "François, in her note to me said that she wanted our help with something and that she would be in touch soon."

"That was before René was captured," I said.

"Yes," replied Luc, "she would not have known about that when she wrote the letter."

"But she knew about it when she gave it to Jacques," André said.

"I don't understand your point," said Luc.

"What I'm saying," said André, deliberately, "is that she had a chance to change the letter before giving it to Jacques. She did know about René when she handed it over. The letter was for you Luc and it was sealed. She could have told us that she wanted us to do something. She didn't. The letter was for you, alone. What else is in the letter, Luc?"

André was probing again. He would not be satisfied until Luc handed over the letter for him to read. Luc was not about to do that.

"There was some personal stuff too," Luc said and he blushed.

This is not something that I had seen before. Luc was a rough, tough masculine man who preferred his relationships without commitments. This was a new experience for Luc too. I thought that André was going to take advantage of Luc's discomfort but, for once, he did not.

"OK, André," said Henri, "I think we are all going into town. Do you know of anywhere safe we can stay?"

"Sure," André replied, nonchalantly and he threw a glance at me as he said this, "I know a guy who has an apartment overlooking the plaza, near the bistro where you met François. I'm not sure if it is free. I can find out. If that fails I know a friend of Maria. Her husband died at the start of the war and she has young children so it will not be as convenient but I'm sure she'll put us up for a night or two."

"Why don't you go with Jacques, André," said Henri, "and see if you can sort us out a place to stay. We'll meet you this afternoon at the bistro. I wouldn't mind something good to eat."

André and I made our way into town leaving Henri and Luc behind. I was sure that Henri wanted a word with Luc on his own though I never discovered what they spoke about.

André led us to a narrow backstreet to a small terraced house with a gnarled wooden door with peeling paint that had once been blue. He used the brass knob to bang on the door and I heard a young man's voice say that he would answer the call. The door opened and an effeminate young man with blond spiky hair screamed with delight. He leapt into the air and his hands waived frantically.

"André! Is that really you? Where have you been?"

He then burst out of the door and put his arms around André and kissed him full on the lips. André did not object and kissed him back.

"Let's get inside, before the pigs see us," said the young man.

We went into a narrow and dark hallway and then into a small lounge. He then led us into the kitchen at the back where another young man was at the sink. The man was tall, muscular and very masculine with dark stubble.

"Who is your friend?  He's very pretty.  Is this your boyfriend? Have you forgotten me so soon?"

"I'm forgetting my manners," said André, "This is Jacques. Jacques, this is Emmanuel."

I shook the effeminate young man's hand.  He had a weak handshake.

"This is Isaac," said Emmanuel, introducing the muscular man at the sink to us.  "He is a Jew.  We are looking after him."

The significance of this statement was not lost on me.  I was assuming that Isaac was both homosexual and a Jew; a poisonous combination in occupied France.  I shook his strong, large hand and he smiled at me with his mouth, but not his eyes.  I was wrong as Isaac was not gay but had simply teamed up with another group of persecuted people.

"Jacques is engaged to be married," said André and raised his eyebrows, "to a woman."

"Such a waste," said Emmanuel and he pinched my backside.  My tolerance was being tested and I think I passed.  Isaac looked on impassively.  Emmanuel was stunning in appearance.  He was short in stature, androgynous with high cheekbones and a pose that many models would have wished to emulate.

"Oh, it's good to see you André.  I was sorry to hear about Jean. Have you seen him?  Is he recovering?"

"That's why we came here," replied André, "but we haven't seen him.  Nobody knows where he is."

"That's good isn't it?  If nobody knows then the boche don't know either."

"Yes, but I would like to see him."

"I've heard he is in a bad way, André," added Emmanuel. "They beat him pretty badly.  They're bastards.  I hate every one of them."

"Emmanuel poisons Germans for fun," said André to me and I must have looked surprised.

"You think, because I'm a puff, that I can't fight. I do it in my own way pretty boy. You'd be surprised how many of the master race squirm with delight when I unbutton them. They think I'm a woman of course and I dress up really well. You would be surprised at how well Jacques."

He smiled at me showing a row of immaculate teeth. I was uncomfortable and he was enjoying my discomfort.

"Actually, Emmanuel," I said, "It is easy for me to imagine you dressed as a woman."

I'm still not sure why I said this but it brought a twitter of laughter from everyone, including the taciturn Isaac.

"Be careful, Jacques," said André, "Emmanuel will think you are flirting with him."

"I spike their drink. I have some wonderful concoctions and I make sure they suffer. It's so much cleaner than cutting their throats like you boys do. And it is so difficult to get the blood out of my frocks."

Emmanuel was a complex person. I looked at his slight frame. It was quite feminine and it was difficult to imagine him as a resistance fighter. Resistance manifested itself in many different ways.

"What brings you here André?" asked Emmanuel, "I'm sure it wasn't just to see me. You must want something?"

Emmanuel looked at André and I could hear the double intent in Emmanuel's question. André noticed it too and grinned at him.

"Later, Emmanuel," André said, "I've some work to do first. We need to use your apartment overlooking the square. Is it occupied?"

"It is such a mess, André," said Emmanuel, "no one has lived there since the occupation."

"We don't mind that," replied André, "you want to see the conditions we have been living in."

"I don't need to see them," added Emmanuel. "Look at you both. You look like peasants and you smell like them too."

I looked at André and he at me. We must have looked a sight. I had not shaved since I left the Martin's farm and André's patchy beard made him look like a goat. Our hair was lank and greasy.

"Clean yourselves up before you go, at least, where is your dignity?"

"There'll be time for dignity when this is over," I said, pointedly.

"He has a sharp tongue," said Emmanuel to André whilst looking at me, "and when do you think it will be over Jacques?"

"Jacques doesn't think, he knows," said André.

"Now I'm interested."

"Jacques is from the future."

Isaac leaned forward now and showed more interest in the conversation.

"Like René?" Emmanuel asked.

"You know of René?" I asked.

"Yes, but I never thought that of him. He seemed so genuine."

I was puzzled now. I had seen René bundled into the Gestapo car and I was fearful of what may be happening to him. Because we had arrived in the same way, I had an attachment to René and I wondered whether the Gestapo thugs had broken his will and he had spoken of what he knew. My attachment to René was about to be broken.

"What do you mean Emmanuel?" asked André, "We saw René's capture."

"You saw his staged capture. René is on his way to the high command in Germany. He is dressed as an officer of the SS."

"What!" I exclaimed, "Never."

"Yes, Jacques, yes."

I was stunned by this revelation as was André. We were both silent in contemplation for what seemed like minutes but was, in fact, seconds.

"Fuck!" André said simply.

"That changes everything," I said, " René knows too much. What made him do this? He must know the outcome of the war; after all he's seen the aftermath."

"That's the point," Isaac entered the conversation at this point having listened quietly. He stepped forward and joined us.

"What's the point Isaac?" Emmanuel said gently as if addressing a child.

"René did not like the outcome of the war, nor what happened to the world afterwards. He wants to change time. He wants to change the future."

"How do you know this Isaac?" I asked.

"I came with René. I was with René when he came through the rift in time."

"He did not tell me!"

"He told nobody," added Isaac, "nobody at all. He lived a tissue of lies. I'm sure he told you about his girlfriend? He told you she was tortured and killed, yes?"

I nodded.

"René was a loner and René and I went through the time rift together by accident; we found ourselves in the wrong place at the wrong time. There was no girl and never was."

André looked at me. We had all been duped and René knew so much. We were all in danger. My mind was racing. The Germans were fighting a battle for Eastern Europe and for France. They were preoccupied so there had been no raids. René knew much of the resistance and its structure. There were many who were in peril. Yet, there had been no captures of resistance fighters reported, or none that we knew of.

Then I had it. It was not René's contemporary knowledge that was of interest to the Germans. It was his twenty first century knowledge that they wanted. René wanted to change the future world and he had chosen the dark force of the Nazi's as a vehicle. A strange choice of partner to my way of thinking.

"What profession was René? What did he do in our time?" I asked of Isaac.

"He was a scientist," replied Isaac, "specialising in nuclear energy and fusion."

"Shit," I spluttered, "this is serious."

André glanced at me and said, "I'm not sure what you are talking about Jacques but I don't like the look on your face."

"There are things happening right now André that make a difference to the world for a generation. We discover how to harness massive forces, those that bind atoms together. René understands the science of this. If the Germans get hold of this technology then everything will change. I mean everything."

"But you know the future, Jacques," said André, "what are you telling me?"

I looked down at my feet and, as I did so, I caught sight of Emmanuel opening a bottle of wine. At that moment I needed a drink.

"André, I don't know any more," I replied, "but if René is right and the future can be changed then we are all in peril. I don't think we can take the chance."

At this point Emmanuel passed us each a glass of rich red wine and I downed the glass in one go. Emmanuel raised his eyebrows and refilled the glass without speaking.

"What are you suggesting we do?" said Isaac in his deep booming voice.

"We must stop him. We must stop René," I replied.

# Paul Smith

Paul Smith is an engineer and Fellow of the Institution of Engineering and Technology. He lives in the wonderful county of Yorkshire and enjoys living there (why wouldn't he). He has had what seems a lifetime working in information technology and now believes it is his turn to become a user of technology rather than its creator. So he has turned his creative skills to writing novels rather than long theses aimed at convincing his customers to purchase from him (oh and some of them were very long) and is enjoying it so much that he wondered why he didn't do it earlier.

# By the Same Author

## No Time for a Retreat

Barrington and Alan both wanted to take a break and separately checked in to the 'Retreat'. Their break was more exciting than they expected when they met a spirit hiding in a drinks machine and were then told by an attractive and enigmatic woman that they had a very important duty to perform.

Another visitor to the Retreat, Nikolas, is embroiled in the adventure. He was not in the master plan but nobody told him so he went anyway.

"Unlikely saviours," Dole said, "they look like wimps to me".

The story is deeply spiritual and asks questions about the very nature of our existence. These are questions that every thinking person has asked at some time.

"An enjoyable read which makes you think about the things that are important in life. Deeply philosophical and quite funny in places. I liked Dole; he was a real character." The Reading Group.

## A Question of Resistance – Part II, René's Story

The follow-on from Part I of this adventure story set in wartime France. Part I explored the story from Jacques point of view and gave a diary of his adventures starting at his unorthodox arrival with his friend Georges and charting his assimilation into the resistance movement. Part II is told by both Jacques and René who provide very different viewpoints. René believes he can change the outcome of the war and change time and history. Jacques is determined to stop René and an epic battle ensues. Jacques is no longer sure that the future is set so the gloves are off as the two of them lock horns, carrying André, Luc and Henri with them and introducing Isaac to the perils of resistance.